IFWG AUSTRALIA DARK PHASES TITLES

Peripheral Visions (Robert Hood, 2015)
The Grief Hole (Kaaron Warren, 2016)
Cthulhu Deep Down Under Vol 1 (2017)

CTHULHU
DEEP DOWN UNDER

VOLUME 1

EDITED BY

STEVE PROPOSCH
CHRISTOPHER SEQUEIRA
BRYCE STEVENS

INTRODUCTION BY

RAMSEY CAMPBELL

A DARK PHASES TITLE

Cthulhu Deep Down Under Volume 1

All Rights Reserved

ISBN-13: 978-1-925496-47-5

Anthology Concept Copyright ©2017 Steve Proposch, Christopher Sequeira & Bryce Stevens

V1.0

Printed in Palatino Linotype and Bebas Neue.

IFWG Publishing International
Melbourne

www.ifwgpublishing.com

This collection is dedicated to Lindsay C. Walker

TABLE OF CONTENTS

INTRODUCTION: LOVECRAFT'S MONSTER

RAMSEY CAMPBELL

What was Lovecraft's most monstrous creation? Cthulhu and Wilbur Whateley must be candidates. The author himself told August Derleth that he'd "spent enormous pains thinking out *Cthulhu*, & still more in devising the two blasphemous entities that figure in my new 'Dunwich Horror'." His purpose in this, as with all his tales of cosmic terror, was to communicate a sense of the utterly alien. He had little time for the standard figures of supernatural fiction—vampires, werewolves—and the mythos he created piecemeal was intended to suggest things vaster and more dreadful than it showed. Traditional occultism failed to engage his imagination—he found it too conventionalised— and his mythos was one of the ways he sought to revive a sense of the genuinely weird. He thought it fell far short of his ambitions and said so in his letters, calling it Yog-Sothothery and inventing fanciful relationships between its creatures. Although he encouraged his colleagues to make use of it and add to it, he could surely never have imagined how it would outlive him. It was his monster—his Frankenstein.

I call it that deliberately and of course wrongly in order to make the point. Just as Mary Shelley's creation has acquired in the public mind a name she never gave it, so Lovecraft's cosmic concepts were given an overall name to aid in their codification. In fairness, while he was alive Lovecraft encouraged other writers to use or add to his mythos; he apparently regarded the proliferation of references as lending it more verisimilitude. All the same, I wonder what he would have made of the immeasurable entity the mythos has become. "The most merciful thing in the world, I think, is the inability of the human mind to correlate all its contents" — by now this may apply to his own creation in a way even that great dreamer could never have dreamed.

August Derleth was the primary organiser of the mythos. He named it for Cthulhu and elected himself guardian of the usage, advising me in a letter that "we generally refer to it as the Cthulhu Mythos, not the Lovecraft Mythos." He was also the originator of the Mythos action tale, creating Laban Shrewsbury to do battle with Cthulhu and assorted monstrous associates for the length of a book. He even reconceived Lovecraft's alien invaders as terrestrial elementals, adding one of his own to make up the set. The reader must decide to what extent this involved the attitude Lovecraft described as earth-gazing.

As the first of the new generation of authorised mythos-mongers, I must take a significant amount of the blame for the blurring of Lovecraft's ideas. I ruined at least one unused inspiration among his fines — from his Commonplace Book, by reconceiving a swarm of alien insects as giant ones, which he hadn't meant at all. Indeed, I was so troubled by the mistake that in my first Lovecraftian novel I did my best to revive the idea in terms of his own dream. Stranger still, my original story was adopted by gamers and by later Mythos writers as their source, and before I knew it my insects had a name I'd never given them.

To come upon your own inventions as developed by others is a weird experience, not necessarily unwelcome but certainly salutary. I would rather folk went back to the original for their inspiration, though — to Lovecraft himself, of whom my mythos tales are but the palest adumbration. If I have a grain of his essential saltes in me, I hope I live to shape up to its stimulus.

By the time I edited a Lovecraftian anthology the mythos and its creatures had burgeoned and multiplied to such an extent that it was impossible to devise a coherent overview, which (so I thought) left writers free to return to Lovecraft's first principles — cosmic awe and "dread suspense." That was nearly forty years ago. What has happened since? Lovecraftian soft toys, Lovecraftian children's comics, role-playing games that may invoke the very entities they seem to turn into pawns of the game, to possess the participants unnoticed... Let us cleave to what sanity remains to us and contemplate the book before us.

In one of his last tales—*The Shadow Out of Time*—Lovecraft tried to grasp Australia. While much of his work is founded on places he actually visited, it can be argued that (like the Antarctica of *At the Mountains of Madness*) his version of the Antipodes gains a special vitality from having risen out of his imagination. Now the Australian Lovecraftians return the creative compliment and people the continent with their inventions. Some tales take the detective aspect of his work and develop it in their own contemporary ways. Some are breathless action pieces that are nevertheless not too swift to leave awe and terror behind. Some offer suspense that encompasses dread, and loathsome fright— Lovecraft's enthusiastic phrase—can be encountered too. The female viewpoint was wholly absent from his fiction, of course, but it's celebrated here. Some stories have dark fun with his concepts without betraying them, and several make his work part of their material, or, not just the man himself, but his previously unknown son. I was struck by the highly individual voices of some tales here—the voices of writers with the confidence to give Lovecraft new life, to express their own visions that extend his.

A final word. I hope this book represents a stage in the rediscovery of Lovecraft—his sense of structure, his care with language (too often carelessly overlooked, not just by his detractors) and the extraordinary modulation of prose that characterises much of his finest work, his commitment to trying out as many forms of the weird tale as he could find in him, his ambitions for horror as literature. Rise up, antipodeans, and shine your light on the path! It leads back to greatness and onwards to the heights of awe.

Ramsey Campbell
Wallasey, Merseyside

A PEARL BEYOND PRICE

JANEEN WEBB

For there are strange objects in the great abyss, and the seeker of dreams must take care not to stir up or meet the wrong ones.

H.P. Lovecraft, 'The Strange High House in the Mist', 1926

Michiko was not afraid. She had heard the monsters singing, each to each, a hundred times before today. She was fascinated, but she did not think the creatures even noticed when she dived into the blue-green deeps of their realm, fishing for pearls on the edge of the abyss.

She knew the monsters were always there, though she could never be entirely sure she had seen one. She had caught glimpses—a tentacle slithering into a crevice, a huge eye peering at her from beneath a ledge, a sudden burst of bubbles at the mouth of an underwater cave—and she did not need to see them to know them. In her heart she understood the cadence of their monster melody. Their music was made in deeper, darker tones than the whale-song that vibrated through her bones whenever the great herds of humpbacks came to the warm waters of the Indian Ocean. The monster song was mournful: the creatures of the deep sang of loss and sorrow. They sang of darkness and death. They sang of despair.

Michiko yearned to help them, to mend their misery. She was barely fifteen, the youngest of the Japanese pearl divers, the littlest mermaid of the Ama group that worked on the Kimberley coast, eking out a meagre living on the fringes of the world. The older women seemed happy enough, glad to live independently in a strong, female community that provided for their needs: they fished, and they gathered the plentiful seafood of these warm waters—crabs and crayfish, prawns, sea urchins, and valuable *bêche-de-mer*—they dived for oysters, hoping always for pearls; they made mother-of-pearl buttons, and they carved exquisite whalebone amulets to trade for other necessities. The women told grim fireside tales of want and oppression in the society they had left behind to come here, left for this peaceful life where one day merged seamlessly into the next. But Michiko had known no other. She had been no more than a babe in arms when her mother had fled Japan. And now she was restless, stuck here in paradise, trapped here on the shore with her all-female family and her strange dreams of the *Akkorokami* that lived beneath the waves.

When the tide was out, Michiko gathered seaweed for the camp. In the inter-tidal area, she marvelled at the footprints of the monsters, creatures so heavy that their feet left imprints in the living red rock. The imprints were so deep they sometimes made little rock pools full of swaying anemones and tiny periwinkles, and she imagined that the legs that belonged to the feet that made these prints must be at least as tall as the masts of sailing ships—the tallest things she had ever seen—and the bodies atop these legs must be vast indeed, bigger than the most enormous whale. She longed to meet such creatures. And when she slept, she dreamed about them, dreamed that they would someday show her the dark mysteries of their hidden, forbidden world.

The morning sunshine was warm on her face as Michiko waded out through the shallows of the rocky headland, preparing to dive. She tightened her linen loincloth, checked her knives, and fastened her woven rope bag for collecting oysters. Then she tied back her long black hair and pegged her nostrils closed. She was ready.

She paused for a moment on the brink, scanning the heaving surface of the sea for signs of danger. She was unafraid, but not unwary: she knew there were risks aplenty for divers here on this idyllic coast. The ocean was full of predatory sharks, deadly box jellyfish came and went in their seasons, and closer inshore there were huge saltwater crocodiles that lurked near the mouth of the estuary. And there were always the *Funayūrei*, the ghosts of drowned sailors, sliding like pale eels through shipwrecked ribs and spars, always ready to suck the souls from the living. Michiko had seen sailor's bones, picked clean by crabs and currents, washed up to lie bleaching on the sandy shore. She always gave the bones a wide berth. It was bad luck to touch such things. She fingered the carved whalebone amulet at her throat, reassured by its curving shape incised with magical wards against the soul-stealers. She never swam without it.

She shook her head, re-focussing her thoughts, then took a deep breath and dived, sleek as a seal. As she broke the surface, the melancholy monster music flowed around her, curling around her near-naked body, caressing her as she arrowed downwards. She swam smoothly, angling through schools of brilliant little fish, yellow and blue, their scales glowing bright in the slanting sunlight that lit waving beds of kelp and seaweed. A giant clam snapped shut as the shadow of a cruising manta ray fell upon it, a huge bass grouper nosed close to her, and in the distance she glimpsed a green sea turtle, hunting. She felt the pull of a different current as she neared the oyster colony that clung to its rocky outcrop on the edge of a deep fissure. She eased her knife from her belt, ready to gather.

Then a single note changed. The monster song was different. Now, the music sang to *her*, promising heart's desire, promising an end to the aching loneliness of her life, luring her towards the edge of the steep shelf where the water was deeper, darker, and colder.

She peered into a crevice. She saw the outlined edge of what might have been a giant octopus, but realised on the instant that this was something more: this creature's sinuous tentacles had long hairs like a sea spider, hairs that trapped air bubbles from the surface of the sea and dragged them down beneath the waves.

A grey tentacle coiled back, then unfolded towards her,

silently offering a single, perfect pearl.

Michiko's salt-stinging eyes widened with surprise.

The tentacle coiled again, changing now through a myriad of iridescent colours, beckoning her to dive deeper, to enter the cave.

Despite her fascination, Michiko was still counting time. She could hold her breath for a full two minutes, and her two minutes was nearly up. She was running out of air. She turned for the surface.

The monster understood. It reached out to her again, this time sliding the tentacle close to her mouth, offering a bubble of air.

Michiko hesitated. Deep in her heart, she felt the vibration of the song, telling her that there was plenty of air inside the cave. She took the chance. She gulped the air bubble.

The hairy tentacle grabbed her, coiling around her with impossible speed as the monster pulled her into its lair.

She reached out with her knife.

But the creature of the deep had already relaxed its suckered grip. And now Michiko understood that the song sang true: the top half of the underwater cavern was, indeed, full of air. She opened her mouth very slightly, exhaling slowly, so that her breath made the familiar whistling sound, the Japanese divers' *isobue*. It sounded strange in her ears, echoing in the silence of this strange place. She gulped air that tasted stale, damp, and salty: but, for all that, it was perfectly breathable. Michiko relaxed, just a little, curiosity getting the better of caution.

The melody changed again. *Welcome, little mermaid. Be assured I can feel your thoughts. You are my guest. I will not harm you. You are safe here.*

Michiko, waist deep in cold seawater, bowed her head in acknowledgement. She shivered.

Thank you, great one, she thought. *I am honoured.*

The song that surrounded Michiko changed to warm her quivering body. She looked away from the circling tentacle and gasped in disbelief at what she saw. The walls of the cave were lined with ledges, and the ledges were heaped with treasure: she saw caskets spilling over with gold and silver and precious gems; there were long ropes of pearls, and bolts of brocade fit for an emperor; there were beautifully engraved swords and knives and jewel-set goblets, the lost bounty of countless shipwrecks, stolen away from the restless sailor-souls, gathered together to line the monster's glittering nest. She wondered if this might be the undersea lair of some mighty dragon.

No, child, said the monster. *Dragons are puny things compared with such as I.*

Michiko was sure she felt the creature laughing at the very idea. She peered further into the gloom, and realised that she could not make out the shape of the monster beyond the thickening of the long tentacle whose tip still circled her waist, holding her steady.

No, child, the creature said, answering her unspoken thought. *You cannot look upon me. I am vast. I contain multitudes.*

Then…

You are young, unspoiled. You spoke to me in your dreams. I heard your longing. It amuses me to reach out to you. Perhaps it will amuse you to visit me again. Will you do that?

The compulsion was overpowering. Michiko knew that there was no other possible answer.

Yes, she said. She did not want to leave, but almost a full minute had passed, and she could feel pressure building in her lungs. She would have to swim for the surface, and soon.

Choose, said the monster. The tentacle swept over the heaps of treasure, offering it to her.

Michiko was not greedy. She passed this first test. She selected a practical silver dagger and tucked it into her belt, delighted at the creature's bounty.

Choose again, child. I feel your pleasure. It gives me joy.

This time she reached into a brass bound chest and picked out a thin gold ring set with a small cabochon ruby. She was thrilled to find that the ring was a perfect fit for her index finger.

Thank you, great one, she said.

Once again, she felt the monster's deep laughter. *You have chosen well, child. Long ago that ring belonged to one of the Elder Race, and it still carries with it the gift of tongues.*

Michiko had no time to ask what this might mean. The sea creature was still speaking.

But the third time pays for all. Take some pearls with you, child, it said. *You have not fished today. You must not disappoint your family.*

Michiko accepted the proffered pouch and eased back the drawstring. She gasped in surprise. She had never seen pearls so large, or so fine. *It's too much,* she thought.

Do not give them all to your mother at once, the creature warned. *One is enough for today. We do not want every pearl fisher on the coast seeking out my cave. Hide them away, for next time.*

I understand. Michiko closed the little silk pouch and tucked it safely into the band of her loincloth, feeling the round smoothness of the pearls pressing against her goose-pimpled skin.

And now you must go. Human beings are so fragile. You cannot risk a longer stay. Farewell.

Farewell, great one.

There was, abruptly, nothing else to be said.

Michiko felt the overwhelming presence of the monster song leave her mind as the ancient turned its attention elsewhere. She was alone in the treasure cave. She checked the carved amulet at her neck, making sure her luck was still with her, then she gulped a deep lungful of air and dived through the cave mouth, instantly heading upwards in a graceful, practiced style that brought her safely to the shallows. She came ashore on the sandy beach, at a familiar spot where the freshwater stream that was the centre of the Ama camp flowed down past spiky clumps of salt spinifex and the waving branches of Boab trees and into the open arms of the sea.

Michiko reclined against a rocky ledge, marvelling at her experience. She knew she had not imagined it. The ring that now encircled her finger was proof enough of that. She lolled further back, letting the warm wavelets wash over her quivering limbs. It had been an exhausting dive. She pulled off her bandana, freeing her long black hair to tumble about her shoulders, its curling strands mingling with the red and brown sea wrack that swirled about her on the sand. She leaned on one elbow, feeling the kiss of the sun on her face, feeling the salt drying on her exposed skin, feeling her nipples harden in the breeze. Her senses stirred. She was still thinking about the monster, re-living her strange encounter, a meeting that had been frightening and exhilarating all at once.

As she lay there, the creature that lived beneath the sea put out a long tentacle to find her again. She accepted its touch, pretending not to notice its questing progress up her white thigh. She did not pull away when the tentacle's tender tip slid beneath her loincloth and slipped between her private folds to find her own little pearl of pleasure. She gave herself up to sensation as the tentacle pushed and probed, slipping and sliding until she arched her back and cried out in delight—her own warm juices sluiced away by the cold salt waves, her soft sighs lost in the crying of seagulls on the lonely beach.

At last the tentacle withdrew, and she rose, reluctantly, to her feet. She splashed her way back to shore and headed toward the Ama camp, following the path of the stream where it meandered between scrubby gum trees and twisted screw palms with their bright red fruit. The ripening fruit reminded her of her ruby ring: she took it off and slipped it into the hidden silk pouch, to keep it safe from prying eyes. Then she withdrew one of the monster's pearls, fingering it as she walked, inhaling the warm scent of the dry eucalyptus leaves that crunched underfoot, their perfume sharp in her nostrils after the damp salt smells of the beach. Michiko bit her lip, fretting now about what, if anything, she should tell her mother about the pearl. For first time in her young life, Michiko had secrets to keep.

She met her mother on the sandy path, and one glance at her mother's anxious face told Michiko something was wrong.

"Where have you been?" Her mother's voice sounded shrill in Michiko's ears after the deep tones of the ocean creature. "I've been waiting for you."

"I dived near the headland," Michiko replied. "There was a rip. It took me a while to swim back, that's all."

Her mother's tense expression softened a little. "I'm glad

you're safe," she said. "I was worried. You know I don't like you to dive alone."

"I'm fine, Mother."

"So I see. I've brought your shift for you. Cover yourself up. We have company."

"Company?" Michiko pulled the simple cotton shift over her head, hiding her nakedness.

"A sailing ship has come, seeking trade. It's moored in the next bay. That's why you didn't see it when you went out."

"Oh," said Michiko. "We weren't expecting traders."

"No. But these are not the usual buyers for our goods. These men say they come from far away, from Norway."

'What's Norway?" said Michiko, trying the feel of the unfamiliar word on her tongue.

"No idea," her mother replied. "It doesn't matter. We don't have much put by at the moment. This isn't the usual season for traders, but the sea currents are running strong, and the winds have been high. The ship was probably blown off course. We've seen men repairing their sails today. I think the Captain is just making the most of a bad situation, trading wherever he can."

"Does he have rice for us?"

"I doubt it. He has offered flour, salt meat, and ship's biscuits."

Michiko pulled a face.

"We take what we can get," her mother said. "The salt meat will make a change from fish. And we need knives, if the Captain will sell them. We have a few small pearls to trade, and the grandmothers have finished carving some whalebone to sell, but we can't spare much else. The mother-of-pearl shell is already promised to the trader who brings our rice."

"Will this help?" Michiko held out her single, superb pearl, still marvelling at its perfect lustre. "I only just found it."

"It's beautiful." Michiko's mother hugged her. "I don't think I've ever seen a pearl so beautiful. It'll more than pay for our goods. You're a treasure. I'll go at once to do the bargaining. The grandmothers will still be there."

"I'll come with you."

"No, Michiko. Go back to camp. These are rough men, and

the captain is an evil brute. I can always tell."

"But…"

"Please, Michiko. The sailors won't bother the grandmothers, and I can fend for myself. But you are young and beautiful. It's better they don't see you."

"If you say so."

"I only want to keep you safe. It's all I've ever wanted."

"I know, Mother." Michiko pouted. "You always say that. And you never let me come with you. The sailors can't all be bad men, can they?"

"They can. Trust me, daughter, they can." She turned away. "I must go. We'll talk later."

Michiko sighed. She watched her mother walk away with the pearl, wondering if the ancient of the sea had known that such a treasure would be needed today to trade with the strangers.

Of course it knew, she decided. *How would it not know?* And then came a second thought, the corollary of the first: *what else did it know to make it want to give me the dagger and the ring?*

She waited until her mother was out of sight before she set out for the headland. She had decided to climb to the cliff top — that way she could look down upon the ship in the next cove and observe the sailors from a distance, unseen. Just looking at them wouldn't break any promises.

The midday sun was hot, and the rocky path to the top of the cliff was hard on Michiko's bare feet as she scrambled to the summit. She startled a brown snake that lay sunning itself on the deserted track, and she stood breathlessly still until it had slithered away into the spiny grass. But when, at last, she reached the top and sat on a sun-warmed rock, the view was spectacular. She gazed out over clear azure water to where the unexpected ship lay at anchor, its white sails furled, its tall masts swaying gently as the sea swell rose and fell. Beyond the bay a flock of white cockatoos wheeled screeching above the darker green of a patch of rainforest.

Michiko took out the ruby ring and slipped it onto her finger, still trying to fathom the monster's riddling words. She pulled her loose cotton shift closer about her body when a light breeze sprang up, but still she sat there, hugging her knees to her chest, daydreaming. The tentacle's touch had left her restless, uncertain, yearning for something she could not yet name. She let her thoughts wander. She wished she could sail away on the ship to see the wonders of the world.

She almost fell off the cliff in fright when the stranger touched her shoulder.

"Sorry," the young man said. "I didn't mean to startle you. I was sent up here to be the lookout." He held out his spyglass, as if in explanation. "Not that we expect to see anyone way out here, but you never know."

Wrapped in her shift, Michiko could not easily reach the silver dagger tucked into her still-damp loincloth. She scrabbled to her feet, ready to run.

"Don't go. I promise I won't hurt you." He smiled, and opened his hands wide, miming harmlessness.

Michiko did not understand the words, but the gesture was clear enough. She stared at the interloper. She had only ever seen a few of the old men who came regularly to the Ama camp to trade, and she had never imagined that any man could be as big, or as handsome, as this young sailor.

"I'm Lars," he said. He pointed to his chest. "Lars."

To Michiko, he seemed as tall as a tree. He had pale, freckled skin and startling blue eyes and bushy red hair that sprouted in thickets all over him: he had a curly red beard, red hairs on his brawny arms and legs, and a tuft of red chest hair that stuck out through the wide laces of his cotton shirt.

He pointed to her. "You?"

She realised he was asking her name. She put her hand to her chest, copying him. "Michiko," she said. "I'm Michiko."

"Pleased to meet you, Mi-chi-ko," he said, stumbling over the strange syllables.

She giggled at the way he mispronounced her name.

He smiled again. He sat down beside her, hitching up his baggy trousers. His shirt gaped open at the neck.

Michiko saw that he was wearing one of the grandmothers' amulets threaded on a leather thong, the whalebone carved with painstaking precision into whorls and spirals and the outlines of a strangely finned creature. She pointed. "*Samebeto*," she said. "Shark man."

He didn't understand. "I just bought this,' he said. "It's for good luck."

Michiko pulled her own *Funayūrei* amulet from beneath her shift, to show him the different carving.

"We match," he said.

She tried again to explain, curving her hand to imitate a swimming shark. "Yours will save you from shark monsters."

Lars just grinned, incredibly pleased that this tiny, fragile, beautiful girl with her long black hair and her ivory skin and her brown, almond shaped eyes wasn't actually running away from him. She was the most exquisite girl he had ever seen. It didn't matter that he couldn't speak her language. They understood each other well enough. He raised the brass spyglass to his eye, scanning the bay.

Michiko had never seen such a thing before.

"Look," he said. He adjusted it for her. "It brings things closer. See?"

Michiko peered through the glass. She squealed with pleasure when a pod of dolphins came into focus, leaping and diving through the waves, their curving fins slicing through the azure waters of the sandy bay. She handed back the spyglass, feeling suddenly shy. She twisted the ring on her finger.

The world changed.

Lars pointed to the dolphins. "Sharks?" he asked.

He used his big hands to mime closing jaws, but he no longer needed the gesture. Michiko understood him. The ring had given her its gift of tongues.

She shook her head. It took a moment before she realised she could speak to him. "No, Dolphins," she said. "Dolphins are safe." The words felt strange in her mouth as her tongue twisted around the unfamiliar sounds.

Lars' grin widened to astonishment. "You can talk to me!"

Michiko shrugged. "Some words, I think."

"That's amazing."

She hugged herself, marvelling. She'd made a friend. Things were going very well. This was turning out to be a wonderful day.

Lars was still grinning. "Share food?" he asked.

He pulled a grubby cloth bundle from his pocket and unwrapped it slowly, careful not to alarm her. The cloth contained a bit of hard biscuit and a thin rind of smelly cheese. He mimed eating.

Michiko sniffed. She drew back, horrified. She shook her head. "I'll come back." She turned him around and pointed up and down the slope. "I won't be long."

"Okay," he said. He picked up the spyglass again. "I'll keep watch."

She wasn't really sure he had understood, but she set out anyway.

An hour later she was back, carrying a little clay pot of seaweed-wrapped smoked fish.

The boy was still peering out to sea. He looked uncertain when she offered him the food, but his hairy face crinkled into a wide grin when he tasted the fish. "Wonderful," he said. "We have smoked herring at home." He untied a little leather flask from his belt and offered it to her. "Drink?"

Michiko sipped cautiously. She coughed, and spat out the fiery water.

Lars laughed, and took a swig himself. "I guess you're not used to strong drink," he said.

She shook her head. She ate a very little of the fish, then offered him the rest.

He wolfed it down.

She smiled guilelessly up at him again, at this enormous, gentle young man. They sat companionably for a long while, warmed by the sun as they gazed out to sea, feeling far away from the demands of their work-a-day lives.

Now that Lars knew Michiko could understand him, he told her about his home in Norway, in Bergen, waving his arms about as he described the mountains and the fjords. "You'd love snow," he said. "The world is so pretty when it's covered in snow." He looked across at her, laughing at her puzzlement. "We'd have to get you some warm clothes, though. You'd freeze to death in what you're wearing."

"This is all the clothing I've got," she said.

He laughed again. "It must be nice to have never been cold," he conceded. "I could get used to that."

Michiko could not untangle her emotions: she was reminded of her strange encounter with the old one beneath the waves, of how it had comforted her and calmed her terror; maybe she just felt safe with Lars. Whatever the reason, she resolved to stay with him as long as she could. The sun was sinking low on the horizon by the time she picked up her pot, preparing to leave.

"Tomorrow?" she asked. "I'll see you again tomorrow?"

He nodded. He touched her hand. "Tomorrow," he echoed.

She did not let go of his hand. She turned to look up at him. She smiled.

He smiled back. And then he bent to kiss her upturned lips.

Their first kiss was gentle, tentative, fleeting.

The second lasted longer. When they finally drew apart, Michiko's heart was beating fast. Her face was flushed, and the sensations kindled by the sea creature were stirring once again in her loins. She had no idea what should happen between a man and a woman, but she was curious to learn. She stared at the growing bulge in Lars' baggy cotton trousers.

Lars blushed to the roots of his red hair when he saw the direction of Michiko's gaze. "We should go," he said gruffly. "This isn't the time." He pointed to the path. "We'll both be missed."

Michiko was perplexed, but she followed his lead. He helped her to her feet, and they scrambled down the steep path together, hand in hand, each heading back to their separate lives, each wondering how they might contrive to be together.

The light was fading when Michiko finally slipped back into the Ama camp. She still had more pearls, and she reckoned that these would more than account for her absence if she had any explaining to do, but nobody questioned her absence. The women were all too busy with the extra chores required to meet the demands of the ship from Norway: there was fish to be smoked, prawns to be dried, and carving to be done. The camp was a hive of activity.

"The ship leaves in three days time, if the winds stay fair," Michiko's mother said. "The Captain says his repairs will be finished by then."

"And then maybe we'll be left in peace for a while," one of the grandmothers added sharply. "I don't know why they can't smoke their own fish!"

"They are men," another replied, as if this was explanation enough.

"True," said the old woman, as she bent her back once more to her task.

Next day, when her diving was done and she had filled her woven bag with sea urchins and abalone for the camp, Michiko slipped the sea creature's ruby ring onto her finger once more and climbed back to the headland. Today she was wearing her favourite cotton shift. She wanted to look her best.

Lars was not there.

She was disappointed. She shrugged, and was about to head back when he came panting up the rocky path.

"Sorry," he said. "The Captain has brought our departure forward. *The Hildalga* will sail on the morning tide. There are a million chores to be done."

"Oh." This was too soon. Michiko did not know what to say.

"But I can stay with you for a while. I'm supposed to be on watch."

Michiko reached up then, and kissed him. "Take me with you," she said. "Take me to see Norway, to see the snow and ice."

Lars shook his head. "I don't think I can," he said. "The Captain would never allow it."

"I can pay," said Michiko. "I have a very valuable pearl. I can offer him that."

Lars thought for a moment. "Well," he said at last, "if you can pay for your passage, that would be a different thing. The Captain is a greedy man. Let me think about how best to manage it."

Michiko hugged him. "I knew you'd want to be with me," she said.

"I always want to be with you, Mi-chi-ko," Lars replied solemnly. He took her delicate hands in his big, hairy paws. "But I thought we would have to part. I was just trying not to hurt you."

"Leaving me here would hurt me," Michiko said. "But now we won't have to be apart."

"I hope not. I think I love you." He bent to kiss her.

Michiko felt her passion rise. She clung to him, returning his kiss.

Lars looked about him at the bare rock face. "It isn't very private up here," he said.

Michiko took him by the hand. "I know a place," she said. "Come on."

She led him back down the headland path and around to a tiny cove, where a cave showed dark against the rock face above a wide lagoon. It was a beautiful place: the shallow water was full of water lilies, their petals open to the warm sunshine; the still air was loud with the croaking of frogs and the shrill cries of wading birds; spectacular red-winged parrots wheeled overhead, their colours bright against the dark green of the surrounding trees.

But Lars only had eyes for Michiko. He scooped her up into his arms and carried her to the cave. He set her down on the sandy floor, fumbling at his clothing. They gave themselves up to desire, coupling with the clumsy urgency of adolescent lust. When at last they lay back, sated, his unruly red curls tangled with her straight black hair.

"Happy?" he asked.

"Yes," she said. She reached for him again, enjoying the newfound sensations coursing through her body. "Very happy, my love."

Later, they swam in the lagoon. Lars floated on his back amongst perfumed water lilies and flitting dragonflies, watching the bright parrots wheeling overhead. He smiled contentedly.

"I could stay here forever," he said. "Maybe we don't have to leave."

"No! Only women live here."

"I'm strong. I could make myself useful."

"You don't understand. My family hate men. They'll drive you away."

Lars sighed. "Then I really will have to take you with me," he said.

"Yes," said Michiko. "I want to see your world. I want to see snow. I want to see it all."

"You won't like it," he warned, after a moment.

Michiko's pretty mouth set in a stubborn line. "We'll see," she said.

In the dead of night, when Michiko made her silent way to meet her lover, she skirted around the sailors' campsite, avoiding the frightening sounds of drunken revelry. The Captain and some of his men were sitting around their campfire, swigging from flasks, swapping yarns and singing lewd shanties while hot sparks drifted upwards into the starlit night sky.

Michiko met Lars close to the ship, but they could not just board—the gangplank was guarded. Two sailors were sitting there at their ease, playing cards in a pool of yellow lamplight, enjoying their last night ashore. There was no way Michiko could sneak past them.

Lars pointed to a trailing rope ladder close to the bow of *The Hildalga*, but Michiko shook her head. And then she stripped off her shift, pulling it over her head in one smooth motion so that she stood naked except for her belted loincloth, smiling at him in the moonlight.

Lars stared at her in surprise, still overwhelmed by the beauty of her body—the body he had so recently enjoyed. She handed him the shift and waded into the water, swimming for the seaward side of the ship, out of sight of the guards.

A few minutes later she reappeared, treading water.

Lars walked casually up the gangplank, nodding a greeting to the two men. Then he crept across the deck and let down a rope ladder.

Michiko climbed nimbly to stand beside him on the deck.

He put his finger to his lips, urging silence.

She nodded. She took back her shift and tugged it on over her wet skin while Lars re-coiled the ladder and stowed it away. She *followed him silently as he led the way to the rope* locker.

"In here," he whispered, holding the wooden door for her. "They won't find you in here until we are well underway, and by then it'll be too late to turn around and take you back."

"You'll need this," she whispered back. She pressed the pearl into his hand.

Lars grinned, his teeth showing white in the moonlight. "A pearl beyond price," he said. He kissed her lightly. "Don't worry," he said. "I'll make sure you're not disturbed. Try to get some sleep."

When dawn broke next morning, the red-faced Captain was still drunk. He was cursing and swearing, roaring orders at his men—unnecessary orders about the clearing of decks and the stowing of cargo. The men mostly managed to stay out of his way. 'The old man', they called him: he was sixty at least, his lined face weather-beaten from long years at sea, his iron-grey hair tied back in a sailor's knot, his curling beard grey and grizzled. But for all that, he was a good navigator, a sturdy seaman, and strong as an ox, broad shouldered and hard muscled from hauling ropes. Still, his foul mouth and bad temper were the stuff of legend, even among the toughs of the Bergen docks.

The ship was barely through the heads when one of the crew pulled open the rope locker. He gasped in surprise. He grabbed Michiko, and hauled her out onto the deck.

She blinked in the sunlight, squinting after the darkness of her hiding place.

"Well, will you just look at this," the sailor said. "Hello, my lovely."

The Captain leered. He grabbed at Michiko, pawing at her chest where the outline of her firm breasts showed beneath her thin shift.

She pulled away.

"What have we here?" he said. "A stowaway?"

Lars stepped forward. "No, Captain," he said. "She arrived last night. It was too late to bother you. She can pay for her passage."

"So why didn't she make the usual arrangements?"

"She didn't want her mother to know she is leaving."

"A runaway, then," said the Captain.

"No," Lars said. "I told you, she is willing to pay her way." He held out the pearl that she had given him. "See? She offers you this: it must be worth a fortune."

The Captain snatched it, eyeing it greedily, realising at once that it was a perfect match for the one the old women had already traded, and that a matched pair of large, perfect pearls for earrings was worth far more than a single specimen. The Captain knew jewellers back in Europe who would pay very handsomely for such as these.

He shoved the pearl into the slit pouch in his belt.

"Fair enough," he said. "The girl can stay on board until we reach the next port." He leered again. "Still, there's no reason we can't have some sport with her on the way," he added. He scratched deliberately at his crotch.

"But she's paid you in good faith!"

"Then it's time she learned the world doesn't work that way," the Captain snarled. "Hold her."

Two grinning sailors grabbed Michiko, pinioning her arms by her sides.

The Captain seized the front of her shift. The fabric tore. "Well, aren't you the pretty one," he said. He ripped off the rest of the garment, expecting to frighten her, expecting her to cry.

But Michiko was angry. Freed from the constraints of the garment, she twisted away from one of the sailors. She grabbed the sea monster's silver dagger from her belt. The dagger guided her hand. The dagger knew how to fight. She slashed at the other sailor.

He yelped in pain and jumped back, nursing his bleeding arm.

Michiko pulled out her oyster knife and stood, defiant, holding a blade in each hand. She scowled at the Captain, daring him to touch her.

"That's enough of that, girl," he said. He drew a pistol from his belt and cocked the hammer. "Now, you just behave yourself, and maybe I won't shoot you. At least not yet."

"No!" said Lars.

"I'm the Captain here," the old man roared. "You can have her later, if you want, when I'm finished with her."

Lars took a step forward.

One of his mates grabbed his arm. "Take it easy," he muttered. "The Captain's in his cups, and she's just a girl. You don't want to start a fight."

"She's *my* girl,' Lars grated.

"Too bad," said the Captain.

Lars moved quickly, putting himself between Michiko and the Captain.

"Fool!" the Captain shouted. "Out of my way."

Lars did not move.

The Captain fired, hitting Lars full in the chest.

Michiko screamed.

There was a sudden shocked silence as the crew registered the enormity of the Captain's crime.

Lars groaned, slumped bleeding to the deck, clutching at the ragged hole in his chest as if to hold in the life that was fast ebbing from his body.

Michiko was afraid.

In the depths of the great abyss, the monster felt her fear.

She backed up against the rail, still holding her blades.

The captain lunged at her. "This is your fault, girl," he shouted.

Michiko did not hesitate. She vaulted over the rail and dived. As she swam for the ocean floor, giant tentacles erupted from the deeps, suckering onto the helpless ship. The *Akkorokami* had come.

A wall of salt water engulfed the sailors as the monster lifted the ship high above the waves and flung it against the rocky headland with the force of a tsunami. The sturdy oak timbers smashed and shattered like matchwood. The ship's spine snapped in two before it fell back into the sea, where the monster was waiting. Huge, hairy tentacles coiled around the wreckage where sailors who had somehow survived the fall clung desperately to splintered spars. These men were already broken and bleeding, and the soul-stealers were upon them in an instant, sucking greedily at their still-living souls as the sea monster dragged the remains of their ship into the depths. And then the sharks smelled frenzied blood, and attacked whatever was left.

Michiko clung to the tentacle that kept her safe, feeding her air bubbles while chaos swirled around her. She could not look at the churning mess of blood and flesh that stained the clean seawater where greedy sharks were feasting. She was shocked to hear the monster's thought: *the crabs will dine well tonight*. She realised that there was no mercy here, no pity. None of the sailors would survive. They would soon join the drowned *Funayūrei* that haunted the wreckage-strewn seabed.

Suddenly, the tentacle tightened, and Michiko felt herself propelled firmly back to shore, back to the place where the camp stream met the sea. The monster released her abruptly, leaving her to stagger to her feet in the surf. When she looked up, she saw that her female family had gathered on the beach, the women all bearing helpless witness to the angry destruction of the ill-fated *Hildalga*, the ship from far off Norway.

But as Michiko tottered up the beach, picking her way distractedly through the red and brown seaweed that swirled around her ankles, the grandmothers backed away from her, fingering their amulets.

"An *Akkorokami* has marked you, girl," one of them cried. "Stay away from us!" She made the sign to avert evil spirits, the sign against hungry ghosts. "A monster has marked you as one of its own. You don't belong here any more! You must go back!"

Michiko was bewildered. She looked down, and saw that her pearly white skin now bore a livid line of raised red welts. The sucker marks stretched from hip to shoulder, where the giant tentacle had gripped her tight.

Only her mother dared approach her. "Michiko," she said. "Can you speak to me?"

"I'm not a ghost, Mother," Michiko said. "I have survived."

Her mother's eyes filled with tears. "I thought I'd lost you," she said. "What happened?"

"The sea creature saved me," Michiko replied. "It threw me clear of the ship."

The grandmothers muttered again, repeating their incantations, but Michiko's mother took the chance: she opened her arms wide.

Michiko ran to her, grateful to be wrapped in the familiar embrace.

"It's all right," her mother said. She turned to the older women. "She's warm. She's flesh and blood. It's all right."

The grandmothers looked unconvinced, but did not demur when Michiko's mother put her arm around her daughter's shivering shoulders and turned back towards the camp.

"Let's get you home, and warm," she said. "I'll make you some broth."

Michiko was shaking now, shuddering with grief. Lars was gone. Her love was gone. Her bright future was gone. She felt numb with loss, deadened by sorrow. Her mind was dark with despair. She was too shocked to cry.

The littlest mermaid allowed herself to be led away, back to the Ama camp, her paradise prison, back—though she did not yet know it—to bear a girl child.

HAUNTING MATILDA

DMETRI KAKMI

Matilda Craddock sat under the apple tree in Uncle Tom's yard, waiting for her parents to take her home. The flesh-like tendril that extended from her right hand and trailed along the ground like a bizarre skipping rope twitched sporadically, as though it possessed obscure remnants of life. It was dusk. In the stillness that settled over the valley, Matilda stretched on the ground and looked through the bare branches at the sky. She cast her mind into the immensity and grappled with the stars that glistened and winked, like sentient eyes, and imagined they sent mysterious messages meant for her alone, though she could not fathom what they would say to an insignificant child. Her concentration was so intense that she almost forgot to listen to the hum of conversation coming from the house.

Her mother said, "It's late, Jervase. Let's get going."

"Righto, Juney," replied Matilda's father and scraped back his chair.

But Uncle Tom wasn't ready to release his guests yet. He said, "How about one for the road, eh?"

Matilda heard the edge of a bottle strike the lip of a glass, followed by the measured gurgle of liquor.

"You two are hopeless," June Craddock said. "It's a wonder you can still stand up."

The Craddock brothers cackled evilly.

"Where is she?" said June Craddock.

"Where's who?" said her husband.

"Your daughter," replied his wife.

"Dunno. Outside, probably."

The question broke Matilda's musings. She stood and smoothed her dress. The skipping rope tightened its grip on her wrist and fed its fleshy substance into the main artery until the entire length vanished in her arm. It wouldn't do to let her parents see. They would never understand. Matilda passed through the back door into the kitchen. Her uncle's house was a basic soldier settlement farm, sat in the middle of wattle and stringy bark scrub.

Matilda's father looked up from his glass and cried, "Here she is." He pulled his daughter close and said, "Sleepy?"

Matilda shook her head, more to clear the alcohol fumes that encircled the table than to answer the question.

Her mother said, "Jervase, let's go." She scooped up the playing cards strewn on the table and secured them with an elastic band. "We've got a long day tomorrow." She stood up and, out of habit, began to clear the table.

"Put on your cardie. It'll be chilly out," she said without looking at Matilda. She piled glasses and several plates in the sink. "Are you going be all right?" she said to her brother-in-law. "We can stay the night if you want." Though there was hesitancy in her voice.

"I'm fine," Tom Craddock replied, rising to his feet. "I'll have to get used to being on me own from here on."

June Craddock gave him a pat on the back as though she were burping a baby and said, "Come a little early tomorrow. Maybe around lunch time, before they arrive."

Tom Craddock nodded, though he was none too sure about the prospect of the solitary life that loomed before him now that his wife Primrose was gone.

Jervase Craddock pushed away from the table and stood. He swayed on his feet before saying, "Juney, you get the hurricane lamp. I'll saddle up the horse."

June Craddock whirled round. "No, you don't. You're not fit to tie your shoelaces, let alone go near a horse. I don't want another death on my hands. I'll do it. You can light the lamp. The wick is new and I filled it up earlier."

In a few short minutes June Craddock returned with a stringy chestnut mare. Jervase Craddock hoisted his daughter on the animal's back and told her to sit tight. The night was dark as a feather on a crow's back. The sky formed a bejeweled dome over the house and pressed on the land an infinity of stars, galaxies, Nebulae.

"You walk ahead with the lamp so we can see where we're going," June Craddock said, shoving her husband between the shoulder blades. "Make yourself useful."

Jervase Craddock faced his brother and said, "See ya tomorrow."

Tom Craddock nodded and leaned against the veranda post until his brother's family passed through the gate and entered the unfettered country beyond.

Home for Jervase Craddock and his family was almost three miles away. The dirt track nudged the edge of the forest. Although there was no wind, the she-oaks made ghost-like sibilant noises to the right. Matilda loved the sound in the day and often lay under the trees to listen to their talk; but she dreaded to think what secrets they exchanged at night, what plots they hatched behind her back. Astride the horse, she focussed on the light that came from the lamp in her father's raised hand. Jervase Craddock was first in line; his wife followed close behind, holding on to the horse with its precious cargo.

Some time later the path dipped down to a noisy creek.

Without turning her head, June Craddock said, "Don't fall off, Missy."

Matilda wedged the remains of her hands between the horn and rise in the saddle—not that she needed to; a slender flexible appendage emerged from both wrists to bind her to the seat, bolting her to the saddle. The horse couldn't throw her even if it took off.

The fingers and thumbs on Matilda's hands had been cleanly sheared off at the second knuckle. It happened so long ago that Matilda could not remember a time when she did not have the full use of her hands. Possibly she had been born like that—the way George Marshall's boy was born with twisted arms and legs.

31

The horse clattered across the creek. Soon after, the family emerged from the hollow on to the plain. Even so, the fireflies that lived beside the creek and filled the surface of the water with light refused to leave Matilda alone. They pranced round her head and spread to the lower branches of trees until the world was festooned with blinking lights. Matilda smiled and gazed in wonder.

The lamp in Jervase Craddock's hand threw light on a lone grave under a stout gum tree. A bunch of daisies wilted on the freshly dug mound. Matilda forgot about the fireflies and turned her attention on her aunt's final resting place. It was peculiar to think of Primrose Craddock under the earth. It did not make sense. So very deep under. The dry soil, filled with crawling things and trailing roots of plants. It's no place for a human being. The funeral, such as it was, had taken place that morning. Matilda had stood at the edge of the grave and looked down at the makeshift coffin and it seemed to her that it was being cast in a hungry maw that could chew up her aunt and spit her out, clean of skin, gleaming with bone.

June Craddock sighed and stopped in her tracks. The horse with Matilda on its back came to a halt behind her.

"Stupid woman," she said, shaking her head. "Stupid, stupid woman."

When the news broke about Primrose Craddock's sudden demise, Uncle Tom had told Matilda that his wife had gone to sleep and never woke up. This rare sign of sensitivity and consideration on the part of her uncle was misplaced. Matilda was no fool. She didn't believe him for a minute. There was no doubt in her mind there was a shattered body inside the rectangular box. It would never walk or talk again. Even so, Matilda hoped that Uncle Tom's melancholy wife had gone to a better place in the end.

June Craddock told her husband to wait and walked to her sister-in-law's grave. Her husband let off an exasperated sigh and, lifting the lamp higher, peered at his wife's back. June Craddock stood beside the grave, a strand of dark-brown hair streaming behind her in the breeze that sprang up and rushed through the treetops. The sound travelled from the topmost branches down to the wildflowers that sprout upon the ground. In no time at all, the world was filled with a malevolent hissing and thrashing of plant-life.

Alarmed, Matilda wrapped her finger stumps round the tentacle that held her to the saddle. It congealed in her hand to the consistency and texture of wood and she used it to rap sharply against the saddle's hardened leather. For some reason, she wanted to warn her mother. All it did was frighten the horse. It threw back its head and whinnied.

After a respectful couple of minutes, June Craddock returned to her husband's side.

"Let's go."

"What was that about?" he asked.

"Paying my last respects, stupid cow that she was. I'll never understand it, or forgive her for doing it."

They set off. The open valley fell behind. Trees closed in again, blocking the wind, hemming in the path that made a steady course for home.

"She's only got herself to blame," Jervase Craddock said after a lengthy silence. His big strong hand gleamed in the lamplight, the hair on his knuckles clearly defined.

"The point is," his wife uttered, "she was your brother's wife and my sister-in-law. It's right to mourn the dead."

"No one forced her to do herself in."

"She couldn't cope; didn't understand. That's all."

Her husband chuckled darkly, but with affection. "We're not all as tough as you, love."

"She just couldn't deal with what we do for a crust," June answered thickly. "I knew she wouldn't even try to understand when she found out. That's why I didn't want her to be involved from the start."

"Yeah, but fancy throwing yourself off a cliff... Imagine finding that— "

June Craddock cast a wary eye on her daughter.

Matilda pretended to be absorbed in the fireflies that continued to swarm round her head, making her resemble the Queen of

Heaven. She knew Aunt Primrose killed herself by jumping off the cliffs that surround Starve Crow. It was a big fall, too. Like leaping off the edge of the world.

"You know what her problem was?"

June Craddock didn't want to know, but she was sure her husband was going to tell her anyway.

"She was mad. She believed all that crap about things living in the hills. You and me, we dish that bulldust out for the sake of the disciples, but Prim believed it. She was off with the fairies." He drew on his cigarette. "Tom shouldn't have married her. Blacks are trouble. She wasn't all there, I tell you." He blew a plume of smoke in the air to punctuate his statement.

His wife backed him up: "Times are tough. You do what you have to do to survive."

"Where there's demand, there's supply."

"If we don't do it, someone else will." June hoped that was the end of the conversation.

But Jervase wasn't finished. "Didn't she know we're in the middle of a depression? The money we make out of our little business put food on her table as well as ours. Maybe she preferred to starve, or eat Witchetty grubs?"

Husband and wife laughed, shook their heads, as if some people are beyond understanding.

Several minutes passed before June Craddock said, "The irony is we wouldn't be doing any of this if it weren't for Prim. She knew about the altar and what it'd been used for. If it wasn't for her, you would have tossed it out with the rest of the garbage in the basement."

"True enough," her husband conceded. "That rock is the best prop we've got."

"Yep. No altar, no disciples. No disciples, no money," June said, rubbing her forefinger against her thumb.

Jervase Craddock snorted. "Disciples my foot," he said. "More like a bunch of perves."

"Ach," June Craddock uttered, "they haven't a shilling's worth of sense between them."

"You know why?"

"Nope."

"They think with their pricks and not their brains," Jervase hooted, giving her a kiss on the cheek.

"And that's fine with me," June said, linking her arm to his. "That's just fine with me."

Husband and wife pressed towards each other and continued to walk as though they were lovers taking a solitary walk in the forest.

There were no houses along this stretch of road. Matilda knew that she and her parents were alone. Should anything happen, no one would have an inkling. The further they walked, the deeper the sense of isolation. The night, the immense silence, closed in like a trap, surrounding the travellers until they and the flimsy bubble of light in which they walked appeared to float in space.

Matilda tensed up on the horse. She had a sense that something stood far back in the woods, watching. The realisation tightened every muscle in her body. Her head turned to the left, then to the right, as though she were a bat using sonar to track down her quarry. She cast out her mind and, by degrees, became aware of the thing that waited farther back in the trees, pacing its movements with the light that bobbed on the road. She couldn't bear to look directly at it. She only sensed its presence and caught occasional glimpses as it flitted between tree trunks with astonishing speed. It was as though it flew or glided, long tendrils reaching out from the body to wrap round trees and pull it along, several feet above ground.

Matilda knew it waited for someone to step out of the light— for a moment. Then it would pounce.

"Gotta take a leak," Jervase Craddock said. He handed the lamp to his wife and wandered into the bush. He didn't hear the whine his daughter made in her throat, or if he did he ignored it.

Matilda leaped off the horse and raced after him, wailing.

June Craddock placed the hurricane lamp on the ground and grabbed her.

"Wait on. Do you want to pee as well?"

Matilda shook her head and pointed at her father, eyes wide with fear.

June Craddock held on. "He'll be back in a sec. Calm yourself."

Matilda shook her head again and struggled in her mother's arms. June held on. The daughter flailed and kicked.

"What's the matter with you? Listen, he's taking a piss. He'll be ba—"

She didn't finish the sentence. The air was torn asunder by a horrific scream.

June Craddock had been married to Jervase for twelve years. They'd been through a lot together. She knew he was nowhere near as tough as he ought to be. But in all that time, she had never heard such exultant terror in his voice. She called his name and turned to dash after him. Matilda wrapped her arms round her mother's waist and held on with all her strength, shaking her head and making a rasping croak in her throat, eyes wide with alarm.

June Craddock yelled, "Let go," and pushed her daughter aside. Matilda fell but managed to wraps both her arms round her mother's left ankle. The screaming in the bush intensified to an unbearable pitch. The panic, the sheer fright of it barely sounded human. Birds clattered out of trees and there was loathsome recoil in the air, as if the atmosphere was disturbed and vibrating to an unknown song.

June Craddock shouted again, "Let go," and delivered a sharp kick to Matilda's head with the heel of her boot. Matilda collapsed in the dust. June ran into the dark, calling her husband's name. In her haste she forgot the hurricane lantern.

Matilda rose to her feet and tried to hook the stumps of two fingers through the metal ring at the top of the lantern. It was in vain. There wasn't enough flesh and bone to grasp the ring. She almost wailed with frustration. As though sensing her helplessness, a fleshy hook slid from her left wrist and attached to the lamp. Matilda hurried after her mother, light tilting madly at her feet.

Jervase Craddock's screams had been replaced by a wet gurgling that reminded Matilda of an overflowing drain in a storm.

In all her years Matilda had not wanted to speak, never

wanted to relate what she saw and thought to anyone. But she wished for a voice now. She wanted to call, 'Stop Mum. Don't go. You're safe in the light. It's too late for Dad.' Yet nothing came out except the lowing of a pathetic cow. She despised herself. She wished she were dead.

Matilda became aware that she couldn't see her mother. She wiped blood from her eyes and listened. Her forehead throbbed where her mother kicked her. She heard June's bulk push through the undergrowth to the right. Matilda raised the lantern and peered in the dark. Her mother was ahead, struggling through the undergrowth. From nearby came the sound of water pelting the ground in a torrent. It looked to Matilda as if her mother was running toward a waterfall. On second thoughts it didn't sound like water at all. It was too luxuriantly thick and creamy for that, full of spattering globules. Matilda heard her father make a final choked stammer, lavish with agony and torment. There came a terrible breaking sound, like a bundle of twigs snapping in two. The silence that fell was worse than the preceding noise.

June Craddock stood with her back to her daughter. A pale gum loomed in front of her and the light, as Matilda approached from behind, threw dancing shadows over the grisly scene. Jervase Craddock had been sliced in half at the waist. The chest was open and blood covered the ground. The gore was a sleek, satiny black, a lustrous steaming alloy that coated rock and grass and tree in shimmering striations. Most surprising was a severed hand that gripped an impossibly high branch and dripped red in a viscous trail along the length of the tree trunk. And it seemed to Matilda that the ground, the very soil, lapped up her father's blood with insatiable lips.

Matilda stepped closer to her mother. She did not dare touch the woman. She did not dare breathe for fear of disturbing her. For the time being it was enough to keep her mother safe in the light.

June Craddock was a tough, practical woman, a roll-up-your-sleeves country type. She lived life with pig-headed determination and performed her tasks with fanatical commitment. Life was about survival, the business of getting from one day to the next without succumbing to hardship. There was nothing else. In all her years she never wavered from that singular mission. These qualities made her invaluable to the Craddock brothers and saw her triumph where others failed. She wasn't one to break up and cry that's for sure.

She faced her daughter. "Let's get out of here," she said. Her voice was final, steely. But she stumbled more than once in the scrub and leaned on Matilda for support.

When they joined the mare on the forest path June Craddock said, "Hold on a minute."

Matilda turned to her mother, blinking tears out of her eyes and doing her best not to wail.

"Do we go back to Tom's or do we keep going to our place?" June Craddock asked.

It was a sign of indecision Matilda had not seen before. Her mother was definitely rattled.

Matilda pointed the way ahead. It made sense to go home. At this stage they were closer to their own house than Uncle Tom's farm. It was safer, faster, to go home. In the morning they'd come back to collect her father's body, if the animals didn't get to it first.

June Craddock glared at Matilda. And before Matilda could see it coming, June slapped her daughter hard across the face. For the second time that night, Matilda fell to the ground. The hurricane lamp tumbled from her hand. The light gutted and went out. Blackness fell on the scene. June Craddock pounced on her daughter and grabbed her by the throat.

"You useless cunt," she cried. "This happened because of you. This is your fault. You know who did this, don't you? The bloke from Bendigo, that's who. He did this to Jervase. He wouldn't have done it if you'd let him screw you. He followed us and he killed my husband, just like he said he would. It's your fault. You killed my mate…the only thing I…" June's voice broke. "You took him from me." She raved and squeezed, bashing Matilda's head to the ground. "But oh no you were too sore. What good are you? Whore. Can't even do that properly."

Matilda didn't fight back. Her mother was right. It was her

fault. She was to blame. She should have let the man from Bendigo put his thing in her during last month's ceremony.

Matilda remembered the disastrous gathering. Rituals were held the first Thursday of the month in the basement of her house, well away from prying eyes. Worshippers gathered from three o'clock onwards. They encircled the altar and stood naked beneath their long grey robes until her father lit candles and performed a cleansing ceremony. It was meant to appease the 'Sleepers in the Hills' before the disciples got down to the business of purifying their bodies for the coming resurrection. On that particular day, however, they'd been interrupted. For some reason, Aunt Primrose came to the house and finally discovered what went on in the underground room. She went berserk when she saw a man on top of Matilda. She screamed and pummeled the man, until her husband Tom hit her in the face and told her to shut up. That quieted her, but she refused to let them continue with 'this blasphemy,' as she put it, 'this evil'. Through tears, she declared her disgust with what was going on, the ugly usage of a child. To make matters worse, it happened in front of the gathering. That was very silly of her. Uncle Tom hadn't wasted a moment. He dragged his wife upstairs and 'kicked the shit out of her,' as he later told his brother and sister-in-law over a beer.

Matilda heard the assault take place upstairs as she lay on the stone altar in the basement. She had been so upset that, try as she might, she couldn't play her usual part in the ceremony. She was very sore after the second man. And four more waited their turn. Even so, Matilda tried not to complain. She knew the family relied on her to make money, and that the men who travelled from all over the state to possess for a few vital minutes a precious miracle, which, they claimed, prepared their weak flesh for the day when 'the Sleepers' stepped forth from the portal between her nine-year-old legs. Nevertheless, Matilda cried out and turned away her face when the third man — the one from Bendigo — climbed atop her. He had been angered by the girl's behaviour. He claimed it was an insult to the gods and showed disrespect for the ritual. He wanted his money back or else. Jervase Craddock refused. "Once money exchanges hands, mate, that's it," he said. "Now bugger off, the lot o'ya. She's crook."

All the same, the man who didn't get his money's worth had been furious. He'd come a long way, he said, and now he was supposed to go without being purified? No way. He'd get his own back, he threatened. Just you wait and see…

But Matilda knew that the disgruntled disciple from Bendigo did not kill her father. It was the thing in the forest.

By now Matilda's face was blue. Her beautiful green eyes bulged from the sockets; eyes she kept shut while grown men pressed her skin, and while mum and dad collected cash from the punters. Matilda's tongue protruded from her mouth. She gasped for air, clawed the dirt. Her mother's enraged face loomed over her. The hard, calloused hands clasped the tender throat. The fingers squeezed tight as she throttled the life out of the 'cash cow,' as Uncle Tom laughingly called his niece.

"Are you a cash cow, Matilda? Are you our cash cow, little girl? Come over here and give us a kiss. There you go. Don't go growing up too fast. We need you. Aunty Prim can't have a baby to replace you. Her womb is barren as the Nullabor."

Matilda nodded and smiled and did as she was told. She loved her mum and dad. She adored her uncle and aunt. She put all her trust in them. They looked after her and she wanted to do right by them. Always. And so the men congregated every month in the basement.

Matilda's eyes rolled back in her head. Only the whites were visible. Spittle dribbled from her mouth. It felt as if her body belonged to someone else. By the minute she was weightless and far away. Floating. Outside her body. Outside the world. It was nice. No fear. No pain. And it didn't hurt so much, this not being able to breathe. Her lungs bursting, throat bulging. And still her mother squeezed. Saliva and tears dripped from her on to Matilda's face.

Matilda's breath came in harsh gasps. Her fingers loosened and the skipping rope slipped out of her wrist. No one noticed when it slithered snake-like away from the mortal combat of mother and daughter. Then everything changed. June Craddock gasped and her grip on Matilda's throat relaxed. She jerked violently back and away from her daughter's prone body, falling hard on her backside. Matilda sat up, coughing and retching, her head spinning. She opened her eyes and saw the skipping rope coil swiftly several times round her mother's neck. Nothing and no one held it. It had life of its own. Then, with an appalling shriek, her mother's body was hoisted up into the sky. Matilda saw June's dark outline, like a cutout doll, rise up against a background of stars. Higher and higher in the firmament she went, until it seemed she was a witch in flight. It was almost beautiful to see. When the body stopped the upward ascent, Matilda saw that it hung by the neck from the highest branch in a tree, the feet kicking pitiably. Matilda gasped. A pall spread from her mother's body to obscure the stars, the moon and the sky. It resembled a storm cloud in February. Then it swarmed down and engulfed her.

When sense returned, Matilda lay at the base of the stairs in her house. Sunlight flooded the grimy windows. Unearthly quiet ruled the world. She sat up and rubbed her eyes. It had been a bad dream. Yes, she will go upstairs and check on her mum and dad. No doubt they are in bed, asleep. She will scrounge together breakfast in the kitchen and take it upstairs for them to enjoy. But why was the front door open and why was she on the floor? A sound caught her attention: footsteps on the floor above.

Here comes Mum, Matilda thought. She'll know what's going on.

Matilda turned and knew from the gasp that escaped her throat that it had not been a nightmare. It had been real, and it was not over.

Aunt Primrose stood at the top of the stairs.

Had he been present, Tom Craddock would not recognise his wife in her current state. In life Primrose Craddock had been a paltry figure, insubstantial, inconsequential. She had been plain, easily forgotten. Death had transformed her almost beyond recognition. Like a sculptor working on putrescent flesh, the Dark

Angel had wrought a creation from beyond the stars, a soaring elongated column of radiant pitch. Had she been carved from darkest obsidian Primrose could not have been more beautiful, more bewitching and more terrifying. Her allure as she stood at the top of the stairs, staring down at her niece, was devastating. She drew the eye and repelled it simultaneously. She was a mirror whose radiance possessed a moon-like coldness. It sucked in light and rejected warmth. She was utterly alien. As she came down the stairs, everything melted round her. The house vanished. The wooden steps and banister were gone. Matilda held her breath. She stood in outer space as her aunt drew closer and closer, sparkling and crackling as unseen particles struck her skin. Where the long hair ought to be, Matilda noticed, was a series of twitching, twisting feelers, stiff tactile barbs and sensory organs with pulpy mouths and suckers. The woman had no legs. She slithered. Half a dozen elongated appendages covered her lower half and propelled her forward in rapid flowing movements.

Matilda had liked her aunt's inelegance; there was something safe and comforting about it. Before this disquieting vision she was humbled, shy, uncertain. She rose to her feet and stared with reverence. That's when she noticed that the entity (for she could no longer think of the stellar being as homely Aunt Primrose) was carrying something.

A glass jar rested in the palm of each hand and as the creature approached, liquid moved thickly inside the containers. One jar appeared to contain pale asparagus spears and the other chunky pink fruit.

Primrose stood in front of her niece. She smiled and in that instant outer space vanished. The room reappeared as if it were a curtain drawn across a stage to block out the vast cosmos. Reality snapped back in place, exactly as it had been. The creature placed the jars on a small occasional table by the staircase.

"My little love," she said, bending down and placing an ice-cold finger on Matilda's begrimed lips. "Your salvation is at hand. Everything will be all right." Neither male nor female, the voice had two tones: a bass and a treble that melded and clashed, weaving in and out of each other to create uncanny music.

Primrose dipped her hand in one jar and placed the peculiar pink fruit in her mouth. Then she leaned forward and kissed Matilda on the forehead. Matilda closed her eyes and breathed in the earthy aroma that came from the thing's skin. Lips moved from Matilda's forehead to the bridge of her nose. There to linger briefly before sealing Matilda's lips with a firm kiss.

In her nine years of life Matilda had known many a grizzled kiss from hoary men. None had been as tender and passionate as this. She opened her own mouth and allowed the creature's tongue to enter and probe. A rigid insistent object pushed into Matilda's mouth. She choked, spluttered, attempted to cry out, tried to withdraw; but the thing had locked its mouth to Matilda's so that they were welded to one another. Feelers, tentacles and claws kept the child in place. Matilda fought to free herself, eyes wide, beating the thing on the shoulders; muffled cries escaping from round their bonded lips. She became aware of a paralysing coldness in her mouth; and when Primrose pulled back and stood smiling icily, Matilda cried out:

"Stop, stop. You're hurting me."

She stared. Who had spoken? Surely that had not been her. Yet the words had emerged from behind her teeth. A tongue that had not been there previously moved inside the cavity in her head.

"Who said that?"

"You did."

"Me?"

"You, my little love."

Matilda waggled the tongue inside her mouth. It was too big, too awkward and invasive. Yet it allowed her to produce words for the first time in memory.

Wonderstruck, she said: "I've grown a tongue."

"Until last night the tongue belonged to Jervase Craddock. Since he saw fit to cut out your tongue, the least he can do is allow you the use of his. He won't need it anymore," Primrose added when she saw the look of horror on Matilda's face.

Primrose gave one of her gelid smiles and picked up the other jar from the table. "Sit. It's time to restore the fingers that were so cruelly taken from you."

Matilda sat on the second stair. Extending a tentacle, Primrose pulled over a chair and sat opposite her niece in the oblong of sunlight streaming through the open door. She produced thread and needle and, one by one, proceeded to sew the ten fingers that floated inside the second jar to the end of Matilda's hands.

Matilda recognised her mother's gold wedding ring on one finger and the scar on the left forefinger where June Craddock accidentally cut herself with a knife not six weeks ago.

Like the tongue in her mouth, the fingers were too big for Matilda's hand. They were wrong. But it didn't matter. No sooner did the creature finish sewing one finger to Matilda's hand then it began to move of its own accord, like an octopus eager for something to clutch.

The seamstress spoke as she worked.

"Once upon a time, there was a little girl. Her name was Matilda. She was the prettiest, most darling child in the world. Everyone admired her green eyes and flaxen hair. But no more so than her parents, Jervase and June Craddock.

"Jervase Craddock and his brother Tom came to this valley after the Great War. The government had given Tom Craddock a soldier settlement, but there was no such kindness for the cowardly older brother. Jervase had spent most of the war years hiding in the mountains. When Jervase Craddock and his wife June decided to squat in this house," Primrose's eyes roamed ceiling, walls, floor, "it had been empty for a long time.

"Soon after, a gorgeous little girl was bestowed upon the couple. As she grew older, stories about her uncanny beauty spread. People went out of their way to stop at the porch and admire her. They said her loveliness was beyond belief, haunting.

"One day, while clearing the basement of the old house, Jervase Craddock chanced upon a peculiar object—a large white rock, covered with mysterious hieroglyphs. Jervase didn't know it, of course," Primrose said, "but this was the heart of the great and winding snake. He fell to earth in the beginning time. His body shattered. The sun bleached his heart and turned it to white rock with his story written on it in a language no one could speak or understand. The great snake is the creator of all there is to see. He is the end of all seeking. Break the code of the stone and you open a doorway for him and all the others like him to return."

Primrose revealed stories of a secret cult that existed many years earlier. "White men all—a good dozen—who still lived hereabouts until a few years ago," she added to her rapt audience. "A man called Walter Whiteley found the altar. He bought the land and built a house atop it. On certain nights he and the disciples went down the basement to talk to the Ancients. But it was a sick, twisted calling. They were playing with fire and did not know it."

The story thrilled Matilda. So much was making sense. So many little questions were being answered. It was funny and scary at the same time.

"Primrose, the former owner of this body, told Jervase and June about the stone. Once they discovered its secret history, they had their pretext. What they'd been looking for all along. They could now open for business.

"The husband put out the word. First came one and then another. At first curious and cautious and only after dark, when the moon had set and shadow lay thick upon the ground; and then in a more daring fashion, during the day. They all came with money. They all craved one thing: to see the famed altar and to possess upon its surface the four-year-old child with green eyes."

Matilda tilted her head.

"Did the altar make them?"

Primrose looked up with a smile.

"Not entirely. Some things lie deep inside a man's heart. So deep and buried that even he may not know it exists. All it takes is for one small thing to bring it to the surface and he will give it free reign." Primrose removed a finger from the jar and continued.

"Word spread. The defilement upon the small child's body continued. One day Matilda's mother said, 'She's getting older.

The law might hear of it. We're done for if she talks. Cut out her tongue.'

"And so, when the girl was almost five and about to enter school, Jervase cut out her tongue with a pair of shears from the barn. It was a miracle Matilda did not die. Business went on as usual. A year or so later the mother said, 'She can't talk, but she can write. What if she writes a note? Chop off her fingers.'

"Jervase held Matilda down while her mother put the little hand on the chopping block and chop-chopped off her fingers with a hatchet. Finally, they had the perfect moneymaker. The girl couldn't talk and she couldn't write, but she could be of service.

"The father convinced his brother Tom to get in on the act. It didn't take much to convince him. He's a bad lot, in some ways worse than his older brother."

Primrose stopped, reached in the jar, removed another finger and continued the tale.

"Tom Craddock's wife, Primrose, did not know what went on in the basement, but she had her suspicions. That's why they kept her away and she was not involved."

Ah, Matilda thought, now we're coming to the interesting bit. Her entire being tingled with excitement.

"Do you know who the Elder Things are?" Primrose asked.

Matilda almost shook her head. Then, remembering her voice, said, "No."

When the creature spoke again it sounded as if several different voices came out of its mouth. "We are the forgone conclusion, whisperers in the Dark Bower. Older than the earth that harbours us in water, air and rock, we are supreme, all encompassing. We are shredders of reality. The eagle on the wing. The cat on the prowl. The breath in the fossil. We live inside hills and wait…"

Next came a crystal note, an utterly feminine voice: "Did you know that Walter Whiteley succeeded in opening the door to the Elder Things?"

Matilda was content to merely shake her head.

"Indeed he did. And do you know what else, my little love?"

The thing that was less and less like Primrose Craddock every minute, rubbed noses with Matilda.

Delighted, Matilda giggled.

"What?"

"You are not your father's daughter." Primrose laughed and clapped her hands, delighted, as if she had told the funniest joke at someone else's expense. "Jervase Craddock had nothing to do with you. His seed was infertile. On the first day of September nine years ago, The Wordless Voice—He who was born without a father—seeded June Craddock. In the throes of passion, the god slipped between Jervase and June and beget himself a daughter fair…"

"Oh," Matilda said, finally catching on.

Primrose was down to two fingers. The thread and needle passed in and out of Matilda's skin, painlessly stitching June Craddock's hard-working fingers to Matilda's undersized hand, one by one, snick-snick went the scissors on the black thread. When the manicurist finished, she leaned back and admired her handiwork.

"Beautiful," she said. "You are complete. Now you can go into the world a picture of loveliness. Remember two things. Always wear black gloves. And never forget that the tongue and fingers will last the passage of one full moon. Then they will go the way of all flesh and must be replaced with a fresh tongue and fresh fingers. Do you understand?"

"Yes," Matilda replied, delighting in the word. "Yes, I do."

This time there was real warmth in Primrose's smile.

"When the disciples gather this afternoon," she said, "don't kill them all at once. Imprison them in the basement and take them one by one at your will. Then you will be sure to have a ready supply of tongues and fingers in the pantry. Keep the spare ones in this solution." She tapped a jar.

"Will do."

Primrose returned her niece's smile. "Time to get ready for Uncle Tom," she said. "He will soon be here, my little love."

What a dump, Tom Craddock thought. What a disgrace.

He spat his disgust at the dry grass. It was high noon. He stood outside his brother's house and shook his head. How had the best house in Starve Crow become the district's biggest eyesore?

The old Whiteley house, a run-down Victorian gothic revival erected at the end of the nineteenth century, had been empty for well on a decade. It wasn't big but it was smart. A weatherboard and brick confection, it boasted two floors and shady verandas front and back. Locals called it the Crooked House, for the simple reason that the edifice was sinking into the ground; or, more accurately, into the basement. The descent caused the bricks to split, the wood to warp and the house to tilt wildly to one side, so that looking at it was a matter of leaning your head to the left and adjusting your vision to suit the skewed perspective. It gave the place an awry feel, as if things weren't right with the world.

As Tom stepped on the front porch, he noted that the shutters over the windows were closed. So was the usually open front door. The total absence of sound struck him. Nothing. Not even his sister-in-law's wireless, or the scratching of chickens. It made him uneasy. Still it was nothing compared to the god-awful silence he endured in the marital bed last night. He didn't want to go through that again. For all her faults, his wife Primrose had been a warm, reassuring presence. He'd grown used to her.

He knocked on the begrimed glass set in the front door and, as was his habit, walked in without waiting for an answer. He passed from room to room. Saw no one.

"Hello," he called. "Anyone here?" His voice echoed in the empty house.

"Down here." The husky male voice sounded like his brother Jervase.

Tom Craddock came down the stairs, ducked at the last minute to avoid a low beam, and entered the basement.

Matilda was alone. Dressed in a handsome black dress, she sat primly on the altar, feet dangling, hands clasped delicately in her lap. A flickering candle lit the gloomy scene. June and Jervase were nowhere in sight.

"Where's your mum and dad?"

He expected no reply.

"Are they out?"

Matilda smiled and looked at him from under her eyelashes.

A grin spread on Tom's face. Hel-lo, he thought. The slut wants me.

He always knew—hoped—it would come to this.

He walked up to his niece and stood over her, looked in her eyes, bit his lip. Then he kneeled and brought his face to her eye level.

"Got something for Uncle Tom?" he said deliberately.

Matilda nodded. Then, with one swift movement, she lifted her skirt and displayed her prize.

Tom sucked in a breath, placed his hands on her knees and leaned forward.

"What have we here?"

An eye opened between the girl's legs and stared at him. Tom Craddock managed a "What the fuck?" before a frenzy of tentacles leaped out of Matilda's groin and attached to his face. His screams were muffled by the appendages that swarmed in his mouth and poured down his throat. A flexible limb tightened round his throat and with the tumultuous wriggling of a squid, more waxen limbs streamed up his nostrils and into his ears. He was lifted bodily from the ground. As he rose into the air, he looked at his niece's face and saw that the attributes of a normal face had been obliterated. In their place flitted the features of his wife and then his niece; his brother and his sister-in-law featured in rapid succession. The faces shot by like images in a flick book, overlapped, merged, formed, reformed and inexorably slowed until Matilda's face coalesced into a semblance of itself. Only now she possessed four mouths in descending order, from forehead to chin. All were lined with sharp, evil-looking teeth. Then a tentacle scooped out Tom Craddock's eyeballs and squirmed into the empty sockets. In the darkness that fell he heard his dearly departed wife say: "Be careful with his tongue, *my little love.*"

WIFE TO MR LOVECRAFT

LUCY SUSSEX

[Found written upon a series of postcards, mainly of South Sea Scenes, c. 1930s, never apparently sent. They were discovered in a San Jose thrift shop]

1. A Tropical Volcano

Dear How,

I meant to write Howard, but got interrupted, as happens. When I came back 'How' looked just fine on the page. It summed us up. Like: How did we ever get married? Blame the words, what we said and wrote to each other, the only thing we had in common. How did we ever think we would work it out? Those words again, mixed with pure blind optimism. How did we part? Without pain, as it should be.

I meant to write you before with my news, but time just runs away sometimes. You did file the divorce papers? [crossed through]. I am now Mrs Doctor Nathaniel Davis. Life sure is something else in LA. See, now I can talk like the natives, but then women always are mimics. I don't do Amateur Press anymore, nor other writing. Nate is a fan of golf, and bridge parties. With different folks—or as the people down here say, blokes—different strokes.

2. Warriors in an Outrigger Canoe

Nate is also a fan of cruises, South Seas this time. He has family in the shipping industry. Remember those postcards I sent you from Europe? These postcards aren't so much your kind of thing, but then neither am I, not any more. Nate asked me to cook kosher, just like my Grandmom did in the shtetl back in Russia. Lucky I can remember the recipes. I never cooked like that for you.

Still, you might get some story ideas from the photos. The volcano is in Hawaii. The canoe full of warriors is from Tahiti, as is the dancer in the grass skirt. They all look fine folk, as if they lead a good life—like I do now.

3. Tropical Island, with Port in Background

We're in Australia now, where Nate studied medicine. Also where those cute kangaroos come from. Like we saw in Central Park zoo, remember that? You said they looked deformed. The island is called Magnetic, because it sent an explorer's compass wonky. If I was still writing for *Weird Tales* I'd use that. Instead I gift it to you. Tomorrow we go fishing on the Barrier Reef, wonder of the world, so-called. I am also told it should be blown up, as it wrecks ships. There's a story in that too.

4. Dancer in Grass Skirt

She looks so happy in her grass skirt and shell necklace. I grinned just like that when I dove into the warm reef water in my new bathing suit. The corals look like some fancy garden in the sea, but not King Neptune's, nor one of your old gods either. Every time I breathed an air bubble and it shot towards the surface it seemed I lost more of my old, unregretted life. Goodbye Russia and its pogroms, goodbye grimy Liverpool, goodbye Brooklyn hatshops. I lolled in a deckchair wearing my raffia hat and shell earrings, and read the only book on board, some murderous

English lady called Christie. Not your sort of thing either. She needs a sea monster or two.

5. Fishermen with Marlin

Nate hadn't caught anything, but when he pulled up his line, there came with it a mass of heavy pulpy red. It clung to the bait, spitting water at us. If you thought a kangaroo looked deformed then this creature was a transmogrification. See, I can still do obscure English words! It had tentacles, or stubs of limbs, and one staring gold eye, with a slot of a pupil, like a goat's. Nate slapped it down on the deck, where it promptly performed some sort of chameleon change, from angry red to decking colour. The crew and us visitors just goggled. Nobody had seen the like before, they said, nobody wanted to try it as tucker (food), and yet nobody wanted to kill it. There was something weirdly cute about it, like you get with kittens or pups. When I thought that, I remembered our baby, that story we wrote together, about horror on Martin's Beach. I said: "Throw it back, it's a juvenile."

6. Conch shells and Tongans

But the other charter fisherman on board said it must be new to science. He wanted to show it to some biologist back at Townsville (sounds to me like a tautology). So two crewmen who were called Karnaks, or Blackbirds (they looked Tongan to me, see verso), got told off to force it into a barrel with some seawater. That was a battle, but finally they had it kegged. The light was going down by then, and so we puttered off to a little island for the night. There was a guesthouse there, but mostly we lounged on the beach by a driftwood fire. The crew cooked up the fish caught on the reef, and served us beer and coconut wine. At the edge of the waves the phosphorescence shone blue, like neon lace.

7. Tongan Warrior Dancing

The fish was the finest I ever ate, but I could only nibble at it, and barely drink. The Karnaks danced in the firelight, beautifully, but I couldn't think of anything but the Martin's Beach story. When we discussed the idea, that night we first kissed, I said: "Beowulf!" You were so surprised. I'd read it in the Olde English, which is practically German, and cognate to Yiddish. We ripped off Grendel's mother, and sold it to *Weird Tales*. Not that I could tell anyone on the beach. Which was worse, confessing to having three husbands, or reading Germanic poetry, or writing for pulp magazines?

8. South Sea beach, with Turtles, Inverted

The coconut wine made everyone paralytic, and I mean that literally. Only the sober walked, or carried the drinkers to the beachhouse. I lay beside Nate, listening to the thatch creak and the waves soughing. No way could I sleep, and after a while I got up and dressed. Outside on the beach, the moon shone, and the fire had reduced to embers. Nothing was in sight but still I had the creepy feeling of being watched. The ship's dinghy was still bobbing at its anchor at the low tide mark. I waded out to it, and rowed for the ship. I had the sense of being watched, and in my mind was a line of people, being drawn slowly into the sea. I didn't want that happening on this Tropical Island, or elsewhere. I needed to stop it.

9. Nature Morte Arrangement of Coral

On the ship, I found the barrel by stumbling over it. It lay on its side on the deck and from the chunks of wood and splinters I guessed either someone had taken an axe to it, or whatever was within had busted out. I couldn't see the creature anywhere, then out of my eye I glimpsed a slow movement. A silhouette uncoiled from the darkness, and I recognised one of the Karnaks: the cabin boy, left to mind the ship. He gestured to me, finger on mouth, and I nodded back at him. His eyes gleamed in the moonlight, and I saw he was watching something on the deck. I tried to follow his gaze, and again could only discern the presence in the darkness when it moved. The creature was inching itself awkwardly across the deck, towards the side of the ship.

10. Bèche-de-mer Lugger

It got as far as the scuppers, and then stopped. I looked for something like a net, in which to get it over the gunwales, but the kid just shook his head at me. He pointed, and I saw the creature come to a drain hole, and squat on it. As we watched, it seemed to diminish, and I realised it was squeezing itself out, like toothpaste, or a baby. It took a long while, but finally we heard the splash below as it hit water. We both went to the railings, and saw beyond the phosphorescence around the reef something huge and dark. It looked big as a whale, but with one gleaming golden eye, the pupil like a slot.

11. Cuttlefish Bone, being Chewed by Parakeet

She submerged, this Grendel's mother, and that was the last I ever want to see anything of the like. It was too close to our weird tale, too close to my old life, which Nate doesn't like me mentioning. The Karnak kid must have known some version of the story, a South sea Beowulf. Here be monsters; and let them be. Let mother and child swim away together peacefully, monsters though they are. If they wrote stories, would we be the monsters?

We might have written more tales together, you and I, but we were too alien to each other for more than just a once-off. And so I let you go, How, to disappear into your personal sea-depths, and you let me go, to mine. How could I do it? Very easily.

With all my affectionate good wishes
Sonia (once Lovecraft but now Davis)

DARKNESS BEYOND

JASON FRANKS

From the journal of the bushranger Alexander Aymes: convicted of Assault, Arson, Robbery and Escape from Custody. Charges of Murder reduced to Manslaughter in plea bargain. Prisoner is sentenced to life imprisonment. Transferred to Port Arthur Prison, on 17th June 1867.

17th June

It seemed a pretty enough place when they led us down from the decks: lawns and trees and cold blue skies. From across the black waters of the bay, the penitentiary building looks like a palace with its towers and adjacent cottages. On the slope above stands a magnificent church, erected in the Gothic style. It would be a credit to any of the towns I have visited my attentions upon these last few years.

But this is a bad place. I felt its misery upon me well before they marched us through the gates. Even the name of it rolls grey and heavy from the tongue—Van Diemen's Land. My sentence is for life, but in this place I am not sure it is preferable to the alternative.

I have seen the insides of more than my fair share of prisons. I have spent far too much time in the company of such rough men as are found there. I have always found them to be boisterous and rowdy, especially upon the arrival of newcomers. But here they are sullen to a man. I have never seen the like.

This is a bad place. I suppose it is no better than I deserve.

18th June

Since my father's ruin I have lived in alleyways and flophouses. I have taken shelter behind bordellos and under porches. I have slept beneath hedges when I could and in open gutters when I could not. I have survived four months in the hold of a prison ship.

Here, at Port Arthur, I have my own cell.

Whitewashed walls and a hammock and a desk and a chamber pot. It is clean and bright during the day, and we are sometimes even permitted a candle at night. I have not seen such luxury since we lost our home and were cast out into the street.

Perhaps I have misjudged this place.

23rd June

In all my years I have yet to work an honest day, but I have certainly lived my share of privation.

When there was no money in my purse, when there were no towns to reave or rob, I survived in the naked bush. I have lived hard all my adult life. But this!

How they work us here. Dawn 'til dusk, cutting and hauling wood. Dressing the timber and strapping it for transport. Loading and unloading the carts. They work us to exhaustion, and then they work us more. The commandant says that hard work and prayer are the surest course to rehabilitation.

My work detail is usually supervised by a trooper named Seamon. He seems a likeable sort, though earnest. He laughs easily, but I do not think he understands the jokes. Perhaps he no longer recognises them—none of the other prisoners have demonstrated much capacity for humour. Hough is usually the other guard, but sometimes it is Walsh. Sometimes it is both of them.

There are five others on the detail.

Leonards is Cornish, to judge by his accent. He likes to give orders, to the guards as well as to the other convicts. His nose has been broken so many times it looks like a sausage that has split its skin.

McKinley is an Irishman, as you might have guessed. A gaunt, hollow-eyed little fellow. I've heard tell that he's here for his politics. I've also heard that he is a vicious fighter, though you wouldn't know it to look at him.

Brown is a strange one; an East End guttersnipe grown to monstrous proportions. He walks with a hunch although there is nothing wrong with his spine, and he speaks to himself constantly in a high little voice. Mostly he talks about the work, other times I do not know to whom he is speaking or what the topic of conversation is. His presence is strangely soothing, although perhaps that is just in contrast to Leonards' dialogue.

I do not yet have the measure of Mitty or Boyd, but I write their names here to aid me in remembering them.

2nd July

This month we have our work on the western flank of the grounds. Seamon lets us walk along the beachfront on our way to the site. Although it is bitterly cold, I feel my spirits lifted by the salt tang in the air and the gentle surge of the bay.

So good was our humour this morning that we struck up an actual conversation. I told them wild stories of my ranging days. Hold-ups and bar fights and shoot-outs and chases. Not all of the stories I shared were my own, and many of the details were not strictly true, but in this place there is precious little entertainment to be had and I felt it my duty to provide as much as I could.

Leonards has not said a word all day, not even his usual carping.

30th July

They call this a Model Prison. That means that there are no floggings. Transgressions are usually punished with reduced food rations.

Good behaviour—which of course means tattling—is reward-
ed with additional food.

Without proper sustenance the work is more terrible than
ever, especially in the vicious breeze that slashes us from the bay.
Today I could not prevent myself from shivering. By the end of
the day, I could not judge where those shivers ended and the
shakes of exhaustion began.

Reduced food is the most usual punishment here, but there
are others. McKinley told me that the worst of these is the Silent
System. Brown began to weep, so I did not press him for more
information.

Leonards has spent the last three days in the infirmary and
his share of the work fell to me along with the blame for his
condition. I am paying for it now, but it has been worth it. I don't
think he will trouble me again.

4th August

Horror on the beach today.
Leonards is back on the detail, mostly recovered from his
injuries, but Seamon thought it best to keep us apart a while
longer. For that reason Brown and I were detached from the main
group and set to the task of repairing a dinghy, which had blown
loose of its moorings during the storms last week and dashed
itself upon a reef. Fortunately the water was shallow.

I admit I was terrified when Walsh instructed us to wade out
and drag the wreck ashore. I cannot swim, and I am deathly
afraid of the waters. Luckily the cold excused my shivers and
the wetness the sweat upon my brow. But I do not think Brown
would have noticed either way: he jabbered happily to himself
through the whole exercise and set to the task with a relish that
convinced me he is quite as insane as everybody says.

It was not until we had driven the boat onto the beach and
relief juddered through my limbs that I noticed the stink, thick
and caustic, like bile spiced with cloves. Walsh backed away,
covering his mouth with a handkerchief while I choked and
gagged on the odour. Brown seemed unaffected.

When I could again breathe, Walsh pointed at the boat with his rifle. "Get to work, Aymes."

Brown and I bent to the task while Walsh retreated further up the beach. After a time I became accustomed to the smell and accepted its presence as another ambient source of misery, along with the icy breeze and the splinters in my sodden hands.

I do not know how or when the beast crept out of the water, but it was Brown who saw it first. He dropped his tools and his whispering fell to the barest susurration.

It was black or dark grey beneath the weak morning sun. A splash of boneless tissue, about eight feet in diameter, although I had the sense that there was more of the thing spread across the sea floor beneath the shallow tide. Its skin bubbled slowly, bursting to reveal luminous green orbs. The eyes then sank back into the flesh and blinked closed, but there were always more of them, bubbling up on some other part of the creature's hide. Tendrils encysted with such eyes would form at its extremities, rolling together and rising from the central mass, waving in the air before losing coherence and collapsing.

I do not know how long we stood, staring at the beast, before Walsh screamed at us to get back to work. I turned my head to him, and then, gripped by sudden terror, swung it back towards the beast, fearing that it had reared up from the sea, reaching for me with those awful tendrils, peering close with those unearthly green eyes.

I do not know if the beast heard Walsh's voice—I am unwilling to credit it with ears—but it was already receding back into the surf by the time I had made my turn. Moments later it was gone from sight, though its stink remained for the rest of the day.

Brown has been silent since the beast made its appearance. When he recovers his powers of speech, I fancy he will have a new topic of conversation to hold with himself.

I am not a scholar, but I am not entirely ignorant. To say one thing for the rough existence I have lead, it has afforded me many idle hours, and I have spent as many of those as I could with my nose between the pages of a book. I am not a learned man, but I fancy that I am better read than many who name themselves gentry. I want to say the beast was some kind of sea jelly, but it lacked the delicate structure of such creatures. Its hide looked thick and porous, more like the meat of a fungus than the translucent skin of a medusa.

We know the sea only by its surface qualities, by its colour and its texture and its clarity. The further one gets from the landmasses that scum it over, the stranger it becomes—and the deeper.

Charles Darwin claims that we dragged ourselves from the sea on fins and flippers. We drove ourselves aground; we grew lungs to breathe the air, and feet to walk upon the earth, and hands with which to climb into the trees. The Devil knows I am not a Christian man, but I have never believed this theory. People are lazy things, attached to their homes and reluctant to change their natures unless forced to do so. If anyone should know that it is I. But, in light of what I saw today, I am coming to believe that Mr. Darwin may have a point after all. If the oceans are filled with life such as we beheld this morning I can scarcely blame our ancestors for fleeing into the trees.

What terrible compulsion has drawn us back to the water's edge?

14th August

I am in the infirmary.

I do not think that I can commit what has happened to paper.

Brown is here also. I should thank him for his deeds, but somehow his presence makes it all the worse.

Brown was there. He saw it happen. He knows my shame.

15th August

The infirmary still. The bleeding will not stop.

16th August

I had hoped they would change the work detail, but they have not. Leonards, McKinley, Mitty, Boyd. Only Brown will look me in the eye.

Seamon does not press me if I am lax in my work. I have not recovered my strength yet, but I do not think that is the reason for his lenience.

29th August

They are treating Brown in the silent cells again. I had never taken him for a violent sort.

We were almost done loading the wood for the mill before anyone noticed that he was missing. Seamon sent Walsh to find him, but he had not ventured far. Brown had prostrated himself by the shore. He was wailing and calling out loudly enough that we could all hear him well before Walsh came upon him.

Brown did not respond to Walsh's demands, even when the trooper discharged his rifle. At Seamon's command, Mitty and Boyd rushed forward to grab him, but he surged up and threw them off in a fit of rage. McKinley charged him and bore him back to the ground, then Leonards had to add his weight to the Irishman's when Brown's thrashing proved more than McKinley could contain. They sat on him while Mitty and Boyd secured his arms.

I did not watch this closely; I was on my knees, puking into the sand.

Hough arrived with another five troopers, but by then the passion had left Brown. He hung limp as they dragged him away.

"Speak to me, speak to me," he cried. "Why won't you speak to me?"

The sea's gentle soughing was his only reply.

6th September

Brown is returned to us today.

He no longer mutters to himself; he barely speaks a word. In that respect he is little different than me, but where my eyes are downcast, his head is always bent towards the sea. His eyes bulge with their strain to see the waves, and I swear his ears twitch for it as well.

The sentiment around the detail is most queer now. Leonards asked what happened to my stories. Of course I did not reply. He barked some laughter, which McKinley and Mitty soon took up. When Seamon told them to shut their holes they did so without complaint.

17th September

Today we rowed out to the cemetery island in the middle of the bay, which the authorities have cheerily named the Isle of the Dead. Each boat towed a small raft laden with shrouded corpses behind it. Many of these have been months in the morgue and the odour of decay was strong even upon the water. Brown and I rowed together, under the supervision of Hough.

On the island we spent the morning digging a wide, square pit, four feet deep and ten yards wide. After our tea break we rolled the corpses out of the canvas sheeting and into the grave. It was too small to accommodate all of the bodies side by side, so we packed them in three layers deep.

Brown was quiet on the island, but once we got onto the water to return to the camp he began to sing. His voice was wild and sibilant, but there was music in it, and language. I dread to know what he was singing about, though I do not believe I would be able to understand it even if I knew the words.

18th September

They had to drag Brown from his cell this morning.

Hough and Walsh were able to march him to the site with us, but they could not make him work. In the end they just left him to wander by the shore, crooning and bellowing and hissing his music. There is no more harm in him, any more than there is work. Seamon says that he will be transferred to the asylum tomorrow.

There is a terrible odour in the cell block tonight.

23rd September

I feel a madness stirring inside me. Not Brown's gibbering lunacy, but something cold and heavy and familiar. As we marched past the bay I could feel it pounding in my head. The bay remained its usual placid self, and I wished it would roar to match the rushing in my ears.

This is the rage that drove me through my ranging days, when I took what I desired and other men looked upon me with naked fear in their eyes. The desire to exercise it thrills me.

Vengeance.

If I only had my guns.

1st October

The Silent System claims that prayer and contemplation are the keys to rehabilitation, and this prison has taken the philosophy to heart. My head was still swimming from blows when the commandant explained this to me. I nodded my comprehension, though the guards had to prop me up on the bed to do so.

The hood is a dome-shaped cap made of felt, with a flap that folds down over one's face. For five days I wore the hood. The jailers would not let me speak, and the flap was only lifted enough to permit them to spoon some thin porridge into my mouth.

If Seamon had been longer at his piss I would have had them. I would have had the rifle out of Walsh's grip and then I would have had them. I am not a dead shot, but these troopers are lazy and ill-trained. I would have had them, if Seamon's modesty had driven him a dozen paces further. Filthy bastard.

Instead ...

Five days I sat, hooded, in darkness and silence. As the sun traversed its cycle, I found that there were more shades in darkness than I had ever imagined.

First there is the colour black, which one can still observe in the broadest daylight. Then there is shadow, where light is visibly blocked from venturing. Then there is true darkness, where no light can venture at all, but that is just an absence of light. There is a darkness beyond that, and it is a far deeper realm indeed. There are depths where the light has never travelled, where it has not the power to exist. There is a place where the darkness is thick enough to snuff out any candle, quench any fire. There is darkness so dense that it could put out the sun; and there are beings that live in that darkness.

The things that Leonards and McKinley did to me on that beach—the violations they visited upon me while Mitty and Boyd held me down, while Seamon stood by laughing—those are nothing to the obscenities I suffered down in the fathomless depths. The beings I contemplated were so hideous that I could discern their forms despite the utter destitution of light. The prayers I offered them were silent, for the darkness was so heavy that it choked the air from my lungs. Loathsome as they were, what else could I have done in the presence of beings of such magnitude?

Silent contemplation and prayer.

The guards removed the hood late yesterday afternoon and returned me to my old cell. I did not protest. Tomorrow they will send me out with my old work detail, but I will not return.

The Old Ones know me now. Beneath the waves, beyond the skies, they know my name. I am theirs. I must attend to them as they make their preparations.

They will wrest this world from the light. They will drown the cities and swallow the mountains. They will burst the moon and drain the sun. They will draw the earth back into the darkness from which it frothed. They will flood the universe until the horizon is abandoned and there is no barrier between the sea and sky. All shall be at peace then: tranquil and still but for their fitful stirrings. Our puny sentience is an affront to them, for theirs is the truest claim upon existence. All lives, all creation, must be extinguished. I understand this, now and I welcome it.

Tomorrow I will go into the water. I will take as many with me as I can.

*O*n the morning of October 2nd 1867, Alexander Aymes murdered two troopers and four convicts in an attempt to escape Port Arthur Prison. Suffering from multiple gunshot wounds, the prisoner waded out into the Bay and soon fell to the current. His body was never recovered. This journal is all that remains of Aymes' personal effects, which were found to be host to an unidentifiable fungus and burned. Convicts in adjacent cells still complain about the terrible odour. It is unknown how far the spores have spread.

THE DIESEL POOL

KAARON WARREN

It took me a while to figure it out, but the difference between men and ghosts is that ghosts don't want sex. They just want to talk. I didn't mind listening. It was more comfortable than the other, especially now I worked out of my car.

I'd figured out that parking at Old Parliament House was a good safe spot overnight. You pull in after midnight when the place is long closed and the security guards are sure everyone has gone home. You park around on the dark side, in the three-space spot that never sees sun. You make sure you're gone by six in the morning when the patrols come, and you're assured of five good hours of sleep. The people over in the tent embassy kept an eye out for me. More than once they'd chased off a shithead moving towards me. You can't always tell a shithead but, however they're dressed or whoever they are, their shoulders will kinda slouch forward as if they're being led — *not my fault*. Blokes from the tent embassy only have to call out to them and they scurry off.

Mostly I'm left alone there. For work I'll park in Barton near the Government offices. Plenty of ghosts there, sitting in my passenger seat, telling me all they've lost. Some of them remind me of my dad so I like sitting there next to them.

Dad was the one taught me how to talk to ghosts, although I didn't know it at the time. It's like that old trick story about the guy who kills himself when he eats turtle soup and no one knows why. It turns out he was once on an island, stuck there, and someone gave him soup they said was turtle. At the same time, yeah, one of the other people on the island disappears and when you hear the story it's obvious, yeah, but the soup he ate on the island was made out of person and it was only when he ate the *actual* turtle soup he figured it out.

It's like that with me and talking to the ghosts. I didn't know until I knew that I could do it.

So what Dad did was train me to listen for things that other people can't hear. Look for images that are there but hidden. It's only when I figured out I had ghosts in my car sometimes, not men, that I realised what he'd taught me.

"Little Jenny Hanniver," he called me, "Little Jenny, you need to wake the dormant organs, so you can hear the things that dogs bark at, that cat's ears prick up at. You'll see pictures from beyond."

I learned later he was talking about the pineal gland and that most people thought he was crazy. But could they see ghosts? Talk to them? No they could not.

That was his secret, I guess, what gave him the inside track.

What got him killed.

I tried parking my car near where he died, hoping he might come talk to me but there were too many others, men who'd died with him in the hotel fire, beating at my windows like moths, and I had to drive away. He'd been led there by a ghost who told him my mother was waiting for him to rescue her, but she wasn't so he couldn't.

Maybe I'll park there again soon.

I'd had a busy week. Lots of men, few ghosts. Ghosts don't pay, although they do try to help at least. I had a bag of Indian food. I got extra to take over the road. I don't mind spending all my cash money. I don't like touching the money in the bank, though. I'm letting it accumulate. I don't want to end up like Mum, homeless at 45 due to poor life decisions and god knows where she is now. I'm technically not homeless; I've got the car.

I took the bag of food to the tent embassy and they asked me to stick around but I don't like to impose. Back in my car I cosied down. The House behind me seemed to breathe; expand and contract, expand and contract, and the rhythm of it brought me peace.

I've got one main ghost who visits me at Old Parliament House. He isn't even a politician, which is weird. He was a tourist to Canberra, although he reckons he wasn't, he reckons Summernats doesn't count as tourism. "We're here for the cars, not this shit-hole," he says, as if there's any difference. He likes my car because it's all done up on the inside and the engine is pretty revved, but you wouldn't know it to look at it from the outside so there are no alarm bells for the cops.

So this tourist ghost, he can't remember his name from day to day but he's got a tattoo that says Gary loves Cindy so I call him Cindy, just for the laughs. So Cindy tapped on my window about 1am. I opened it a crack but it was bloody freezing outside so I didn't want to let too much air in. The crack was enough of an invitation for him because there he was, in the passenger seat. His hands were filthy with grease so I didn't like him touching anything but he never left a mark.

"How are you, Cindy?" I lit a cigarette. Smoking in the car probably wasn't a good idea but I actually liked the smell of stale smoke. It reminded me of the pubs we went to when I was a kid and Mum was already gone. Dad'd park me at a table in the corner where I'd get attention from the patrons in ebbs and flows.

Cindy nodded and rubbed his nose. "It's down there, I swear," he said. He was always on about these mythical pools of diesel they kept in the basement, for emergencies in wartime. He only found out after he died and he was bitter about that.

"I coulda been a rich man," he says. He wants me to go tell his brother. Never crosses his mind that I might like to get rich, too. I told him that and he says, just get him here and I'll show you both where it is. You can both get rich. "You might even like each other," he says, and he gets this look, this man-look.

I finished my smoke and pulled up the blankets to doze off. I quite liked having Cindy next to me; he was good company.

At around 2 am, though, I awoke to a kind of thrumming in my ears, like when you drive fast with only one window open. Cindy was clutching the dashboard, trying to stay put, but it was like a vacuum cleaner sucked him away from me, and he flew backwards, through the car door, through the great white walls of Old Parliament House.

I watched in the rear view mirror and saw nothing. I should have stayed put but I like to know things so I climbed out and walked to the wall where he disappeared. It was solid, firm. Although I thought I saw a smear of diesel.

The next day I managed a shower and went back to the place as a tourist. It was pretty empty; it'd been in the news lately, rumours that it was full of asbestos or something. Whole classes of children who'd gone through on tour were coming down with respiratory issues, they reckoned, so the kids were staying away in droves. I dropped my $2 in the donation box and smiled at the volunteer, a nice lady who looked like she knew a lot.

"Can I ask a weird question?"

"That's mostly what we get! We do know the answers to most of them," she beamed.

"I've heard that there are diesel pools in the basement. Like from the war or something."

"Ah. You'll have to talk to Lance about that. Lance is our resident conspiracy theorist."

I thought that was a bit rude.

Lance was about my age and quite sweet. He really did care about all of it and gave me a private ghost tour, full of gossip and stories of murder and demonstrations of how the chairs would be pulled out when no one was there. He had odd stitching all over his hands and arms, around his neck, as if he'd been in a terrible accident and sewn back together. I didn't ask him.

He reckoned he didn't know about the diesel pool but he said, "Why do you want to know that?" which was odd. I told him the truth, that the ghost of a man who'd come to Canberra for Summernats told me so. He said, "Under Old Parliament House there are tunnels and doorways and rooms. Some of the tunnels go nowhere but the deepest dark. Some of the doors open onto rock and dirt, flat and hard as any concrete-laid surface. And some of the rooms go on forever. Down there a monster lives."

I asked who wrote that and he said he did. He wouldn't say

more about the monster but told me he'd show me one day, if I was brave enough.

Meanwhile I'm noting all the doors I could get into. All the old empty offices, warm and protected. I didn't mind the ghosts I could see in the dark corners; they seemed happy to walk back and forth on their own.

Only one of them beckoned me. It could have been Cindy but he was too far away for me to tell.

"It's warm inside," Lance said. "You could make your home here and no one would know." He took me down four floors, where I wasn't supposed to be. Down there, they kept old files. Old chairs and furniture, boxes empty and full. Doors and windows. All these forgotten things.

Lance said, "No one likes to come down here. Every door hides a ghost. If you open a door the ghost will take you." He licked his lips. "You'd like it at first, is the thing, because it comes like a kiss, gentle and passionate at the same time. But before long you're lost. It's why I don't do that sort of thing."

He'd do it if I convinced him to; I knew that for sure.

"I can hear footsteps," I said.

"There are always footsteps," he told me. I asked him about the monster, how it got there.

"It came from the inland sea a long time ago. What I've heard from my grandfather who knows all this stuff is that it lived in peace in the centre of Australia until men tried to find water there. They dug it up, disturbed it, and so it ripped one of them apart. Then they shot it, almost killed it, but it drifted and swam and survived until it made it to the lake that exists under the House."

I didn't believe in monsters, not that kind anyway, and thought I could live with the ghosts and the footsteps if I was going to crash in here.

I didn't dare for a week but then some mongrel pinched my car. A paying customer who didn't pay. Luckily I had my bag with me but he got everything else. I had the name he gave me but with no rego, no insurance, I wasn't seeing that car again.

I wished I hadn't left my clothes in there but I raided the charity bins, found myself something to wear.

It was going to be cold. I wasn't getting any work that night, not dressed like that, not with nowhere to take them, so I hiked to Old Parliament House and around the back, under the construction sheet and found the loose corner Cindy had told me about. That's where he and his mates had snuck in. He never told me how they got out again though; he didn't like to talk about how they died.

I saw dark footprints in the carpet and bent down to sniff at them.

Diesel.

"Looking for a place to stay?" I heard. It was Lance.

"Don't you ever go home?"

He said, "Can you come quick? He says he needs you."

They always say they need you but usually it's not for anything they can't find anywhere they look.

The House felt like it was breathing in, and out, and in.

"Who? Cindy?" I hadn't seen Cindy since that night in my car.

Lance led me though a doorway with hinges present but rusty, the door removed. Then through a short corridor, so dark I couldn't see my own fingers. I'd lost my phone in the car, one of the many things I lost, so I didn't even have that. In the darkness, the gloom, my eyes were dim and you couldn't see in that light, not even a cat could.

I turned to go back but couldn't even see a chink of light where the doorway was.

Why did I keep going? Why do I do anything? Most of my decisions aren't that, they're compulsions. They're *what's next*, or *why not*.

Like my mother.

And my father, too, in the end before he died. Still alive, clinging on but dark on the inside, filled with the ghosts he'd seen, his barriers down too far. And then he wasn't

Another doorway with a thick door I had to shoulder open. After I was through, the door snicked shut like a sigh.

"Where is he, Lance? Are you taking me to Cindy?"

"Not a man," Lance said. "Not that. It's the visitor from the Inland Sea. The one who made me what I am."

His voice was reedy but deep, and he spoke as if he had bubbles in his throat. "We searched all our lives for water, and what did we find? What did we find indeed. A great and wondrous creature with claws like swords and teeth like diamonds." He gurgled at me and I stepped back, but there was none of that.

"Come quick," Lance said. "Chance of a lifetime! This is an opportunity not many get to have. You're a lucky young lady."

I felt pulled along, sucked in, dragged, and the sound was a giant inhaling.

This way, this way, further and further down. There were old signs of habitation, a cigarette packet, a beer bottle, a calendar dated 1952, a bucket, a pile of rags.

There were old lights glowing dully here, yellow and feeble, but better than pitch dark.

"All he wants is your breath. Just the smallest breath," Lance said. The next door opened, and there was a suction of air like a vacuum, and a blow back. I found it hard to breathe. There was the smell of deep, murky waters, or an old dishrag left to dry in the dark. I've always had a phobia of deep, murky waters, at least since we did the Mekong River at school. There are catfish in that river three metres long. There are stingrays 500 kilograms. The thought of it freaks me out.

"There's gold. There was gold in the desert and we brought it with us. Dragged it underground stuck in his flesh, like an orange at Christmas time my nana used to make. With the cloves."

He was a ghost all right, with the bloody talking. "We were foolish," he said. "So very foolish. But at least we had an adventure!" He exhaled, as much as a dead man could. "He's a poor lost creature from the sea, found his way via the actions of foolish men. Fools and thieves and liars and..." he stopped talking. I felt a sharp prick at the base of my throat as if someone held the point of a knife to it, but no one was there.

"He'll make your throat hurt as long as you're alive," Lance said. "After which you'll feel blessed relief. It's as good for you as it is for him," he said, and that woke me up because I'd been hearing that bullshit for half my life. It was hardly ever true but they didn't care.

"I call him the Sea Monk," Lance said. "He's like that. He swam in here when he was small then grew so large he couldn't escape. He's grown long arms to reach out for food so sensitive it's like he's got eyes on them. He's losing his breath."

The smell of diesel, now, so maybe Cindy was right. I'd have to tell his brother. Maybe he was a nice guy. Dull but nice and he wouldn't notice my shit maybe. I'd tell him that there were pools of diesel for us to make our fortunes.

At the end of the hall I saw a little girl, dancing like she was rolling a hula hoop. I thought *shit, I hope I don't have to save anyone* because I didn't feel capable of much at all, really, apart from walking on.

"Cindy's waiting," Lance said. Only he didn't say Cindy, he said some other name.

The smell of fuel, like Summernats burnout night, without anyone wanting to see my tits, and something else, salty, was it called briny? I remembered the word from school. There was a deep intake of breath, almost like I imagined a tidal wave would sound, then a whooshing like a plane leaving or something.

The little girl was joined by a dancing bear, which made no sense at all. I wondered what I'd taken. You don't always remember (kind of the point) and you never really know what is real.

Life's like that.

More creatures danced now. I heard music, like a tinkling piano or something, or an old music box lost at sea, water-logged, but still playing a tune.

"Come quick," Lance said. I didn't care about Cindy any more. I wanted to find that music box and take it away with me. It was comforting.

As I neared the end of the hallway (I must have been a hundred metres underground. No carpet here, no wallpaper, just dirt floor and rough wooden walls.) I thought I saw bones lying in neat piles. We walked on, and those I saw dancing were not people at all, not bears or cats or anything but long, grey, mottled, encrusted tentacles.

Beckoning me.

I felt Lance hiding behind me. The in out, the suction, and he's protected behind me. "Go quick," he whispered.

I went. The smell of diesel made me feel ill but if I breathed through my mouth I could taste it so nose was best, through the jumper I'd taken from the charity bin that wasn't washed and smelled of dog.

A tentacle, not the long arm of a loving man helping me to my seat kind sir? Not the tiny fingers of a baby in mine? Not that. It took me around the waist, gently at first then tightening until I lost my breath. It lifted me off my feet and drew me through one final door to the great pool of diesel.

Fumes off it like mist but a solid, gelid layer.

This stuff was old.

"So lonely," Lance called out. "All it wants is a friend. He just wants to be petted until he wastes away." Then under his breath, "And a bite to eat"

I saw Cindy and he was a ghost of his former self, barely there. Missing the centre of himself, existing as a shadow.

The tentacle was slimy, slippery, and I'm skinny and agile so I wriggled myself out of its grasp. My lungs ached with it; I'd been smoking too long, my lungs were shit. I'd have to give up. I WOULD give up.

The tentacles rose out of the water, dozens of them, some holding what was left of a skeleton, skull and spine, some waving other things. In a pile in the corner I could see wallets, bags, gold in a tipped out pile at the edge of the diesel pool. The tentacles dripped with the thick black stuff and were lumpy, scarred.

I saw a sea of faces, so many lost at sea and dragged with this beast as its constant companions, drawn back with what they've gathered, the breath of fresh air, the scent of outside.

was in the doorway. I didn't want to be seen again, so no sudden movements. I backed up but Lance was right there behind me, and he was a man after all. No ghost ever had a hard-on.

"Go on," he said, nudging me forward with his groin. I couldn't pass him; he was twice my size.

"Do you think," I said, turning slowly and pressing into him, "that every room's been christened?" His eyes widened and he let me lead him away. I was disappointed with how easy it was.

"Come on," I said. "We can come back and see your pet later." How I even spoke I don't know. And once he got my pants off he'd be disappointed because I'd pissed myself, unless he liked that kind of thing. A lot of them did. He wouldn't let us get too far, stopping at an abandoned office about fifty metres from where the monster breathed. "In here," he said. His breath was laboured. He was overweight but, when he stripped off his shirt, surprisingly athletic. I was the one who was out of breath.

"It'd be better in my car," I said, wanting out of there, but he shook his head. I hoped he'd be the type to get sleepy afterwards, and while he was at it I looked around the room for something to whack him with, not too hard, just so I could push him away and run, get the fuck out of there.

He was breathing hard, eyes squeezed tight, when a tendril found him. It attached to his face, like a gas mask, or a filthy face washer, and it dragged him away by the head. I think it killed him right there, or knocked him out at least, because he was dragged away like a rag doll, his arms and legs limp, unresisting.

Then the House fell silent.

spent a year living in the House. I'd bring someone every now and then. It preferred athletes to public servants (bigger lung capacity). I wondered if that's why it took Lance and not me that day. Did it understand how much better I'd be at bringing friends in for sleepovers?

All it wanted was breath, so I held mine when I was nearby. You have to exhale to do this, even when instinct tells you to keep air in your lungs. You need to exhale so air bubbles don't escape into your blood. The monster took their breath and let them go, most of the time. It didn't like bodies rotting. Ghosts were something else; ghosts could hang nearby and not take up any room at all. Lance crouched in a corner, rarely moving, or he wandered the archives, entering every door he could.

There were so many rooms and corridors no one ever knew I was there.

There were a lot of ghosts in the Old House.

The tentacles started getting braver. Reaching further. Making their way out into the hallways. It wasn't long before they'd reach the main hall, the entrance way, somehow making us think they were children, dancing around like finger puppets.

Then circumstances changed.

It was foolish men. It's always foolish men. They wanted to change the place, rebuild, redesign, wanting it done fast so they're down there with masks on, welding guns, sparks flying, and they never knew what hit them.

The monster's eyes like burning lamps; the first time I saw the rest of it, beyond its tentacles, was the last, before the diesel took fire and burned for a year and a day. This, not before the monster had spewed a thousand skittering worms. I watched them wriggling through the cracks and away, and I felt a visceral nausea.

I liked to think the monster found its way through the underground waterways to a lake somewhere, or out to sea, some place where it could draw in great lungsful of the fresh air it so craved. As for all those worms, seeking breath themselves?

They're in the water.

DREAMGIRL

STEPHEN DEDMAN

Can't fall asleep… Even more tired than I am thirsty, but *must not* sleep…

We'd been driving for over an hour, and the terrain hadn't noticeably changed; the only thing that a normal person could have called a landmark was the plane, no longer visible in the rear view mirror. It made it difficult to be sure how fast we were going, and I was startled into whistling when I looked at the speedo. "Remind me to take you out in the Lamborghini sometime."

"It's okay," Rachel replied. "The last thing we have to worry about out here is getting a ticket. Not much chance of running into anyone, either.

"Don't bother," she added, as I glanced at my watch. "It won't tell you anything useful."

I'd intended to check our position with the GPS function, not the time. I shrugged. "I hope you know where we're going."

"Of course. We have a mystical psychic bond with the land; it's in our blood. Right?" She grinned, and her perfect white teeth made her face look slightly darker; if she kept her mouth shut, nobody ever would've realized she was part Noongar or Koori or whatever abos call themselves nowadays.

"Don't give me that bullshit," I said. "You were born at least a thousand miles from here. How long has it been since anybody actually lived in this godforsaken place?"

"Godforsaken?" She seemed to consider this. "Forsaken by *your* god, maybe."

"Do you actually have any fucking idea where we are?"

She was silent for a moment, then stopped the Land Rover and opened the door, stepping out into the full blast of the sunlight. She walked just far enough that she seemed to shimmer in the head haze, and picked up a small stone. Judging from the way she was juggling it from hand to hand, it must have been hot as the hobs of Hell, but she brought it back to the car and showed it to me. "Do you know what this is?"

"Gibber?" I said as she closed the door, then looked at it more closely. It was black, smooth, about the size of a ten cent piece and about as perfectly round. I turned it over and looked at it more closely; it resembled a flying saucer from a fifties B-movie, convex on one side, the other domed and flanged, a bit like a jam tart. I rubbed it between my fingers. It felt more like glass than metal. I'm an MBA, not a rockhound, but I've had to learn a little geology. "Obsidian?"

"Not quite. Ever heard of australites?"

"Not that I remember."

"Darwin glass? Blackfellows' buttons?" I suspect I looked blank. "Tektites?"

That rang a faint bell. "Bits of meteor, aren't they?"

"Close. When a big meteorite hits and forms a crater, sand and soil and rocks get thrown up into the air. Sometimes they get thrown up so high that they have to re-enter the atmosphere coming down, and they melt into the shape that can best survive re-entry. NASA scientists copied the shape of australites like this one to make the heat shields for spacecraft."

I looked around the flatness. "We're in a crater?"

"A huge and incredibly ancient one. So old that the rim has all but eroded away; even satellite photos don't pick it out."

"But you did?"

She grinned again. "I had some help from the MAD."

I nodded; the plane was fitted with a Magnetic Anomaly Detector as well as other geosurveying gear, and she was incredibly good at pattern recognition. I'd had her background checked before I started sleeping with her, of course. She wasn't just a pilot or a tech, though she was more than competent as either; she had a degree in geophysics and her PhD supervisor swore she was a genius. My PR people had even suggested leaking it to one of the gossip columnists that we were dating, especially if I was serious about going into politics: Dad had said some pretty negative things about abos when the idea of native title first came up, bad enough that even the Coalition had felt the need to distance themselves from him, though there were lots of stories that suggested Dad hadn't been averse to a bit of dark meat in his younger days. Rachel wasn't the first of my employees I'd picked up, but unlike most of the others, she'd kept me coming back for more. She was something of a rags to riches story herself, in a small way; youngest of three girls raised by a single mother, scored a scholarship to a good school, and then to uni. Licensed pilot, no criminal record or history of drug problems despite having some pretty dodgy acquaintances and relatives, and still (just) on the right side of thirty. The only hints that she hadn't grown up in a nunnery were a tattoo on each wrist—a tree with five branches, and some sort of crooked five-pointed star with an eye in the centre, which she'd explained as souvenirs of her goth phase—and her ability to twist that superbly toned body into more sexual positions than I'd ever tried before. Add to that amazing legs, a gorgeous arse, and eyes so dark and deep that you barely noticed her nose was just a bit too flat and wide to be beautiful, and you could understand why I'd let her drag me out here to the middle of nowhere without my usual entourage. Besides, there was the sample she'd brought in; it contained enough gold, as well as traces of palladium, platinum and iridium, that I didn't want to risk some other company filing a claim first, so we'd let everybody think we were just heading off for a dirty weekend.

"Have you found the meteor?" I asked.

"Not yet. The meteorite would have disintegrated on impact, but there may still be a good chunk of it buried near the centre... wherever that is."

"The MAD hasn't picked it up?"

"No. The range on your plane's not much more than two thousand kay." She started the car again, and continued heading roughly north-east. "If it flew over where I think the centre is, based on the data points I do have, it wouldn't have enough fuel left to get to another airport."

"Where exactly are we?" I asked, with another glance at my watch.

"If I told you we were in the Gibson Desert, would it make you feel any better?"

"Not much. How big is this desert?"

"About 155,000 square kilometres. Roughly the size of England, plus GST."

"Wonderful. If I'm going to apply for a mining lease, I'm going to want something a bit more precise than 'somewhere in England'. I hope you can find your way back to the plane, at least."

"Of course. But we have a way to go, yet."

"Not too much longer, I hope."

She shrugged. "Your money makes money, whether you're awake or asleep—more in an hour than most of us make in a year. But if you want more…"

"Hey, I'm here aren't I? Wherever the hell that is." Sure, I could afford to sit back and hire people to run the company—I inherited enough that even I'd have trouble spending it that fast, and I sure as hell wasn't interested in giving it away—but Dad didn't get to be a billionaire without taking chances, and it's not like he never made mistakes, either. I'm not ashamed of being a gambler. And if this find was as big as she was claiming, it would beat any single discovery that Dad had ever made.

"You didn't answer my question earlier. Does anybody live here?"

"Not as far as I know."

"Nobody who's going to claim land rights?" I'm not a racist, but I'm just as keen as Dad was to put an end to all this 'native title' bullshit.

She shook her head. "I doubt it. It's been too long since anyone lived here; the place is too dry."

"I hope you're not going to blame that on global warming."

"Only if you go back to the Cretaceous, when this whole area was underwater. A lot of explorers came out this way, looking for an inland sea. They were only about a hundred million years too late. In geological time it's hardly worth mentioning."

"Was that before or after your meteor hit?" I asked, after she'd been silent for what felt like a few minutes.

"I don't know yet. Time…time doesn't mean quite the same thing out here as it does in Perth."

"Try telling that to somebody who wants overtime." I looked around. The landscape didn't seem to have changed at all, even though my arse was telling me that we'd been driving over gravel and sand dunes for at least an hour. "Who was Gibson? The guy who discovered this place?"

"Not exactly. He was a member of one of Ernest Giles' expeditions, back in the 1870s. Giles named the desert after him after he disappeared. Ludwig Leichhardt and his party were also heading in this direction when they were last seen; no-one ever found *their* bodies, either."

I snorted. "You make it sound like the Bermuda Triangle, except without the water. Next you'll be telling me you that you think you've found Lasseter's Reef, or that you believe in R'lyeh."

"You've heard of R'lyeh?"

"It's an occupational hazard of spending time with palaeontologists and anthropologists. Every time something goes wrong on one of the offshore rigs, some joker mentions the *Emma* or the *Alert* and says we disturbed Cthulhu. How big was that fuckin' city supposed to be?"

"We don't know that R'lyeh was only a city. Nearly everything we know about the Elder Gods comes from dreams, and the translations aren't completely reliable. What if it was an island, or an entire continent?"

"Oh, great. The last thing we need is a team of amateur archaeologists tromping over my mine sites looking for non-Euclidean geometry. What the hell *is* non-Euclidean geometry, anyway?"

"Short answer? In Euclidean geometry, parallel lines never

intersect. In non-Euclidean geometry, they can."

"Meaning what?"

"Euclidean geometry assumes that two-dimensional planes are completely flat. Non-Euclidean geometry adds extra dimensions. If you look at a page on a map book, the parallel grid lines never meet. But if you added an extra dimension and some distortion, by, say, folding the page, the lines *could* cross each other. People who've been to R'lyeh have noticed that there don't seem to be any straight lines and everything appears distorted, even time. That's what makes me think we may be closer to it here than anyone's ever realised."

I shivered despite myself, and wondered if we'd cranked the air-con up too high. "That's just heat haze. Mirages. Do you have any evidence that this place is anywhere near where R'lyeh was supposed to be? I mean, I know your people take dreams really seriously, I've heard about the Dreamtime and all that...but you're a scientist too."

"All that we see and seem, is but a dream within a dream."

"That's from *Picnic at Hanging Rock*, isn't it?"

"Edgar Allan Poe."

I chuckled. "You can recite poetry, too?"

"'Out on the wastes of the Never-Never,'" she intoned, "'That's where the dead men lie. There where the heat-waves dance forever. That's where the dead men lie.'" She was silent for a moment.

"Is that what your ancestors call the place? The Never-Never?"

"No, that was Barcroft Boake. A surveyor from the Eastern States; he committed suicide during the Great Depression. But it's a good description, Never-Never." She stopped the car and climbed out.

"We're close."

"How can you tell? It all looks the same."

"Not to me."

"This is where you found those samples?" I glanced at my watch; the hands didn't seem to have moved since the last time I'd looked, and the digital readout was blank, no matter how many buttons I pressed.

"Yes. If my calculations are correct, the meteor would be dead ahead, or as close to a straight line as is possible out here."

"What makes you so sure?"

"The samples, the MAD readings that show the curve of the crater rim, and an old story my people tell of a great star that fell from the sky and destroyed a city that was home to creatures that lived here even before us, in the Dreaming. Some Cthulhu cultists say it was a deliberate attack, that an asteroid was aimed here, at R'lyeh. Others, that it wasn't an asteroid, but some other sort of weapon, one powerful enough to transmute elements and warp time as well as space. That's what keeps Cthulhu sleeping, a bubble of distorted time which even he hasn't been able to escape. You don't have to believe that, but keep walking, pick up some rocks, take samples back to the lab…"

I looked around at the shimmering red landscape. "You're sure you can get us back to the lab?" I said, only half joking. I was already becoming tired. She still had a spring in her step, but she did triathlons for fun. "It sounds like a hell of a lot of people disappeared out here."

"More than anyone remembers…but there's enough fuel to take us back to where we landed, and I know the way."

We walked for several minutes, stopping occasionally to pick up a rock. The ones that glistened, I stuffed into the pockets of my cargo pants. "How much further?"

"You see that shimmer up ahead?"

"Yes."

"That's Lasseter's reef."

I blinked, then shaded my eyes. "Are you sure it isn't just a mirage?"

"Keep walking."

I trudged along for what felt like another hundred metres, wishing I'd remembered to grab one of the bottles of water from the esky. The shimmer didn't seem any closer, but the rocks in my pockets seemed to be getting heavier, as though gravity was increasing. "Plane, car, foot…it feels like we're travelling back in time."

"That's because we are. We've passed into the Dreamlands, or the Dreamtime; time and space don't mean the same thing here. If we turn back now, no time would have passed. A few more steps, and we'd get back to the road in time to see the plane land. Go a little further, and you'll be back to a time before you were born. Can't you tell?"

I stared at her. She sounded perfectly serious, and maybe it was the heat haze, or maybe it was because I was almost ready to drop from exhaustion, but she looked slightly younger. "Very funny."

"Don't believe me? Keep walking."

I took a few more steps, then turned around. The Land Rover was nowhere in sight. "If I don't get back in time for the board meeting tomorrow, there'll be hell to pay."

"They won't miss you."

"I bet they will."

She shook her head. "You've already come too far. If you returned now, it would be to a world where no one remembers you, because you've never existed. Non-Euclidean geometry; parallel timelines intersect. Your father died childless and left everything to his second wife. By rights, of course, we should have brought him here, not you; we tried, but he never took the bait. You did."

"What? Who's *we*?"

"People who don't like what your father and his cronies have done to our land, our world. I'd say it's nothing personal, but for me it is: your father also fathered my eldest sister—well, half-sister, Celia. Of course, he never acknowledged her, never agreed to a DNA test, and she died a few years ago in a car crash outside Kalgoorlie. We could never prove that wasn't an accident.

"I came here hoping I could travel back in time to when she was alive, maybe even far enough to stop your father, undo the damage he'd done, but it doesn't work that way. Maybe these—" she held up her hands to show me the tattoos on her wrists, "—allowed me to escape. Or maybe it's because I understand non-Euclidean geometry, or maybe it was that I never fell asleep. Some of the stories say that that's the worst mistake you can make, out here. Fall asleep, and you're part of the dreaming forever, completely lost to the waking world. Just you and Cthulhu." She grinned. "'And his eyes have all the seeming of a demon's that is dreaming / And the lamplight o'er him streaming throws his shadow on the floor / And my soul from out that shadow that lies floating on the floor / Shall be lifted—nevermore!' Never. Never."

"What?"

"Would you prefer some T. S. Eliot? There's a passage in *The Waste Land*, 'The Burial of the Dead'..."

"This isn't funny!"

"No," she said. "Look, you have three choices. If you don't have any way of committing suicide quickly, you can try to stay awake until you die of thirst. Or you can fall asleep, and become part of Cthulhu's dream forever. At least it will seem like forever, with a billion years of alien memories trying to squeeze into your mind, showing you just how insignificant you really are, what *real* power is and how little your family and money and the politicians you own actually matter."

She shrugged. "But time doesn't really mean much in this place, and you'll probably go mad fairly quickly from the heat and the thirst and trying to stay awake, long before the shoggoths find your body. If you're lucky."

Then she was gone, though her grin seemed to hover there in mid-air for the fraction of a second it took me to react. Even without the rocks in my pockets, I couldn't have kept up with her, but I stumbled onwards until I saw her reach the Land Rover and lock the doors. The car vanished into the heat haze a moment later.

I dropped to my knees and patted my pockets. The satellite phone had been too bulky to carry, so I'd left that in the car along with my phone. The hands on my watch had frozen, and the digital readout was dead. My wallet and keys weren't going to be any use out here.

Fuck.

I don't know how long I lay curled up on the hot red dust and gibber; the sun beating down on me didn't seem to have moved at all, and my shadow seemed to be both in front of me and behind me. But, at last, I picked myself up and walked towards that distant shimmer. Maybe it was nothing more than a mirage, or maybe it was Lasseter's Reef, but it wasn't like I had anywhere else to go. If I was lucky, I might find water, or a relatively quick or painless death. A sharp stone, a cliff to jump from, a poisonous snake…a nice, clean, natural death. And if I wasn't lucky, then at least walking might help keep me awake a little longer…

Can't fall asleep…

Even more tired than I am thirsty, but *must not sleep…*

THE THING IN THE BIDET
A TALE OF THE SHRDLU MYTHOS

WILLIAM TEVELEIN

As the incautious excursionist approaches the malodorous *purlieu* of the legend-haunted village of *Dumpwick*, Massachusetts, his initial impressions do not infrequently bear striking similitude to those one might reasonably expect to be engendered by such mythically horrid vicinities as Tartarus, Erubus, Tophet, or much of New Jersey. The earliest indications of the rapidly enveloping noisesomeness of the district reveal themselves immediately upon one's traversing the oozing sludge of the Ginnantonic River via the structurally questionable Badonsky Bridge, whereafter the road abruptly becomes rockier, more copiously pot-holed and more profusely littered with dead woodland creatures of diverse species and degrees of putrefaction. Grim, shadow-shrouded outcrops of decayed basalt begin to burst carbuncle-like through the sallow, sparsely vegetated fields; wind-whipped aspens and shrivelled willows fling out their anguished limbs as if to direct one's attention to something rather revolting happening just over the horizon; gaunt, listlessly grazing ruminants wheeze and cough out buttery phlegm as one whisks past; there are intermittent rains of toads. One hesitates before asking directions from the few microcephalic, chainsaw wielding bucolics one discovers interfering with bloated ewes in roadside ditches, and one drives away terribly quickly afterwards.

Once passing beyond the township's many decrepit, outlying gasoline stations, one observes that a more quintessentially urban blight commences sullenly to assert itself and that the incidence of gunfire increases markedly. Ramshackle but unfortunately not wholly derelict hovels lean unsanitarily against one another, half-hidden by dense clouds of outsized houseflies, mosquitoes and peculiarly unseasonable vultures. Small hillocks of rancid and not instantly identifiable refuse appear surreptitiously to stir of their own accord, drawn perhaps by the mephitic vapours writhing from the multifarious open drains. Obese, eczematous urchins snarl abuse whilst casually nailing defunct rodents to comatose dipsomaniacs; ravaged dowagers in faded paisley morning dresses amble across the streets like stupefied elks, pitifully soliciting nickels, dimes and traveller's cheques; syphilitic clergymen micturate from balconies and blow raspberries at the dumbfounded wayfarer, while leather-clad nuns dart out and attempt to steal his still moving hubcaps. Not surprisingly, then, nobody in his right mind ever so much as considers visiting the place.

Given the choice, by capricious fate and two senescent Deans, of an academic sinecure at either Dumpwick's ill-reputed Histrionic University or that of Farkham, a small town in the Australian region also bearing the name New England, the decision required less cerebral rigour than the extemporaneous composition of a parodic villanelle on the theme of oratorical periphrasis. Farkham, as I discovered through a perfunctory Google of the said municipality, was a rather quaint, temperate, Neo Cymric Meridionalis settlement, and one about which I had no qualms apropos my relocation thereunto.

It was scarcely a month after Farkham University had first written to me, offering me the post of Associate Professor of Crypto-theology in their newly inaugurated school of Comparative Eldritchness, that I found myself settling into my new home, Fatclover Cottage, barely a thesis' throw from the college library. The cottage was a comfortable, well-appointed residence, an unostentatious and harmonious blend of Gothic, Tudor, Georgian, Bauhaus, Huang Dynasty and Adobe, and had been constructed, according to my groundsman Ed Softly, in 1869 by Lord Philip Shaw Fatclover, a former Admiral who had emigrated to the antipodean New England from auld Ireland under what Softly described as a cloud of dark muttering. Wiping his squash with a Swiffer (I ought perhaps to mention that Softly's conscientiousness as a gardener approached mania and that one was apt to encounter him at any time of the day or evening engaged in dusting the vegetables, vacuuming the compost heap or brightening up the dahlias with a little food dye), Softly went on to describe the mysterious and unutterable circumstances surrounding the erstwhile Admiral's demise. According to local tradition and a television program entitled *Australia's Most Offensive Unsolved Unpleasantnesses,* Lord Philip had been discovered on the morning of All Saints 1871, thoroughly dismantled, his component parts having been rearranged so as to form a grisly, though commendably accurate, circled heptagram with a diameter of twenty-three feet.

"His head," said Softly, stabbing a spot of turf with a certain gruesome merriment, "they found right here, on the topmost tip of the great seven-pointed star, facing north and looking a bit pissed off, quite frankly."

I voiced something to the effect of it being perfectly natural to exhibit a degree of indignation were one a former Lord of the Seven Seas thus reduced to a mere geometrical configuration. So saying, I went in to lunch.

As I perched precariously on the kitchen stool, devouring my barramundi and Bovril chowder, I wondered whether the late and tragically unravelled Lord Philip would now have recognised the interior of his former residence since it had clearly undergone substantial renovations at various points in its history. What might the unfortunate Admiral have made of the computerised microwave oven, the light dimmers, the gas-powered barbie or the inexplicable proliferation of lava lamps, I asked myself, but ere I could formulate an answer or swallow down my most recent mouthful of noisome chowder, my concentration was interrupted by an ominous and preternatural susurration from behind the downstairs lavatory door, a vile liquid swooshing noise as of a regurgitating manatee, after which silence once again reigned.

For a moment, I chaffed myself rather uncomfortably, insisting that the sound had been but the product of my overwrought imagination. In my feverishly palpitating heart, however, I knew this was not the case. After all, was not my newly acquired house cat Enigma correspondingly agitated? His hackles were raised, thereby enlightening me as to me what hackles actually were, a matter vexingly elusive from infancy, and he growled testily as if taunted by an impertinent mouse across the room armed with an electric cattle prod. Nevertheless, the habitually inquisitive feline exhibited not the least tendency to investigate the matter more thoroughly. That unenviable task, evidently, fell to myself.

Creeping tremulously towards the half-opened entryway of the now minatory restroom, I was startled by a second dispiritingly raucous swishing sound, this time accompanied by an abrupt blast of virulently odoriferous air. There was nothing for it: the conundrum required confrontation. For one brief but alarming moment, it occurred to me that what might assault my eyes upon flinging wide the portal could very well turn out to be the unlovely sight of Softly, his nefarious lower garments crumpled about his Doc Martens, crouched upon the porcelain throne. Forcing this unpalatable fancy from my mind, I staggered onwards, grasped the heavy bronze handle of the lavatory door and thrust it open. Then, choking on the bile which rose unhesitantly to my gorge, I had a fleeting instant in which to reflect that, perverse as I am aware this may sound, the particular horror of a trouserless, debriefed and straining groundsman would have seemed a vision of sheerest enchantment compared to the spectacle that flashed before my eyes ere consciousness mercifully fled and I fell into a swoon. For there, rising from the bidet, was a wildly writhing mass of translucent, gelatinous tentacles in the midst of which could be discerned the abhorrent caricature of a human face on whose repellent, slime-encrusted brow was inscribed a pulsing, crimson, two-dimensional representation of a great stellated dodecahedron!

Night had fallen like a vast, Stygian absence of daylight by the time my tormented senses returned. With a sudden sickening thud, recollection of my proximity to the besmirched bathroom and its unspeakable denizen reinstated itself, and with a yelp of consternation, I scrambled across the overly waxed floorboards, floundering for the nearest table lamp and sending it crashing to the floor. The next most contiguous lantern similarly escaped my fumbling grasp and shot across the room to splash into the tropical fish aquarium. Three fragmented table lamps later, I succeeded in illuminating the room and gazed about it in a frenzy of trepidation, fully expectant of discovering one or more of those foul prehensile tentacles groping with fulsome purposefulness and propinquity. It was with no small degree of relief that I found that this was so far from the case as not to be happening, and subsequent exploration (and two more broken lamps) proved the lavatory and associated sanitary fixtures to be similarly free from supernatural inhabitation.

Crossing to the bar, I switched on a lava lamp, reached for the heavy crystal decanter of whiskey, poured myself a healthy measure, and whilst replacing the vessel, accidentally knocked the lamp to the floor where, oddly enough, it did not break. I gulped the Scotch down in a single gulp and again reached for the decanter, knocking it onto the prone lamp. Both promptly shattered. Lest the reader become convinced that he (or, not entirely inconceivably, she) is reading the words of a complete prat, I must at this juncture explain that it had not been the mere sight of the spectral and noxious obscenity in the bidet that had thus unmanned me, but rather it was the amalgamation of its hideousness and its blood-chilling familiarity! Alien to all earthly biological configurations as the abomination had been, its form was one with which I had become all too familiar throughout the previous eighteen months. During that time, I had been engaged in the celebrated, if spiritually disquieting archaeological excavations on the detestable island of R'lyecch of which the reader has no doubt acquired an awareness from the innumerable contemporary newspaper and television reports or, perhaps, from a motion picture, allegedly inspired by the events, entitled *The Fun Guy from Yuggoth* (in which, inexplicably, I was portrayed by a performer named Tawny Cypress, who is not only of neither my gender nor ethnicity, but was also irrefutably both too short and slightly too young for the role. Still, that's Hollywood for you).

R'lyecch—for centuries submerged, then startlingly thrown up from the seas a few miles south of Newport, RI, like a vindaloo after a Scottish soccer fan's fifteenth pint of lager. (This emergence was a singularly horrible shock to residents still devastated by the antecedent discovery that most of Rhode Island isn't an island after all.) R'lyecch—with her morbid vestiges of a long (and very sensibly) forgotten culture, her disquietingly asymmetrical architecture, and her miscellaneous related infringements of any sane planet's basic building requirements. R'lyecch—with her weirdly suggestive hieroglyphs, gynecological graffiti and troubling bas relief depictions of a once omnipotent calamari cult, the squid motif of which so strangely echoes the mollusc-oriented symbology of the South Sea escargot cults. It was this last mentioned feature of R'lyecchian decor that was to inspire my research, PBS reality series and subsequent nervous collapse. I became obsessed with this perplexing antediluvian correlation of theology and seafood appetisers, much to the derision of many of my so-called academic peers. In retrospect, I will allow that I might have exercised poor judgement in titling the paper outlining my discoveries: *Was God a Shrimp Cocktail?* But what, after all, is in a name? I remain steadfastly confident of the veracity of my findings and, indeed, could hardly believe otherwise, having witnessed the ghastly circumstances through which the doomed island of R'lyecch came to sink once more to the ocean bed for another millennium's marination. I shuddered to bring the event to mind, an event so far-reaching in its consequences, so deleterious to the sanity of all mankind that the mind reels and bumps into things at the subtlest suggestion of its enormity. A nameless foulness of such inexpressible inconceivability that there is absolutely no point in attempting to discuss it further. So, moving on…

It was shortly after three in the morning when I awoke from my fitful repose, filled with the direst dread and too much chowder. From the floor below my shuttered chamber came a faint but repugnant chattering sound, interspersed with a guttural droning as if my withdrawing room had been taken over by a number of gigantic stick insects who were attempting a vocal recital with Leonard Cohen. Dubious that this could be the cause, I crept noiselessly from my four-poster and into my wardrobe, not, I should stress, from pusillanimity but merely through a momentary misidentification of my boudoir's point of egress. Emerging almost at once, festooned with a profusion of wire coat-hangers, I sprang for the correct door and burst forth into the hallway, whereupon the unnatural tumult below assaulted my eardrums with increased savagery. Now it seemed that the shrill, tittering sounds were resolving themselves into words, albeit of no human tongue which had ever played a part in my own intercourse.

Who could say from what extraterrestrially spawned quasi-larynxes those terrible utterances were wrenched, in what cosmically reviled vernacular they warbled, or whence came the unnerving similitude of their grim cadences to the chorus of *So Long, Marianne*? If such interrogatives left me beflummoxed, I had at least no uncertainty as to the source of the appalling gibbering (I call it gibbering, but never having heard anything gibber before, this remains conjectural). As I forced my timorous way down the steep and perilously tenebrous stairwell, it became ever clearer that the maddening disturbance emanated from no less foreboding a locale than my ground floor lavatorial amenity and more specifically, I had little doubt, that wraith-haunted perversion of a bidet.

Mindful of my earlier precipitant descent into unconsciousness upon observing the blasphemously loathsome thing in the fixture, I determined not to subject my ocular organs to further defilement, but rather to take up pen and paper and attempt to transcribe the more linguistically recognisable syllables that commingled with the execrable chanting and tittering that poured forth from the malignant sanitary appliance. This proved a far from effortless enterprise, since the more human sounds were overlain with the howling of my cat, the crazed piping of the currawongs from the bushland surrounding the cottage, the suggestively bestial cachinnation that compounded the bidet-born cacophony, and the Cramps CD I'd negligently left on repeat play earlier that evening. However, by the time the infernal discordance subsided into silence with the coming of dawn, my small notebook was filled with unfathomable notations which, to one unacquainted with the circumstances of their origins, would appear to be the ravings of one irredeemably insane or at least very, very dyslexic.

"Ygnaiih…ngh'aaaaa…Yog Eggnog nyet flobbagobmob… Na'mdaird nuh eem'n ert…linbinwhinbim…fnord" and so on for a hundred and twelve pages of tightly spaced script. With a dismal exhalation, I flung the notebook into the fire still smouldering in the hearth. What a complete waste of an evening.

I would not, however, fritter away the hours of daylight. Taking advantage of my professorial status, I knocked up the old librarian Alberta Willie shortly before seven o'clock and demanded expeditious access to her restricted area. Although still a newcomer to Farkham University, I was cognisant of the fact that the institution's library included in its collection an immense number of exceptionally rare and decidedly bizarre grimoires. Indeed, many believed it to be the most formidable such aggregation outside the Vatican State and various Byron Bay bookstores. Miss Willie obligingly ushered me to the quaint old athenaeum's nether reaches wherein were stored the "Limited Access" volumes which, even excluding the uniquely comprehensive Victorian perversions section, numbered into the thousands. With what agitation did my groping fingers fall upon such legendary and justly berated tomes as the shunned *Unerwünscht Krampfadern* of Baron Van Maurizon, Comte d'Erlgré's frightful *Culottes des Ghoules*, the critically vituperated *Pnarcotic Manuscripts* and a decidedly queasy-making boxed set of Al Azif, Al Getreel and Al Odutriteh'bezerius.

The specific volume for which I sought I soon descried, mashed in between the emetic *Liber Ebonis et Eboris* and a presumably misfiled copy of *Doctor Doolittle's Puddleby Adventures*. Flinching at the insalubrious quality of the binding, morbidly suggestive of the epithelium of a corrupt and glabrous marmoset, I drew forth the damned treatise, opened it to the title page and felt the blood drain from my countenance as I realised that this was indeed one of the few remaining copies of the *Necrophilicon* of Abdul Alhazbihn (or the "bipolar Iranian" as he was more commonly known by his few friends, innumerous victims and the Book of the Month Club). Digits shaking like continental frankfurts in an earthquake, I flicked through the pestilential pages, shocked beyond all precedent by the sheer relentlessness of the degradation, profanity and utter disregard for personal hygiene that unfurled before me. The spiritual implications were likewise atrocious in the extreme, insinuative of an entire alternative and wholly malevolent universe, unperceived yet coexistent with our own. Reeling in consternation at such a monstrous prospect, I was of a sudden entirely overcome with terror as a quivering, skeletal hand descended upon my shoulder. Thankfully, at that moment my senses sped away and I was plunged into an abyss of darkness.

As the tide of consciousness flowed back like a flowing back tide of consciousness, my eyes fluttered open and beheld the wizened visage of Miss Willie hovering with uncomfortable proximity above.

"Strewth, are you all right, Professor Whibble?" she asked in her irritatingly coloratura contralto. "I only tapped you on the shoulder to ask if you'd like a nice cup of English Breakfast and you got taken queer. Didn't he get taken queer, Doctor Elliott?"

"Dead queer," a masculine voice agreed, and upon raising my slightly throbbing head, I gazed full into the somewhat batrachian features of Farkham's Dean, Shane Elliott. "But don't distress yourself, Whibble, old mate. The writings of the bipolar Iranian often affect first-time readers like that."

Allowing Elliott to assist me to my feet, I recovered the heinous volume, noting that to my chagrin the thing had fallen open to a page illustrated with demonic figures disporting themselves in the most provocative and physiologically arduous of manners. By now distinctly discomforted, I decided to inform the good Dean of my purpose in consulting the wretched grimoire.

"Doctor Elliott," I blurted forth, "what I am about to disclose to you may give you cause to doubt the wisdom of your appointing me to my new post. In fact, it may very well cause you also to question my sanity…"

"I reckon he's still a bit queer," Miss Willie interjected, and Elliott, very considerately, asked her if she wouldn't mind toddling off to make that pot of English Breakfast, discerning the theme of my disquisition to be of no small delicacy.

"Righto," Miss Willie pronounced. "I can take a hint, and I can see when there's queerness brewing. You listen to our Dean, though, you hear, Professor Whibble. He's a deep one and no mistake."

"Only on my mother's side," Elliott confided cryptically. "Now, Whibble, old cobber, tell me, what's gotten your knickers so bloody knotted?"

Later that evening, the Dean and I sat before the commodious hearth at Fatclover Cottage, sipping Tequila Slammers and smoking Havana cigars through a Moroccan hookah. To my relief, far from assuming that he had offered a position in his illustrious University to an unmitigated fruit loop, Elliott had been entirely sympathetic and even compunctious about my plight and the pall of perniciousness that issued from the bedevilled bidet. It was, he stated, the University's responsibility to provide its faculty with clean, pleasant and cosmologically stable living quarters and that the onus was unarguably his own either to rectify or to oust this peccant appliance forthwith. Consequently, he had had the unit examined that very afternoon, engaging a rough and ready looking plumber named Strigby to perform the labour.

After twenty minutes of tinkering, swearing and wriggling about on the lavatorial floor, the tradesman proclaimed that he had located the source of the problem and that it was not uncommon in this particular model.

"The Splatamat HPL93," he declared, "now that's a foolproof piece of bottom-abluting technology. But what you blokes have here is the HPL92 which, to be frank with you, is a load of ferret's tadgers. All sorts of problems with the 92."

"Of the sort Whibble here's been mucked about by?" the Dean wished to know.

"Well, not as a rule, but it wouldn't surprise me," the artisan replied. "Well, all right, it would a bit. But you'd never get it in a 93."

"I see," Elliott suspired cholerically. "And what do you propose we do about it?"

"Well, s'pose I'd better whip it out and get you a new one," quoth Strigby. "A 93 if you like."

Thus, it was that the original appliance was returned to its manufacturer, along with a very harsh note requesting recompense for the inconvenience and speculating at length upon the probable consequences of an inter-dimensional intrusion whilst some unsuspecting houseguest was attempting to deploy the bidet in accordance with its intended function.

"So, then, Whibble, old digger," the Dean articulated, "correct me if you like, but I reckon that's pretty bloody well that."

I smiled and raised my glass of Balmain Bock in concordance, and from that moment my life at Fatclover Cottage was remarkable for its utter paucity of nauseatingly insidious nocturnal jabbering, grotesque and uncannily phosphorescent amoeboid intelligences, and all such demented, flagitious and otherworldly intrusions into the rational realm of college existence. However, while it was undeniably with a certain relief that I returned to a life bereft of metaphysical exigencies associated with post-eliminatory purification, somehow I couldn't help but feel just slightly disappointed. It's funny what you miss.

THE RETURN OF...

CHRISTOPHER SEQUEIRA

Gary, or George, or Charles—or whatever the name of that part-time receptionist and word-processing scribe that Bill Carliss had hired was—came into Vic Chandra's office. Vic was trying to get his head around a fairly complex and correspondingly dull chain of ownership from a merger, and although he was under time constraints he only feigned irritation at the interruption. Avoidance of the mind-numbingly boring project, even if it put him a bit behind, was welcome.

"Oh, Mister Chandra? I've got a bit of a problem," said the receptionist.

"It's Vic, um, mate," said Vic, waving his hand at a chair. "I'm sure it's not that we're working you too hard, I hope? What's up?"

"It's this man in reception. He wants to see someone, but I know Mister Carliss doesn't want to see him, because they spoke yesterday and Mister Carliss told him to go away," said the young fellow, timidly.

Vic almost sprang out of his seat with enthusiasm. He was slender, and had never been in a fight in his life, and this sounded like drama in a life usually without it. "God, his name's not MacKernenny, is it?" Vic's memory darted to a former client of Carliss & Carliss who did not like the advice they'd given him—which MacKernenny ignored; the consequent total of his bill—which he didn't pay; and the various judgments against him—which were State and Federal judicial decisions, not Carliss & Carliss's issue at all, since the lunatic finally chose to represent himself. After the last judgment MacKernenny had come in and threatened to beat Bill Carliss up, but Carliss had called the police and had him dragged out (he took a brand new door with him as he went). But that was almost three years ago, they'd understood MacKernenny was in the nick after that…

"No, he's not like that. No, this guy is not dangerous, he's *old*. I told him Mister Carliss said we weren't taking his case, but he doesn't seem to understand, he's just sitting out there, he wants to see him, and when I told him Mister Carliss wasn't here he ignored me."

Vic almost melted back into his chair. Now the issue was sounding like it wasn't going to be more than a very brief distraction. Just a senile lost dog.

Still. He pulled open his right-hand drawer and tossed the increasingly unattractive merger file in there.

"How about you just bring him in here and I'll have a chat with him. Do you have his name? Are you sure he's not a former client?"

"It's, oh, I forgot his name, I wrote it down at the front desk, but he's not on the database, I'll bring him in?"

"Yes, thanks," Vic said.

Vic straightened a few other things on his clutter-field of a desk, to no real outcome. That was all the time he needed to fill before Gary / George / Charles brought the man in.

He was tall, lean, and, no two ways about it, he *was* old; wrinkled like a sun-dried tomato, but still, only a tad stooped with age. He was dressed too formally for a spring day in sunny Mermaid Beach, and the suit was old, but spotless. He had a sombre face, big wing-nut ears, large eyes and a long nose. If he was soft in the scone, the eyes didn't suggest it; he looked at Vic piercingly, like he was a piece of fruit in a 'Must-Go-Today' bin.

"Sir, I'm Vic Chandra, junior partner with the firm. Our young fellow said you wanted Mister Bill Carliss, but I'm afraid he won't be in until Monday. What is it you wanted us to help you with?" Vic held out his hand.

The old man studied Vic's hand, then took it, giving a brief, gentle shake, quickly released. He remained standing, and unsmiling. When he spoke it was with an American accent, but softened by something; some years living here, perhaps?

"Mister Chandra. I have come two thousand and three hundred miles because I need a law firm to lodge an injunction, or some sort of legal delay or obstacle—I don't know what you people call it—against a motion picture that is being worked on, at a location both near my home, and also at a location here, at facilities on the Golden Coast. That is why I traveled here yesterday, and then inquired with a library about the addresses of local law concerns. Your firm was nearest my hotel."

Vic talked whilst doing some quick mental arithmetic. Two Thou and Three was the span of the entire country—the guy must live in Western Australia—Perth?

"*Gold* Coast, you mean, just south of here? They shoot a bit of TV and films, there. We've done some work for those types of companies, so we could have a client conflict problem. But I'm getting ahead of myself here," Vic said. "Sit, please, sit."

The old man finally sat down, in a chair opposite Vic. He seemed tense, as if he would happily stand up again if he didn't get his way, a look Vic knew from repeatedly seeing it on his father's face when the old man was still alive and sober.

"You're upset by the film production? Noise, disturbances? And if they're shooting where you live, where is that?" Vic said.

"Mister Chandra, yes, it is a disruption, but not noise, as such. But that is not the basis upon which I wish the matter stopped. I wish the work halted because they—they being a company named Paragon Pictures, you would have heard of them, a very large American operation—have no right to make this film, unless I say so. I told Mister Carliss this and he shooed me away. To be frank with you, I suspect him of regarding me as psychologically infirm."

Vic looked at the man, and, a visual echo of Vic's dad, a face Vic had missed these last three years flittered across his mind. Because of that, despite years of honing his professional instincts, Vic grinned, and spoke words he knew weren't really representative of a detached legal persona, but what the Hell, they were true.

"You seem alright to me, sir. You come on, maybe, a bit strident, shall we say, but my Dad was that type. I can cope with it, I think."

The old man's reaction was a surprised stare, but he quickly shook that off. "I see. But back to my situation. My objection, I want that film shut down."

Vic now really knew he was wasting company time on an old loon who thought he was either God or a movie studio mogul, and Bill Carliss had already told the guy to piss off. It was fun, though.

"Umm, so what right do you have to tell the studio what to film? Are you a shareholder?"

The old man's eyes flickered, and was his nose actually wrinkling with disdain?

"Mister Carliss asked me that! Indeed! Shares were the ruination of the United States economy when I was a boy, and they tell me that is a repeated problem today! No, I do not own the studio, but, as I told your Carliss, I have the right to stop them."

Vic nodded, and the old man's voice actually raised in volume. "He told me not to come back unless I had proof of my own name, my own identity, as if I were some sort of drooling incompetent. When I said my things were at the hotel, quite some bus-ride away, he would not relent. But I am no incompetent. I can substantiate my rights."

Vic groaned inwardly. He actually opened the right-hand drawer, quietly; time to get back to work, fun never lasts forever. "Rights." he thought. If this guy was rich his next phrase would include the all-hallowed "It's a matter of principle!" If he was broke he might invoke Jesus. Or Charity.

"Rights are often quite finite things, sir, governed by local statute. What your rights are in the city of Perth, about quiet enjoyment of your home, might not be impinged upon by a movie crew here in Queensland with proper permits, observing the conditions of those local permits," Vic said.

The old man reached inside his coat and a sheaf of documents was extracted.

"Tsk, I am not from Perth, from Western Australia, you misunderstand. My passport, my birth certificate, a driver's license, albeit long expired. The deed to my current abode. Other papers."

Vic took receipt of the bundle, with pessimistic curiosity, but he could tell the old fellow thought the provision of the documents would have some sort of impact. Damn Bill for giving the old guy even a shred of false hope by suggesting the production of any paperwork might shut down a blasted film company! Bill should have just told the old fellow he was barking up the wrong tree and had no capacity to shut down a bloody mega-million dollar-job-creating local bonanza because the schedule interfered with him feeding his budgerigar, or whatever silly thing it would involve.

The old man crossed his arms, but one hand extended from that gathering like a decrepit cobra—wagging a skinny finger. "Mister Chandra, I am not bereft of my senses. I say the filming people have no right to make a motion picture called "H.P. Lovecraft's The Return of Cthulhu" because *those* rights belong, exclusively, to me; Howard Phillips Lovecraft, Junior. I am the son and heir of the original author of the literary rights being adapted for the film's story, being as I was, born to he and my mother, Mrs. Sonia Greene Lovecraft, in 1924, in Chicago, Illinois, in the United States of America—you can see that, yes, from my papers?"

Vic was flipping back and forth through the sheaf, frowning. "Um, yes, although there's a lot to digest here, Mister...Lovecraft. You're saying your father was some sort of writer?"

For the first time that long, lined face relaxed, and a thin razor-like smile emerged. "You have it, Mister Chandra, you have it, at last. The creator of the story and characters used in the film that is being filmed here on the Golden-*Gold* Coast—I beg your pardon—and also being filmed at my current home, which is the island of Pohnpei, in the Federated States of Micronesia, six hours airplane *North*, not West, from here; *that creator was my father*. No one has sought my permission to make this film with my inheritance, which is to say with the fruit of his creative labours. And I do *not* intend to give my permissions. What I intend is to exercise my rights to make those filming people cease their motion picture immediately."

Vic slid the right-hand drawer closed. "I'm saved," he thought.

Vic's interview with the old man continued on a little longer, culminating in him taking copies of all of the documents. He explained to the old fellow that if what he was saying was true, this might be a case beyond the Carliss firm's resources—taking on an international studio like Paragon—Carliss might need to refer him to another firm. HPL Junior (as Vic found himself humorously thinking of the old fellow) didn't really react to that, but thanked Vic and left the office.

Vic had indeed landed something much, much bigger than anything in the experience of his own career, or his company's. HPL Jr was a walking entertainment industry copyright bombshell. He was a Da Vinci Code of author's rights' gold, a discovery worth, literally, millions.

It transpired that his father, Howard Phillips Lovecraft, had been an early twentieth century American writer, who had died relatively young, at forty-six years of age in 1937, in poverty, but not before writing a few dozen, short horror stories and a novel or two that involved completely original style and plot elements. Senior had been a contributor to the booming fiction market of his time, the 'pulp' magazines that crowded newsstands in those pre-TV days, and some said that what Raymond Chandler was to the detective story Lovecraft was to the horror tale, and university Literature departments aplenty would attest to this.

Senior's crowning achievement was the creation of a horror 'series' or 'universe' of tangentially connected, though self-contained stories. These tales centered around inhuman monsters from another dimension that had lived on Earth in pre-history, but if you were unlucky you might stumble on them awakening or get in the way of their human acolytes—read crazed Cultists—and the acolytes' plans to see these Uglies return. Of all the beasties 'Cthulhu' was the marquee monster; a Godzilla-sized, octopus-headed, bat-winged biped that was set to rise again atop a long-sunken Pacific island to take over all, and the mere sight of this thing, or even just the tapping into his powerful dreams, could make a person go stark, staring mad. Lots of folk in Senior's stories ended up on the last page dribbling and cackling incoherently just upon the discovery of this awful back-story of 'The Old Ones' being out there set to return and chew us all up when they arrive (usually upon an occasion forecast to occur 'when the stars are right').

This potted history was presented in summary to Vic, Bill Carliss and the other two partners, Sandra Kerr and Deidre Boorman, on the very next Wednesday morning at Carliss & Carliss's offices, at an urgently convened meeting.

This get-together was scheduled at the request of Deborah Worth of Worth and Co., a copyright law firm in New York that Bill was friendly with and who he'd sent the HPL Jr paperwork to on Sunday night. Worth herself appeared via Skype on a large screen Carliss organized for the conference room, a woman in her forties with tight features and a bronze hue to her skin.

Worth explained she had 'had her people on this straight away' and the findings were highly significant. Cthulhu, his island home of R'lyeh, and Lovecraft's many other creations were the subject of *hundreds*, if not thousands of items of spin-off stories and related merchandise: books, toys, games, action figures and collectables. These ranged from comedy-themed Cthulhu coffee cups to name-check gags on hit TV shows—about the only pop-culture territory not over-saturated was feature film itself, and that was mostly because the Lovecraft literary monsters translated poorly to cinema, being horrors only ever really intentioned for a reader to use their own imagination to depict.

But regardless of that, it was generally understood that all Lovecraft copyrights had now expired, that there was no estate and no legal inheritors as such. No one had even known Lovecraft had a son, but, yes, a check on Junior's Birth Certificate had authenticated it and led to a finding that Worth had now verified: Lovecraft Senior and his ex-wife had decided to spare their boy embarrassment about their divorce and the reputation of a father who was a 'horror-man' (and a very impoverished one), so they agreed to protect him by having her relatives primarily raise him in early years. Lovecraft's own death in '37 made that discretion about the boy's father a permanent choice, so 'Howard Greene' completed his education and commenced a school-teaching career very unobtrusively (and his mother later passed on in 1972).

With this summary presented to the Carliss partners, Howard Lovecraft Junior was escorted into the conference room and joined the group discussion. Vic Chandra wasn't fooled by Worth's rapid adoption of a kindly demeanor as old Junior was brought in; the woman smelled a payoff, a big one.

And indeed, that was what she laid out: Worth revealed to a stunned Vic Chandra, Bill Carliss and their peers, and Junior, that HPL's documents had created an uproar in the last twenty-four hours State-side, particularly copies of letters confirming his ownership of the material in HPL Senior's (heretofore never seen) Will, and very old letters indicating Senior had in fact lodged proper documentation with the United States copyright office; a claim that no 'Lovecraft Scholar' (of which there were dozens, amongst them many lauded literary academics) had ever heard of.

Naturally enough Worth's staff had wanted to test the authenticity of the letters, and that was when things had taken their most dramatic upward swing this very day, when, using contacts Worth had in the copyright office, an astounding confirmation had been forthcoming: The copyright office had *mis-filed* the documents decades ago, but a File Cross-Reference Number on the very documents Junior had in his possession immediately enabled the originals to be located and authenticated in the Library of Congress! Worth crowed gleefully that she now had an email from the director of the copyright office verifying this situation, and indicating the office was conducting a review to establish their legal position in relation to the matter.

This, Worth proudly announced, was "enough to assure a tactical position for us to pursue."

"Mister Lovecraft, we are so glad you had the intelligence to bring this matter to professionals. If you had called or emailed us from Pohnpei we would have flown you over to Los Angeles, though, but no matter, perhaps we can meet soon enough. I'm thinking of a trip out to Australia myself soon."

Vic put his hand over his mouth, to stifle a gasp. *What is going on here? This is worth HOW MUCH cabbage?*

"So, I think you ladies and gentlemen understand what I'm saying?" Worth said. "Mr Howard Phillips Lovecraft, Junior is indeed the holder of correctly lodged copyrights. The failure of the US Copyright office to correctly indicate this in their various catalogues and searchable databases is their fault, and does pave the way to a series of actions that Mister Lovecraft can take, via us, to immediately shut down production on the hundreds, by our estimate, of websites and merchandise manufacturers infringing upon his intellectual property. And, we can seek an immediate accounting. These outfits owe you, by the most conservative reckoning, multiple millions of dollars, Mister Lovecraft.

The old man had sat with his head on his chin, eyelids closed. Vic grew worried, he looked like he was asleep, but Vic knew he wasn't. Junior opened his eyes.

"I can't believe people are doing all this nonsense, but I'm sure you're not lying, Ma'am, otherwise we wouldn't be all here around a big table talking. I've lived on Pohnpei since 1964, and none of this was going on when I still lived in the USA. Mother told me she got the occasional letter from Father's old friends, a writer fellow or two, especially, in California and New York, but that was it. Now all this falderal, as well as the movie that they want to film near my home. Quite amazing."

The old man swallowed, and frowned. "And that's the main thing. The movie. They have a huge ship, a cargo tanker, it is, pretty much. Anchored near Kolonia, near home. Not to be critical, Mister Carliss, Mister Chandra, you others; you think this Gold Coast is a lovely place. But my home, Pohnpei, that's a true paradise. No screaming teenagers and their hideous noise and stupid clothes that look like plastic bags. No cars and trucks driven so recklessly you can't cross the street without dying, killing people so regularly it's like a daily slaughterhouse. Pohnpei is clean, and it's quiet. The waters in Truk Lagoon, you've never seen their like. We have deep sea divers come from all around the world to see them. Not to mention the old undersea ruins of Nan Madol. Breathtaking. Inspiring."

"And the folks there. I've been there fifty years. I was a school teacher for forty years, I was married for thirty-five until my wife passed on. I know these people. Decent, family folk. Everybody knows everybody, there's only thirty thousand of us. Even now, a fellow my age can walk about and he's safe, not like this place. I read your papers in my hotel; you get robbed, you get stabbed, people hit and curse you for no reason. Like the USA is, now, crazy, disrespectful, a mad place ever since poor old President Kennedy was killed, if you ask me.

"That ship is full of movie folk and their equipment, hammering and building props for this movie. But it's not the noise, it's the attitude. They think money makes them better than other people; they think they have the right to be rude, uncivil, and tramp around the place talking to locals like we're cretins. I don't like it. My friends in Pohnpei don't like it."

"When I found out what it was all about, that my *own father's work* was the reason they came—all because a couple of silly lines in one story he wrote mention Pohnpei, and they decide they now have to film some big movie climax scene with giant rubber monsters, and fireworks—well, I became upset, very upset. I'd managed to keep my poor old dad's business to myself. He tried, you see, but he was a weak husband, and not a father much to talk about either. He could have come good in time, but he didn't live too long. He died when I was twelve. Never told his friends, but he wrote to me, and I saw him maybe once a year. That Will, those copyrights, he gave all of them to me before he passed. Was kind of sheepish about it, but it was all he had."

"Anyway, that's all been history, until now. I have been happy to be plain old Howie Greene for my life. Teach school, like I said, and I swim, and I play a little music. A pretty good life, if a quiet one.

"But this movie stuff is wrong, and realized I have the ability to do something about it. And at my age, you don't often have such options. I knew I was going to attract some attention. But this isn't for me, this is for the people in my community. I can't be delicate about my past, now. The movie needs to be closed, and those workers sent back to California, or wherever. They can make lots of other films, I'm sure, or just make one in a big studio, make it look like they filmed on Pohnpei. I know they can do that."

Carliss smiled and addressed Junior.

"We sincerely admire the brave step of coming forward to us, Mister Lovecraft, some people might be intimidated at the thought of challenging a big company like Paragon. Ms. Worth and her people are amongst the best firms in the world, they have lawyers with specific expertise in cases like this. Your approach to us was very kind, but we think you'll be in very good hands, and, if you are willing; we'll serve as intermediaries to any interactions they need to have with the on-shore efforts of Paragon filming the main sequences of the film here on the Gold Coast. We understand the executive producer and director are in town right now, in fact."

Vic was silent. He wanted to laugh. Bill Carliss had never said 'we' in relation to a project of Vic's before, Vic knew it wasn't out of respect for Vic, it was in case Vic stuffed it up, he wanted deniability. But now, 'we' are all one big seamless machine working to Junior's needs, collecting big bucks for doing nothing. The kind of gig Carliss liked best, and, thought Vic, if I have to be honest, I suppose I don't mind that either.

"Indeed," Worth chimed in. "I've sent some waivers and an agreement to Mr Carliss, and he'll walk you through them, Mister Lovecraft, and with your permission, if you sign, I can tell you this: Paragon will not be filming "Return of Cthulhu" in Ponhpei or anywhere else, unless they agree to your terms. And based on the publicly known salaries of the actor and directors who are working on this picture, I think they have in excess of one hundred and fifty million dollars riding on this. If they have to shut down it will cripple them for next year's release schedule. I think you can almost name your terms and they will accede. If

113

that includes things like a curfew for staff working in Ponhpei, well, you, sir, might succeed where the local government of Micronesia could not." At this last, Worth displayed a smile that was so big her gleaming white teeth looked like a shark's.

Junior looked up, nodding a bit like a dog that was watching a man wave a bone. Carliss smiled again. Worth smiled again.

Junior wasn't smiling as he spoke. "No. I want it stopped. All of it. No more stories, no more toys, no more games. And no movies. No more reprints of my father's work, and definitely none of this crazy other stuff."

Carliss licked his lips and leaned over. "Mister Lovecraft, I can promise you, we reached out because we cannot represent your interests from here. Ms. Worth can. Ms Worth's company are experts, and they are willing to take your case on free of charge, you can pay them out of the proceeds. But just understand, this is a significant exercise, these studios are ruthless, they will ignore you and plow on, wouldn't that cause you greater distress?"

Lovecraft was so swift in response that Vic almost gasped, Carliss certainly physically flinched. The old man leaned across the table, again the metaphor of a striking reptile came to Vic's mind as the man wagged a talon at Carliss, then at the Skype screen.

"No. I listened very carefully to what you said. I'm worth a lot of money now. And these movie people have invested heavily, and stand to lose everything. Well, then I have the cards, haven't I? Me. Not them."

"And not any of you. Mother used to say the only reason a lawyer doesn't charge you is if your case is going to get the shirt off the other guy's back, just like any business.

"So here's what you lawyer-folk are going to do. You tell Paragon I want that movie shut down; not one single frame of film is going to see a cinema screen. You tell those toy people to get their accounts in order and start figuring out what they owe me. We're doing this my way. I'm very old, but I am not very stupid. I've seen faces like yours, Mr Carliss, and yours, Miss Worth. I've seen them at a barbecue when someone's carving up a roast hog. That's what I am to you people, or so you think."

Worth's voice cut through the air, ice hung on every syllable.

"Mister Lovecraft, I can see you are distrustful, and I understand that, you've lived away from big city interests for a long time, your Mother's name is at sta—"

The reptile man pounced and gobbled his prey. "Her name is not your worry, young lady! I mind you to never speak of her again unless I give you leave to."

In the fragile silence that followed the old man kept the room's attention. He took a slim piece of paper out of his pocket, and waved it, it looked like a recently written list of names and phone numbers.

"I told you that I got the name of this company from a library. Now there's twelve more names on this list. I'm going to get the bus back to my hotel room and call one of them up, unless you actually get the wax out of your ears and listen to what I'm actually asking you to do? Is that clear as day?"

Worth's face was stone. "Would you mind if we spoke alone for a brief while, Mister Lovecraft?"

Lovecraft stood "I assuredly don't. But one thing whilst you have your pow-wow, if I may. If you folk want to keep me as a client there's one other thing I want."

He pointed to Vic. "This fellow is the only one who talks to me from now on. Only one shows me paper, only one asks me questions. I'm too old for the wiles of you others. If you stick to just him we might get somewhere without me losing my temper. Mister Chandra, he actually listens, and he did exactly like I asked, not what HE wanted. If he's not in this, I go somewhere else."

"I'll be downstairs in that café you got. They got coffee like I haven't drunk since I was in Los Angeles in '58, very nice."

Vic was in one of the more awkward situations of his professional life. It felt bizarre, but also wonderful. Worth started in on Carliss almost straight away.

"Bill, my office has expended quite a few billable hours on this since you contacted us. If you think we're a charity of some kind I can assure you we're not, I—"

"Deborah, it's alright, you can calm down," said Bill. "You'll get remunerated for your efforts so far, probably out of the proceeds of Mister Lovecraft's future actions. But let's make something clear on my end—I never authorized you to run around doing all the research you did. You smelt a significant bonanza, and you acted, and I gotta give you credit, it was very valuable; great instincts."

"Well, yes, but I am very concerned about Lovecraft's attitude to my company and his strange affinity for Mister Chandra. What's being said down there?"

Vic stood up. "Look, Bill, Ms. Worth, I should let you have privacy... "

"Vic, that would be good. But before you go, listen, both of you," said Bill. This Lovecraft is a cranky old guy who distrusts lawyers. Not my typical client profile, and probably not a kind you deal with at *all*, Deborah. Now, get over it."

Worth actually blinked. Her mouth opened but Bill plowed on.

"Vic's done what we *should* have done, not assumed what the client wants. Now he thinks we're snakey. Fine. He likes Vic, he's worth a small fortune. Let's just discuss how we'll move forward most efficiently with that, but really, that's a huge win, he's committed to us via Vic. Vic, leave the details to us, and go and see that our aged friend is OK in a strange town. Take him to his hotel, get him lunch or something."

Vic wasn't sure whether Lovecraft would still be outside in the waiting room, but was pleased he was. His offer to drive the man back to his hotel and share a meal was met with polite agreement. It was a bright, clear day and the breeze was strong and cool, so Vic had the air con off and the windows down as they drove about fifteen minutes away to the Crystal Sands on Pacific Drive. His passenger opened the conversation.

"Got you into any trouble with your bosses, Mister Chandra?"

Vic smiled. "Nah, Bill's a good egg. He just has to be the boss, but then, he does own the company."

Junior nodded. "I think it was the woman who was the problem, I suspect. Very smart, very strong, but pushy. I don't care whether you're my plumber, my accountant or my doctor. You don't make decisions for me, you ask me first, and the only exception should be my undertaker. You get to my age, even the nicest people can be irritating, because they think you can't decide anything for yourself. Well, I'm not senile, as yet, far as I know."

Vic chuckled a bit. "Yeah, well, I don't think those two will be making that mistake again."

The two of them got out as Vic parked in a carpark adjacent the Crystal Sands, a twenty-storey, fairly modern affair. Again Vic admired the fact that Lovecraft moved very ably for someone of his age, Vic's own dad hadn't been seventy-five and he hobbled like a war wounded.

They decided to eat in the hotel restaurant; it jutted out from the base of the hotel and had nice, open air settings. A pleasant waitress with green and purple hair and three nose rings served them and Vic watched Junior shake his head as if he was trying to get water out of his ears as she set their food down. Vic kept his smirk to himself, but was pleased to see Junior acting like a perfectly regular old guy at the sight of the current youth culture's brand of self-expression.

Junior's hotel room was apparently up on the tenth floor and he pointed it out to Vic. "Nice—they got a swimming pool up there. I know I rag on about Pohnpei, Mister Chandra, but I do admit the view from my room, the coast, the city skyline, it's all quite impressive."

Vic spoke around a bite of a sandwich. "This must be costing you a lot of money, the trip, the bills?"

Lovecraft smiled. "Appreciate the concern, but I was wise with my money before retiring. Have to be, the cost of living in the Federated States of Micronesia is a little sharp on some things, compared to the USA, but I own my own home and rent another, so I'm OK, even if I don't teach regularly anymore. But, my life has never been extravagant."

Vic was interested. The conversation continued to amble along on such cultural comparisons and Vic found this odd, old fellow more and more likable; he had a didactic manner that certainly did scream 'ex-school-teacher', but it carried a charm, and inspired a confidence.

Vic was just finishing his sandwich, and had decided to order a second cup of coffee, when he noticed a man with an I-pad, sitting at another table, watching them. The man was maybe thirty, thin, wearing a dirty white shirt and dark pants, and kept looking back and forth from Vic and Junior to his tablet. Vic had a sudden thought.

The guy could be some sort of internet freak, and Vic thus wondered if the 'big Lovecraft story' had gone viral. That some pop culture fanatic had leaked the issue from Worth's office, or the Copyright Office, or the Library of Congress—who knew, maybe one of Carliss' kids was a 'Call of Cthulhu' role-playing game nut? Vic might be lunching with a nerd's version of a literary celebrity.

"Your father was pretty famous, in his own way, I understand," Vic said.

Junior couldn't smile, and gave up trying. "Yes, but really only after he died. Like a lot of famous painters, I suppose. Artists whose work is only valued after they are gone."

"Do you like his work?" said Vic, then added, "I'm sorry, I shouldn't ask, I—"

Junior held up his hand as he finished his own lunch. He swallowed.

"No, it's a good question. Truth is, some of it I like very much. He was an extremely well-read man, and had strong adherence to a form, a structure. His writing was peppered with exotic ideas and wonderful little historical and geographic references. He was very original, too, 'way out' the youngsters say, or maybe they don't use that term anymore?"

Vic laughed. "I haven't qualified as a youngster for a while, but I might still use that term."

Junior grinned at that. "Truth is," he said, "when I was young I read everything Father wrote that I could get my hands on. I didn't see him a lot, and he wasn't a gregarious man, in some ways he was painfully shy, although when you got him going he had too many opinions on too many things if you ask me. But most of the time he just lived in his own little world inside his head. And I wanted to understand that, because Mother raised me very differently. So, I read his stuff in the magazines and elsewhere, probably memorised every word. I won't say I idolized him, I just thought about him a lot, since I didn't see a lot of the man."

"Really?" Vic said. "Memorised? From what I gathered looking some of his material up on the weekend, that's quite a feat, he liked a long sentence or two!"

Junior's eyes rolled back a little and he wiped his mouth with the paper serviette that had accompanied his lunch. "The most merciful thing in the world, I think, is the inability of the human mind to correlate all its contents.' That's from *The Call of Cthulhu*," he said.

"Well, I'm impressed. You could add orator to your list of talents," said Vic.

"You stand in front of a classroom of unruly kids every day for fifty years, you learn to project your own voice, or you at least get used to it. If you don't show some degree of authority, the kids will run crazy on you. They'd do whatever they want."

Vic replied. "From the way I saw you handle Deborah Worth and my boss, Bill, I don't think your kids would have got away with anything."

The old man dipped his head, and avoided eye contact, then lifted it again.

"The good kids are easy, they teach themselves. I used to like it because I had a soft spot for the troubled ones, because, no surprise, I was in trouble a lot when I was young. I reacted to a lot of loneliness and frustration from the situation with my father, then blamed my mother, then blamed him, then myself, and so it went. Alternatively worshipped and hated him; then her. It's funny, your boss and the lady lawyer say there's so many fans of father's work making all kinds of foolish trinkets and gee-gaws based on it…" Lovecraft's eyes were staring at something decades past.

"I was twelve," he said finally. "I did a pottery class, and I tried to make a ceramic ornament, something for him, as a gift. I decided to make an 'Elder Sign'; a thing out of one of his stories that the good guys have to use like a crucifix against a vampire, but it chases away much bigger monsters! I fretted over this thing for days, and it turned out alright, a fist-sized, flat stone with a weird-looking tree-branch-like design drawn on it; three prongs one side, two on the other, just as my dad himself had designed and sketched it for me one time. I hoped he'd love it. I made it, black design on gold painted background. I was really proud of it."

The old man pulled a pencil out of his shirt pocket, and scribbled a design idly on the paper serviette that had accompanied his meal. Vic looked at what he'd drawn.

"**B**ut I never saw him again, and mother had become completely frosted towards him, said we were better off without him. I kept that thing on my bedside table for months. I'd almost forgotten it when I was a young man, eight years later and we heard he had died, back when I was twelve! So I made it for nothing. When I saw kids going a bit wrong, I often just thought of myself. You never know — what's that boy's story? That girl's? What troubles, and sadness have they had?"

Vic could see the old man was anything but maudlin, he was as calm and assured telling the very personal account as he was about anything else, and Vic knew that such honesty came with advanced years; here was a man with no time to waste on shame or falsehoods.

Vic decided to change the subject. "How about some more coffee, or a dessert, Mister Lovecraft?" he said and turned his head to look for their waiter.

That chance turning of Vic's head was the thing, later, that made all the difference, as terrible chaos overtook the two men.

The man in the white shirt had approached them both, so quietly and unobtrusively, that Vic hadn't seen him, and he was now standing right next to them. In a split second Vic instantly flashed on the idea he'd want an autograph from Junior to sell on ebay.

Then Vic saw Whiteshirt had a knife in his hand—a hunting or fishing knife—it was huge and deadly-looking.

Vic just reacted. There were lunch trays on a stack behind him, and Vic grabbed at them and picked one up.

Whiteshirt screamed and lunged at Junior with that knife, but Vic's tray got in the way for two seconds. The knife shimmied off it, but stayed firmly in the man's bony fist.

Junior was old, but not incapable of moving; he slid out of his chair and with reasonable agility he stepped back, and back again; away from the danger. The knife wielder now had to lean forward to get at him; he tried, but Junior was too far away.

Whiteshirt's face contorted—a strange, childish rage manifested itself—and he looked towards Vic. With hate, he lunged at Vic, the knife caught Vic's sleeve and sliced through his suit-coat and shirt effortlessly. Whiteshirt then pulled back, straightened up, preparing to have another slash.

Vic thought, "Fuck, he could have cut me if I was any slower." And he glanced at his arm.

His coat sleeve was hanging loose like an open-skinned sausage and a line was open in his skin, blood was flowing a bright red, little drops evenly hitting the floor. He *had* been cut, and only now was there a slight sting of pain.

Vic looked up—Whiteshirt had the knife raised, he looked like he was going to embed it in Vic's eye.

Then there was a horrible wet and dry crunch and Whiteshirt was face forward, pitching to the ground; and another horrible crack as his face hit concrete. He'd been smashed in the back of the head by the waitress, with a chair.

Vic sat down.

Vic sat up in the hotel room with Junior and Bill Carliss and Tom Forbes, a security consultant that Bill had engaged. There was a steady hubbub of noise outside, which was understandable. A hundred emails had filled Vic's inbox, and there were reporters— more than a dozen—outside.

The incident, a quick trip to the hospital and few stitches for Vic, then the rounds at the police station, it had all been totally surreal, but mostly like a soap opera. Vic felt guilty but elated, and he was amazed at his strange, soaring emotions. Fear, joy; all the attention from concerned police, hotel staff, his boss, and round and round.

Sylvie, his wife, a plump and baby-faced woman, had come in from work to see him at the hospital. She was introduced to Junior and was absolutely taken with him and his story. Once she was satisfied that Vic was OK she spent the afternoon looking after Junior. Junior, for his part, was clearly unequipped to deal with such attention, but Sylvie had a knack, she just ignored all that and kept fussing, whether the recipient liked it or not.

The police finally completed interviews and reports and Vic's worst fears were confirmed. The Lovecraft story had hit the Internet *before* he, Worth, Carliss, and Junior had their Skype conference. Whiteshirt was apparently a known ice-user and musician from Hervey Bay, well north. He had read the speculation and done some very clever online sleuthing; then he'd rung several hotels and pretended to be Junior's nephew. The deskman at the Crystal Sands had revealed Junior was staying there. Whiteshirt had then climbed into a rather decrepit Holden Commodore and driven for four hours, arriving at the hotel at ten AM. Then he just waited for Junior to come back.

The security implications were obvious. Tom Forbes was a dark-haired man with the neck of a regular body-builder. He was calm and quietly spoken even when his word-choices were emphatic.

"You can't stay here, it's been all over the damn news, practically named the friggin' room number."

"But there's not likely to be many more loons, are there?" said Vic.

Tom frowned. "The police said as much, but the problem is, why was there even one? You're not a writer or a rock star, Mr Lovecraft, you're a dead writer's son. I wondered why this guy was so set against you. So I fished about online, and as it turns out our crazy friend had a blog."

Tom dragged out a laptop and showed the others. "The End of Cthulhu!" was the title of a purple and black page.

"It seems that this nut felt that Mister Lovecraft here would put a stop to the masses of, umm, 'Cathoolo' related books and merchandise, or as HE describes it, in his own charming way: 'tributes to the dark gods whose purpose was handed to the world by the teacher; his father, the great Apostle, Howard Phillips Lovecraft, Senior.'

"Then it gets a little weird," Tom grinned awkwardly. "'Know all, his son is the Apostate, the Betrayer, and the Elder Gods demand a righting of this grievous slight against them!'"

Everyone looked sombre. Junior looked frustrated. Sylvie patted his shoulder. Vic groaned.

"Yes, but that's got to be a rare...'condition', shall we say? Can't be too many people who are that messed up."

Tom was shaking his head. "Agreed, but now the problem is that Mister Lovecraft will be media fodder for every strange or stupid notion a 'fan' has. Carliss had a call today about some guy who wants to rent the Gold Coast Convention Centre for an entire weekend and fill it up with death-metal bands and kids playing dress-ups as Lovecraft monsters. He offered fifty thousand bucks for Mister Lovecraft to sign t-shirts for a weekend! I'm sure the money is tempting, but the risks, after an incident like this, could fire up a bunch of copycats who originally had *no* interest in Mister Lovecraft's father's writing! They just become obsessed with the violence and the potential to become front page news."

Junior looked at Vic, frowning. "I had no idea my father's work...I knew there were loyal fans, but thought they were mostly quiet types, readers..."

"It's not all bad news, sir," piped a cheery voice, and the group looked up to see Bill Carliss walking in, a folder of papers in his hand.

"I know this could have been a tragedy, and that's why I arranged for Tom to come in, but we can't change what's happened. However, a ray of sunshine is that Paragon Pictures just got off the phone—they want to talk."

Junior seemed a little disturbed at this news. "Mister Carliss, I'm more worried about Mister Chandra, and a bit about myself to be honest, right now."

Vic put his hand gently on Junior's shoulder. "It's alright, sir. I'm fine, and you'll be fine, if we learn the lesson from all this. But let me talk as a lawyer, now, too. You came all this way for a reason, and these movie people will never be more open to talking than right now, when their project is sitting firmly in a news-cycle. Now's the time to see them."

Lovecraft looked at him doubtfully, so Vic added, "I'm fine, really."

"Enough of all this gloom, you need a cup of tea," said Sylvie and she busied herself on the counter-top of the hotel suite, sorting Lovecraft out, getting him comfortable on a chair and explaining to him the various virtues of a selection of biscuits she had bought for him to sample.

Vic looked across and two thoughts crossed his mind; one was that his wife really had that domestic-comforter thing down pat, and, second, he wondered whether 'H. P. Lovecraft Master of Wafer Creams' was a title the legion of horror fans and genre literati would approve of. Maybe: 'Son of Lovecraft Meets the Tim Tams from Down Under' would be better…

The meeting with Paragon took place in yet another hotel, the Connaught Towers, in Brisbane city, just to be safe, and both parties were happy with this. Apparently Paragon now had a small troop of horror fans congregating outside their local production offices on the Gold Coast, and to avoid a PR disaster they had placed security guys everywhere, and were trying to put a positive spin on things. Most of the fans were hoping for glimpses of the young star, Robert Black, but whilst they waited they were making their vigil lively, by walking around with placards shouting HELL, YES, WE WILL, GO—TO HELL!, or CTHULHU R'LYEHS, OK? The TV, of course, loved all this, and the story quickly went international.

Steve Holder was the executive producer and director of *The Return of Cthulhu*. He was a small, quiet man, about fifty, very calm and precise. Josh Conroy, the director, was thirty, big and loud, with heavily tattooed arms and a bushy beard; and Vic was worried. He didn't think Junior would like the guy's manner.

Conroy was enthusiastic to begin with. "Man, it is such a privilege to meet you, Mister Lovecraft, I'm a huge fan of your father's work!" the fellow shook Junior's hand a little too vigorously.

Holder must have read Vic's mind because he started to take control of the conversation. "We were extremely surprised to discover your father's properties had an inheritor," Holder said, "but let me be very frank, Mister Lovecraft, Paragon has absolutely no interest in unlawfully exploiting those works. The studio has a seventy-five year history of dealing with authors and we will do what is needed to make sure you are happy with the situation."

Vic jumped in, as Carliss had instructed him to.

"Mister Lovecraft appreciates that. However, what he wants is the cessation of filming on Pohnpei. It is causing him some degree of concern; Pohnpei is a quiet community with much natural beauty. He is very unhappy about what your film crew is doing to that."

The burly director piped up again. "I promise you, we'll respect what your father wanted, in fact we will bring his visions to life anew, and although there's a couple of months of inconvenience, think of what we're doing for the local economy! I mean, people aren't mad about that, are they? It offsets a little extra noise, I'm sure!"

Holder intervened. He showed a satellite hook—up to Pohnpei on his iPad. Dozens of crew were busily dressing a set near the edge of a lagoon-like setting where big, strange, stone temple structures jutted out of the water.

"That's Nan Madol, the old ruins on Pohnpei, as Mr Lovecraft would know very well. Fascinating, eye-catching, a vast network of ruins. It was a handful of words your father used in a story he co-wrote when he referred to it, but to fans of his work it's very well known, and even other writers picked up on it after that. It was a brilliant literary filigree; like putting Sherlock Holmes in an actual street, Baker Street; like having Dracula be based on a real Transylvanian warlord."

Conroy was almost bursting with excitement as he added, "So, we scoped the joint and it was awesome, just awesome! And the climax of our movie depends on it being there! I'm tryin' to get a certain kind of *resonance*."

Junior's arms were folded.

"Mister Conroy, you think you're doing my community a favour, but you're not. I had two ladies in my house crying because of the way some of your crew talked to them at the local markets. These people know when they are being made fun of. You people might have got permits, I hear tell, but that doesn't give you the right to treat people like dirt."

Conroy's mouth was open. Vic marveled at the way the old man could establish a parental authority.

"Wait a minute! That isn't fair; you can't expect us to worry about every local that takes offense to some minor interaction. Seriously! We're *not* gonna—"

The producer interrupted.

"Josh, zip it for a second. Mister Lovecraft, I think that I understand your concern. We might have come in without sufficient concern for the locals. We clearly didn't do our homework or adequate consultation and your fear is that our project will leave a further negative result. Well, sir, we have expended a fortune to get this far, and if need be we can simply go back and complete the film in a studio, and use CGI to make the place look like Pohnpei. But that would be a shameful waste. I think there's a win-win here."

Lovecraft shook his head. "What, a curfew? No, no, that won't do anything. Your staff will just be bottled up with nothing to do after a long day's work, it will be broken in five minutes, and probably make things worse."

Holder's eyes were keen. "I think that's a good expectation. So, what about something far more practical and far more in keeping with your actual complaint: We film the final scenes on Pohnpei, as planned, but not until we provide you with certain guarantees around a Code of Conduct—that *you* would help us write—that all our staff and contractors have to sign and carry out. One strike against us, and we get out of town immediately."

Lovecraft rubbed his chin and Vic looked at him, wondering what was going through the guy's head. There was no way the old man would trust them on this. Vic felt a celestial clock ticking.

Conroy, the blunt instrument of a director, killed the moment. "Hey, I've got an idea, maybe we could open a temporary nightclub of some kind, too, and keep all the crew in there after shooting."

Holder turned to Conroy and with a quietness that cut through the air with more ferocity than anything Vic had ever seen in his life—and in his lawyering time he'd thought he'd seen it all—the producer said, "Go and get yourself a cup of coffee, Josh."

The director's eyes looked like they were going to fall out of his head in shock. "Sh-sure," he said, "I'll just go downstairs," and he walked out of the room as if he'd been hit with a two-by-four.

Holder leaned forward. "I'm sorry, he's young, and abrasive. But I control the purse strings on this, completely. If he gets out of line—I *will* fire him. The Code of Conduct is my idea, and not one single person on my crew will be allowed back on-shore unless they sign it. One breach and they will *never* work in the business again. These people are professionals, they will know what I mean. The cast for this are mostly B-Listers, this is a big break for the majority of them, so they mess me with they are out of there and their character dies so I can put a secondary actor on the plate. I can make this work, gentlemen. And you, Mister Lovecraft, would have constant access to me, and to the set. Anything you're not happy about; I will be there. You want to meet actors, see special effects tricks, introduce your Pohnpei friends to people, I can do it."

Lovecraft looked at Vic, and the Aussie lawyer was surprised to realize Junior's question was aimed at him. "What do you think? I would be happy if they could enforce a thing like that, I'm not trying to make it impossible for people to do their jobs."

Vic replied. "I think it sounds great in theory. But what about the movie's plot, story, characters, the way they are adapting your father's material?"

Junior cocked his head; wistful. "You know, that's not so much a bother, but you film people will have to pay me a little something, might be good for emergencies, and the rest, well, we can donate to the local community, build a new library or classrooms at the school."

Holder was beaming. "Happy to do so. Name your price."

The next couple of days were busy. Vic and Junior met every day, with a schedule of items to be dealt with. Vic would follow their morning meetings with a report to Bill and Deborah Worth on Skype, but after a couple of days she relented and Vic just checked in with Bill. The main issues were the daily list of requests and offers of money from parties to have their Cthulhu cottage-industries legitimized; it seemed that people who had been turning out 'sincere' product and art were often happy to pay a percentage if it meant they could still operate. For now, however, Junior wanted all of these enterprises to continue to do business until a final decision was made, but Carliss & Carliss engaged an accounting firm to log and track all the approaches and build a database of merchandising, and the first cheque from Paragon covered those costs easily.

The Code of Conduct was carefully negotiated with Vic, Junior and a Paragon lawyer assisting Holder. Things went surprisingly smoothly; Vic was surprised; the old man no longer seemed so demanding and relentless. In two days they had a workable document and signed on the third.

Vic's moment came when Bill Carliss offered him a full partnership. Vic was flattered, especially knowing how Bill was planning to sell the business to a nephew when he retired. Vic very carefully declined without declining, saying his head was too full of this Lovecraft stuff, and they could talk about it after the Paragon issue was wrapped up.

The truth was, the experience with the old man had made Vic wonder how he was going to feel when the eccentric adventure was over. He wondered if he could stomach looking at a merger file again, and he was terrified he couldn't. Then what? How would he cope with an existence that he loathed—yes, loathed, he knew that was the truth. He hated being a lawyer. In ironic contrast, Vic noted that Gary / George / Charles the temp receptionist guy was made an offer of a permanent job by Bill and was overjoyed to accept it.

The outer office at Carliss & Carliss became the repository of more cards, cuddly Cthulhus and prank deliveries than any other office in their building, which initially had Tom Forbes in a flap, but he eventually settled. Various paperback Lovecraft collections now filled the coffee tables in the waiting room— they seemed to appear by themselves. Vic's favourite was a joke version of *The Australian Women's Weekly*—'The Australian Human's Shriekly'—with Cthulhu wearing pearls and a twin set on the cover, and the feature article being 'Cooking with Friends: Literally'.

Finally the flight to the movie set was arranged. Vic and Junior flew two and a half hours to Cairns thence they waited half a day for the eleven-hour trip from Cairns to Kolonia, the tiny airport at Pohnpei.

Holden met them at the plane. They all went out to Junior's house, in Kolonia: a simple but spacious concrete bungalow. A modest place, its main features were a library and a music room. Many photographs of Junior and his late wife, Isabel, littered the place. She appeared to have been a thin-featured woman of African ancestry, and it seemed there were no children from the union. Vic felt sorry for his strange client. Fatherless, childless, and put in charge of other people's offspring for fifty years.

As the three of them and one of Holden's assistants sat in Junior's living room, it was clear something was troubling the producer. As before, he got to the point quickly.

"I fired Josh Conroy. Frankly, he had a bug in his shorts

from the moment I started to get more involved, I don't think he likes his 'creative choices' questioned. But film-making is collaborative, and I answer to the studio. He wasn't willing to guarantee the Code of Conduct, and it wasn't negotiable."

Junior actually stammered. "I-I said I was prepared to shut things down, but I never thought it would be permanent, or that you couldn't finish your film somehow, some way, I never wanted to cost a man his job."

Holder waved it away. "You didn't. I think, to be frank, Josh brought a bad habit with him. A habit involving white powder he liked to stick up his nose. When things got challenging he resorted to it, and it compromised his judgment. When I fired him he said he was glad and stormed off."

Vic didn't hide his relief. "Well, I think that's probably for the best, but what about your movie?"

Holden answered. "Second Unit Director Jenny Swan is stepping up, it's a great opportunity for her, and she has a lot of good ideas. She's been in the trenches and knows the chain of command, and has people's respect. She personally walked every crew member through the Code of Conduct, in groups, and they signed in front of her. We haven't had a peep of trouble. I have copies of every declaration, Mister Lovecraft."

Junior steepled his fingers and looked out a window at the green, swaying trees and quiet street, where there were more people than vehicles. "Let's go for a walk, Mister Holden," he said.

Junior took them on a tour of his neighbourhood. They met the current Principal at the local schoolhouse, some storeowners and local government representatives. Vic watched as the old man wandered about, very quietly, very gently, and asked his friends what they thought of the proposal. The respect they had for him was genuine, you could see it. They indicated the gratitude they had, that some of the rowdier Americans had since curbed their behaviour and were a little more 'respectful' of the locals, and apparently some of the rowdier locals had taken a few cues from them!

When they were done Junior turned to the producer and said,

"You're a man of your word, Mister Holden. I'm a man of mine. Let's see your movie set."

The set was even more ordinary—for the most part—than it had looked like on the iPad. If it resembled anything it was a building site. Lots of people standing around with equipment, safety gear, in little groups; a lighting team here, sound guys there, special effects crew here, costumes and make-up there.

The new director, Jenny, a tiny blonde woman with a big, musical voice, seemed to move around like a small rubber ball; her eyes saw a problem, she bounced over and helped people attend to it, fixing things everywhere she went, but Vic noticed she never had to browbeat anyone to get them to do what she asked. Junior whispered. "I think the folk here are glad of their new boss?"

Finally they went down to the lagoon facing the ruins in the water, the strange Nan Madol temples made from interlaid slabs of basalt that were partially submerged like some lost city poking out of the water in this lush setting. The current shoot of the closing scenes was arranged around this spot, a natural water theatre-stage, so crew and equipment were on the rocky shore and on flat barges shipped in especially for the shooting, as the water here met rock and dirt rather than sandy beach.

After a general tour of the location, Holder explained they had been doing character bits and more 'normal' scenes and rehearsals since the Code of Conduct was signed, but as per an instruction that Vic had included at Junior's request, the big climax had been held back, just for them to see.

"We've been waiting for you gents. We intend to shoot tomorrow. Are you good, Mister Lovecraft?" Junior said "Yes," and a triumphant cheer went up from the crew, and folk lined up to shake the old man's hand, much to his amusement.

While that occurred Vic noticed a small stack of locals looking at a table that had been set up well away from the shoot. A studio staff-member manned this table and chatted enthusiastically with them, and she was giving out paper flyers. Vic took one. It explained what they were filming on Pohnpei. On the reverse, it had a picture of Junior's father and quotes from some of his stories, including *The Call of Cthulhu*. Right at the bottom, in small print, it said, *"Paragon wishes to acknowledge the Heirs of H. P. Lovecraft."* Vic stuck the paper in his pocket. He wandered back to Junior and Holder. When the crew had finished meeting him, Vic and he were driven back the ten kilometres or so to Junior's house, where Junior insisted he stay.

Before turning in Vic saw Junior looking at a photo of his wife. He said goodnight. Junior's answer was a non sequitur and Vic shrugged it off, attributing it to the old man having mis-heard him.

"Tomorrow is as good a day as any," he'd said.

Tomorrow started at five am.
Vic and Junior were picked up and taken to the lagoon. They were sat on canvas chairs next to Holder. Lovecraft's chair had his name stenciled on the back in black letters.

Jenny had things moving. The operators of a giant remote-controlled Cthulhu puppet monster, the animatronics crew, did a rehearsal of the scene with stand-ins for the lead actor and actress; and it was inspiring. The performers and operators were incredibly regimented, and paid careful attention to Jenny. Actors made up as startling fish-men and fish-women also showed immense energy as the scene was repeated. Junior was intrigued by this and was delighted to receive a quick revelation of the secrets of various appliances and costume design elements by a British couple, Dave and his wife Lou, who were the 'creature-shop' experts. Dave nudged Lovecraft and smiled "I hear it's thanks to you we've got a better schedule on this thing and a more focused director. Nice one, mate."

"Yes," said Lou, "and it's an honor to meet you. Your dad's stories are part of the reason we got in the business; very creepy, very atmospheric. You don't know how sick we get of horror movies where all they want to do is have us mass-produce severed limbs!" Vic wasn't sure how this would go down with

Junior, but he watched in amazement as the old man blushed, and he seemed about to say something more, but he just looked at the woman and said, "That is very kind of you, young lady."

Back in their chairs, the procedure was explained. They took their places, and watched it happen. On cue, Cthulhu would rise from the waters, first one scaly hand would break the surface, then splash down on a basalt slab; then another. Water pumps would force up a great spray, and then the tentacular feelers would appear from the sea, followed by the rest of the big, octopoidal head. The plastic-lensed eyes would issue a dazzling, kaleidoscopic laser display, as Cthulhu cast his gaze upon his subjects. Then the entire creature-structure would be pumped, up and up, and the arms would raise, steam and light were blasted through special vents as the thing assumed a frightening, powerful pose.

The show-stopper was a complex series of pulleys and servitors that allowed massive articulated wings, half insectoid, half bat-like, to unfurl and flap in triumph as the creature's head tipped back and a foghorn-like gurgle erupted. The actress would take her position, and begin screaming as one massive hand would swipe down and she would begin to run to camera, the hand just missing her, setting the scene up for pursuit by the great beast-god.

It was sensational. Vic was more impressed by the patience and the diligence of the operators than even the ability of the actors to slip into character at a second's notice. He watched them run though the effort three times. The stand-in left the mark, and the lead actress herself came on.

Jenny readied everyone for the first real take.

"Action!" someone yelled. The scene went perfectly. Scaly Hand. Tentacles. Head. Creature. Actress. Screaming.

Then the animatronic puppet shuddered, and became completely still, as if its joints had become frozen.

Holder stood up in his chair and literally screamed into a walkie-talkie. Vic and Junior now saw a different side to him.

"What the fuck is going on? This is costing me a million dollars a fucking minute! The run-through was fine, what is going on?"

"*Shit!* Josh! It's Josh!" screamed one of the crew.

Josh Conroy had walked onto the set, and as he strode, people ran screaming. He was naked from the waist up and the upper half of his body was covered in cuts and slashes, relatively fresh, with blood dripping from them. The cuts looked like, no, they were, *words*, carved into his flesh, and this notion was reinforced by the sharp, blood-caked knife he held in his left hand.

His face was filthy, mouth dirty and bloody as if he'd eaten something and smeared the remains over his face. His eyes were dark and hollowed, and unnaturally bulbous, staring. His hair was a matted mess.

Ordinarily, Conroy would have been an intimidating enough figure, a big man such as he, looking so degraded, but what sent the crew scattering away from him was the fact he held an automatic pistol in his right hand.

Conroy stood in front of the Cthulhu puppet and started to yell, the crazed yell of a man who thinks he's alone. He tucked the pistol into the waistband of his jeans, and, using the knife, he stabbed at the giant puppet, and he began to climb, using the knife as a piton.

If Conroy's words meant anything to anyone no one stepped forward to explain them.

"THIS IS THE ART, THIS IS THE SACRED CALLING. THIS IS THE FATE OF MINE, TO INVOKE THE GREAT OLD ONES. LOVECRAFT GAVE THEM HISTORY, BUT THEY HAVE ALWAYS LOVED THIS PLACE, SO CLOSE TO THEIR OWN DOOR. IA! IA! CTHULHU COMES, HE COMES!"

Then Conroy was at the top of the creation. He perched precariously on the head of the puppet. A fall from that height would mean broken limbs at the very least. Holden was screaming into the walkie-talkie, but Vic got the feeling there was no one answering, a theory substantiated when Holden angrily slammed it into the ground.

But Conroy did not fall. He stood upright and plunged the hideous knife into his own neck.

A wide arc of blood erupted from his severed arterial ways

and the crew that had stayed to watch were screaming and gasping, unable to look away.

Conroy teetered, and started to fall. But only started. There was a massive flash of black motion. Conroy's body was caught, safely, from hitting the basalt platform of Nan Madol.

Caught by one of Cthulhu's hands.

The giant animatronic figure stood, higher, steadier, than before. Crew that had been operating the masses of cable stations at the statue's foot were nowhere to be seen, but that didn't matter.

The thing held up the dead body of Conroy and a beak thrust out from the tentacled face. Conroy's body was stuffed into that razor-edged entry. There was a sucking sound and it was gone, in three bites, three horrific flashes of dismemberment.

Cthulhu stood and screamed in tones no human ear could describe in aught but horror.

A swirling of black mites began to spew out of the monster's eyes, strange, buzzing particles. They rose like a cloud and began to spin above the Elder God's head. And as they spun, dazzling light flitted betwixt them. Finally there evolved a huge spinning vortex of black particles—no, not particles, a maelstrom of cosmic, eternal space-night, the void, filled with billions of alien stars. A literal pulsating cloud opening to a dark universe was in the sky above Cthulhu, above Nan Madol, above Pohnpei. The sunlight was cut to less than half. It was like twilight on the beach.

Vic was spellbound, as was every other person on the shore. Vic wasn't sure what he felt, and then he understood, it wasn't calmness, it was existential horror. It was certainty. He was about to die. The world was going to die. It was all ending.

Then a small movement caught Vic's eye.

Junior stood in the water. Up to his knees.

The sea was boiling around the feet of Cthulhu, and ozone burnt in the air, assaulting the nostrils. The gigantic creature flapped and howled as the cyclonic blackness spun, larger and larger, above it. Junior waved at the impossible horror, and the thing noticed him.

It lowered its great black head, and stared at Junior, the laser beams from its eyes lighting Junior and the water around him like a surreal dance-floor.

"You go back where you came from," said Junior and he held up his leathery, bony arm, and opened his fingers.

In Junior's hand was a big, black, flat stone, cradled into his palm, almost filling it. It was black and gold, glazed colours of some kind. A weird design stood out in it, like a tree branch, two leaves one side, three the other. As Vic looked, the stone lifted up, out of Junior's hand, by itself, and hovered there, and then it began to spin.

Vic then went blind, as a whiteness, no, an absence of vision and sound, exploded like a silent shockwave. He saw nothing, heard nothing, felt nothing for many, many long, frightening seconds.

When his vision returned—and it returned completely, with no blinking or shuddering after-effects—the beach, the sky and Nan Madol were returned to as they had been before. The air was clear and clean. Actors, crew and extras wandered about, all a little unsteadilyly, but none the worse for wear.

Cthulhu, and Josh Conroy, were gone.

Holden was talking into a mobile-phone. Vic caught a sentence or three. "CGI can fix it. Yeah, yeah, talk about it at Spago's—next Tuesday. Fuck, no, not the lobster, I'm sick of fucking seafood after the last two weeks."

Junior was sitting in a canvas chair with his name on the back the studio had provided him. He looked very, very tired. Vic sat next to him.

Vic stared at Junior. Stared at H. P. Lovecraft.

"You knew this was going to happen. You engineered this whole thing, to be here. Why; how did you know?"

The old man replied, not without kindness in his voice. "I'm his son. Maybe that's why. Why I knew things about his...other children, you could say. Can't say I'm a religious person, but I guess I believe in a destiny, of sorts. When they started work on the movie here, my brain just couldn't let things go, there were dreams, too, until I got the idea about threatening to stop the production, get them to agree to me being wherever I felt I needed to be. And I wasn't even sure about that. I can't say I ever had all the pieces straight in my head."

He looked at the ocean, then back at Vic. "I guess if I had, I might never have done anything, I would have been too damn scared, or convinced myself I was damn crazy, finally senile, and checked myself into a nuthouse. Lucky I didn't do that, I guess. Lucky I didn't try and make the pieces make sense, instead I just did what it seemed like I had to."

Vic nodded. Then, as if stung by something, he stuffed a hand in his pocket. He pulled his fist out, and unscrunched the paper flyer he'd grabbed the day before. His eyes darted over the text until he found what he was looking for. Then he read it out loud. He was partway through when the old man chimed in and they finished the words exactly in unison. *"The most merciful thing in the world, I think, is the inability of the human mind to correlate all its contents."*

THE ELDER THINGS

B. MICHAEL RADBURN

Darkness slipped over the pale world, grey clouds eclipsing the horizon's Antarctic noonday sun, the temperature plummeting in a heartbeat. Jack Sandford looked up from the lichen sample he was peeling off the exposed rock face, a breath of glacial wind brushing his cheeks on the cusp of the approaching storm. He slipped the snow goggles to his forehead, frowning, noting the substantial density of the clouds.

"What the...?"

He crouched at the open laptop on the groundsheet beside him, the radar image streaming via satellite from the British Rothera Station three hundred and twenty kilometres away. The rapidly moving storm front was blanketing the mountain contours on the screen faster than he had seen before.

"Where did *you* come from?" he asked, tapping its deep red centre with his finger. An hour ago the peninsular was cloudless and the forecast clear for the next two days. It didn't make sense. The weather was unpredictable down here, but this was unprecedented for the summer months. The image froze for a moment as the reception display at the foot of the screen dipped to one bar before rising to three. He glanced at the cloudbank again. It was only a matter of time before his contact with the satellites—and the outside world—would be gone.

Jack felt time pressing down on him. He dug the sat-phone from his pack and selected the Rothera speed dial number, zipping his coat to the neckline as the dial tone purred in the earpiece.

"Rothera Antarctic Station, over."

Relief! Jack recognised Lewis Pritchard's Welsh accent over the static. "Lew, it's Jack Sandford. Do you have a handle on this storm across the research area, over?"

There was a pause of dead air, the Comms Officer no doubt checking his screen. "Jesus-H-Christ, where did that come from, over?"

"That's what I'd like to know." Jack shook his head in mild amusement. "I don't suppose the chopper is anywhere near my location, Lew, over?"

"Afraid not, Jack," he replied swiftly, the transmission broken as the sky darkened. "I'm gonna have to ground all air traffic until this weather settles down. You'll have to haul your Aussie arse to shelter ASAP. Ride it out as best you can. I'll send the bird as soon as there's a break, over."

Jack was watching the churning colours progress across the laptop screen as he listened, already resigned to the fact that he was on his own. *What a monster*, he thought. He blinked, and the reception fell to two bars.

"Okay, Lew. I noticed an ice cave at the ridgeline on my way up here from the landing zone. I should be able to make it back down okay, over."

"Don't take any chances, Jack. I'll monitor the storm and arrange an extraction just as soon as it's practical. Rothera, out."

The radio silence was replaced by the buffeting wind. He surveyed the patchwork of snow and sodden earth leading down to the base of the mountain where the cloud's shadow rolled across the fractured Ronne Ice Shelf in the distance. Jack suddenly felt insignificant against the five thousand metres of mountain towering above him, the Vinson Massif, tallest peak on the continent.

He stowed his samples and equipment into the forty-kilo pack, conscious of the increasing wind speed, groaning at the weight as he slipped the straps over his shoulder. Slipping gloves over frigid hands, he stepped carefully on the decent, using his poles to steady himself against the rousing elements. The chilled wind carried a flurry of snow that needled the exposed flesh of his face, visibility reduced to three metres in a heartbeat. Pausing to catch his breath, he lifted the jacket hood over his head before replacing his goggles. He knew keeping the rock face on his right would get him down the mountain okay, but blindly stumbling around for the ice cave at the base would be risky. Then he remembered the GPS.

He took the Garvin from his belt pouch, cupping his hand over the screen as he selected the tracking mode. One, two, satellites winked to life on the screen. All he had to do was reverse the tracking and follow it back to the landing zone at the base of the mountain. That should get him within a hundred metres of the cave.

Frustrated, he watched the second satellite icon wink in and out. He needed at least three to triangulate his position. "Come on, come on," he said stepping away from the stone wall for a clearer line of site. The third winked on. "*Yes!*" But just as quickly disappeared, the remaining two following suit. NO SIGNAL filled the screen. "Piece of shit," he spat.

He knew that his options were limited. Shelter against the rock face up here, or risk finding the ice cave below. *I'm not dying up here.*

The pack's straps pressed through his jacket and into his shoulders with each laboured step on the descent. His tracks from the morning's climb were still visible for half the trek down, but were eventually wiped clean by the wind. He peered through the driving sheets of snow, occasionally glancing at the GPS in the vain hope it had made contact with the heavens. *The cave must be close*, he thought, just as a fleeting shadow appeared through the pallid shroud ahead. He stopped, eyes straining. *Was someone there?*

"Hello," he called, the sound whisked away by the gale.

He crouched on one knee, stable against the buffeting wind. Then he saw the others, images so faint that at first he doubted them himself, each dissolving into the background as quickly as they appeared until only one remained, tall and slender, a grey patch in the colourless space ahead.

Jack drew a short painful breath. He didn't scare easily,

confident in his own ability in this environment. But this was different, an air of dread sifting through his resolve, his imagination fraying at his usual calculated response to the elements. Then, within a brief break in the sheets of snow, he made out exactly what the dark image ahead was.

The cave!

As he drew closer, the opening in the mountain's ice façade grew clearer, a bastion of safety. He focused on the breach, afraid he would lose it in the next wave of driven snow. But then he tripped and stumbled over a mound in the snow, dropping the GPS. When he turned to retrieve it, he made out the body in the snow, face down, jacket torn in places and splayed open, no gloves, fingers black from frostbite. He brushed the dusting of snow off the bare hand, stone cold, rigid.

His heart raced. The storm front was harsh, but had not been raging long enough to cause this kind of exposure to a man, particularly one so close to shelter. And who was he? Certainly no one from the British Rothera base.

Slipping off his pack, he eased the body over, peeling it away from the frozen ground. The man's beard was a mess of blood from the gunshot fissure where his nose once was, black frostbitten lips curled back in a macabre grin.

"Jesus!" he spat, letting go of the body as he stumbled against his pack.

He took a steadying breath, his attention drawn to the sealskin coat and boots; the waxed canvas pants and leather belt. The clothing was antiquated, yet in remarkable condition. Searching for ID, he forced the rigid jacket closed to inspect the pockets, noticing the corner of a small book protruding from one. Perhaps a notebook, but Jack was perplexed to find a dog-eared copy of *Astounding Stories*, the publication date printed in the corner: February 1936. He slipped it back, patting the clothes, finding a wallet on the inside breast pocket. The leather case was the same as the clothes, old, hand stitched, but in mint condition.

"Where the Hell are you from, stranger?" he whispered.

There were no credit cards, just a library slip and Californian driver's license dated 1930, both on paper, both in the name of

Seth Bartlet. It didn't make sense. The man was too well preserved to be lying here that long, and too far from the American's McMurdo base to have trekked this far.

Tucked in the back of the wallet was a black and white photograph of a small group of men and two dog teams standing on the ice, holding a crude hand-painted banner. Huxley Expedition Summer '36.

"Don't touch him, mister," called a voice from behind.

Jack turned, startled, staring into the barrel of a revolver, the bare white-knuckled hand a patchwork of frostbitten circles. Dressed the same as the dead man, a wind gust drew the fur lined hood from his bearded face, his eyes glazed, wide, afraid.

Jack instinctively raised his hands as he stood, stepping away from the body. "Take it easy," he said above the storm. "I was just trying to help."

The man glanced down at his companion. "He shot himself," he said in a broad American accent. "Couldn't take it no more." His hand lowered with the weight of the gun, his expression near exhaustion. "How do I know you're not one of them?"

Jack frowned. "I can guarantee we're alone out here."

The man swayed, staring past Jack, straining his focus into the snowstorm. "I wish that were true, mister," he said before collapsing.

The gun fell at his feet, Jack digging it out of the snow and placing it in his map pocket. He had to move fast, dragging the unconscious man into the cave, the ice façade opening into the stone cavern beyond. The light was dim, but he could see the packs and blankets scattered around, evidence that the two had sort refuge there. Jack lay the guy down, gathering the blankets over him, checking his breathing and pulse, both faint but regular.

Returning outside, he thrust his walking pole into the snow beside the body to mark its location, already covered in a centimetre of snow, and bound to be well buried by the time the storm broke. He dusted off his own pack and carried it inside before collapsing against the wall to catch his breath.

"Just another day at the office," he whispered, considering the shallow breaths of the stranger across the way.

Within the hour Jack had the man's hands bandaged and his body wrapped in the foil thermo blanket from his first aid kit. There was no official ID on him or in the canvas packs, just meagre supplies including hardtack biscuits and some kind of jerky. There were however another two issues of *Astounding Stories*, March and April of '36, and a tattered notebook with the initials JH after each entry.

He placed the old magazines on his pack. "Are you our Mr. Huxley in the photograph?" he said flicking through the notebook's pages.

The wind moaned outside as if to answer, Jack wriggling into his own sleeping bag, back to the opposite wall, his attention bouncing from Huxley to the darkening cave entrance. The obscure images of those gathering shapes in the snowstorm when he arrived were not forgotten. He pulled the revolver from his map pocket, rolling it over in his hands. *Another antique.* Two rounds left in the chambers. *Comforting*, he thought.

His attention was drawn to the GPS placed on his pack, NO SIGNAL still glaring at him from the screen, reminding him of the isolation. He closed his eyes for a moment, thinking about the local beach he surfed back home, remembering the kiss of sunshine on his face before revisiting the notebook. It was a collection of ramblings; names and phrases he had no understanding of. Necronomicon, Shoggoths, Elder Things and Cthulhu, the handwriting so scribbled and rushed, it was almost impossible to read.

"You should have left me out there to die."

Jack braced, startled, instinctively clutching the gun's handle. The stranger was awake. "That's not how I roll, JH." He waved the notebook in the air. "It is *JH*, isn't it?"

"The name's John Huxley." Pained, he stirred, shifting his weight. "The last of the Huxley expedition," he added.

"Huxley expedition?" Jack smirked. "You look awful good for a man over a hundred years old."

"I don't understand."

"I don't pretend to know why you and your dead buddy decided to come out here in fancy-dress, John Huxley, but it's two thousand and fourteen, and you sure as hell haven't been plodding around here since nineteen thirty-six.

Huxley's expression shifted from concern to understanding in a heartbeat, tearing away the thermo blanket as he sat against his pack, eyes welling with shallow tears. "All ... dead ..." he murmured.

Jack recognised the grief in his expression. "Your expedition?"

He shook his head sombrely. "Everyone I ever knew," he said, meeting Jack's stare. "That damn labyrinth has stolen everything from me." He collapsed back into the blankets, his resolve draining into its folds.

"I don't understand?"

Huxley lay staring at the stone ceiling.

"Ten of us trekked into those mountains in the summer of nineteen thirty-six, mister. Three days later, two of us escaped into two thousand and fourteen. An hour ago, the only other witness to this madness shot himself in the face."

"I admit your clothes and equipment are convincing, John Huxley, but I find the whole time-warp thing a little hard to swallow. I'm sorry, but it's just not possible."

"Neither are the Elder Things!" He exclaimed. "Neither is that damned city of giants beyond the mountains." He nodded toward the copies of *Astounding Stories* on Jack's pack. "It all began with a letter from Howard Lovecraft, the author of that confounded story serialised in that penny dreadful."

Jack frowned, not knowing what to think. He was a scientist, here to study the effects of climate change on microorganisms, not the effects of time travel on twentieth century man. Jack shook his head, bewildered.

"Hear me out," said Huxley.

Jack rested back into his gathered sleeping bag, conscious of the taunting wind outside, his weary body seeking warmth and sleep. "Looks like we've got the time, Huxley ... Go on."

"The *Boston Post* had published a feature on my 1930 Antarctic expedition. A year later I received a letter from Lovecraft who was researching a story he was working on." Huxley smirked. "I was flattered, and saw no harm ... If only I had known."

The name seemed vaguely familiar to Jack. "Can't say it's anything I've ever read."

"That surprises me." Huxley composed himself. "Lovecraft was at the height of his writing career then, his series of so-called Mythos stories growing in popularity, and many like-minded writers using the same platform and seeking his counsel. I suppose I was grateful for the attention, so I answered his questions. I thought that was the end of it until many years later when I received the three copies of *Astounding Stories* in the post."

Jack grabbed the nearest copy and read the featured story's title. *At the Mountains of Madness*. "Apt title," he said.

"More than you know. Although he didn't name the place, it was right here, at the Vinson Massif, that Lovecraft set his tale. Not from the details I sent him, but rather from what he called a most realistic vision—a recurring nightmare—that both haunted and inspired him. The research he requested was to confirm his vision, nothing more, and from that he wrote the story."

"How do you know all this?"

"In the spring of nineteen thirty-five, Mr. Lovecraft called at my home in New York. I had been out for the day, and found him sitting on the steps of my building when I returned. He was a polite man with a quiet disposition and a focused intent, but quite pale and thin—sickly, in fact. I invited him inside, and he wasted no time in presenting his proposal; an expedition to the mountains, funded by Lovecraft and his circle. Like minded authors like Howard, Derleth and Long. Lovecraft was convinced that the geography and photographs from my earlier expedition was so like his vision that he could not rest until he could either prove or dispel his obsession."

"There's a fine line between obsession and madness."

Huxley shrugged. "Both are a sickness."

"But you indulged him nevertheless."

"You must understand that such research endowment can take years to procure, and here was someone all but forcing it upon me. I decided I could explore his mountains and continue my research at the same time." He sighed deeply, Jack recognising the despair in his eyes. "I didn't think for a moment that such things could be true."

"What *things*?"

"The Elder Things—or perhaps their spirits, their life source—I'm no longer certain." He paused, distant. "I had planned to leave the dog team and ascend the sheltered north face. It was a clear, windless day, hard going until we reached the ridge that took us to the summit. The mountain range was indeed like a wall, but the alien city described in Lovecraft's story was nowhere to be seen, just a vast field of blue-iced crevasses."

Jack thought of all the surveys and satellite mapping conducted of the area. "I hate to tell you this, Huxley, but there's not an inch of this globe that hasn't been mapped since thirty-five," he said. "I think such a city would have been discovered by now."

"Do your maps show what lies *beneath* the ice?" he said sombrely. "Standing on the summit that day, I considered Lovecraft's theory had been dispelled, and so decided to descend into the rim to explore the exposed crevasses and their relationship to the geology."

"Sounds like a fixed glacier to me."

"So it would seem, but the builders had used the resources to create a cloak of ice to hide the city." He shook his head, his chin trembling with emotion. "The expedition had camped at the base for the night, exhausted. We were settled in our tents when they came, on the cusp of a storm just like this one."

"You saw them?"

Huxley's expression turned to stone. "Yes. And yet ... no ... We were besieged by monsters unseen, taking us one at a time. It was as if the night and these creatures were one in the same, but you could sense their power—a malevolence far worse than anything our mortal souls could understand. Guns were useless, for how does one shoot the night itself? By morning only Seth Bartlet and I were left, our equipment shredded and twisted beyond use." He gestured to the oilskin pack at his feet. "What we carry is all that is left."

Huxley's rambling was rapidly becoming incoherent as Jack fought the weariness overcoming his body, almost drunkenly, his eyes slowly closing against his will. *No!* His eyes blinked open, fixing on Huxley's, focusing on their conversation. "If those things were so destructive," he said, "how did you and your buddy elude them?"

Huxley shook his head. "I don't know. We were never targeted, and I now believe it was their intention to let us discover their city." The wind bayed in a sudden crescendo, wisps of frigid air exploring the cave. Huxley glanced toward the opening, a weary resolve masking his face. "And now," he said gravely, "I fear that our salvation may perhaps have a greater rationale."

"I don't understand."

"I don't believe Seth and I escaped the siege," he said. "I believe we were spared and guided into that Hellhole." He tapped his temple anxiously, his eyes beaming. "They can get inside your head," he said fretfully, "when you're sleeping."

Jack had no reason to believe a word of what Huxley was saying, yet the extraordinary circumstances of their paths crossing in such a desolate place and the condition of their clothes and antiquated equipment made it difficult to dismiss as fancy. And now, to add to his bewilderment, he could feel his weariness slowly overwhelming his senses. *They can get inside your head ... when you're sleeping ...*

"You must know how this all sounds, John?"

His shoulders slumped, exhausted. "I know how it must sound to a sane man," he said. "But we must remain guarded."

Jack thought of the figures he saw in the storm moments before he stumbled upon the cave. "So how did you and Seth make it here?"

"We no longer had the equipment to climb out, so when dawn broke we descended into a gaping ice ravine near our camp, hoping it would lead us out. That's how we discovered the city beneath its glacial dome. Immense stone citadels of cubes and cones covered in hieroglyphs and portrayals of creatures not of this earth, the images drawing me back to Lovecraft's story. How the Elder Things—the engineers of life's genesis—travelled to Earth after the Moon was pulled loose from the planet, building vast metropolises with the aid of Shoggoths, biological beings created to accomplish their tasks, adopt any form, and reflect any thought."

Delusion or madness, Jack was certain Huxley believed every word. "It's one thing to tell *me* about these things, but when we get out of here you've got the world press to contend with."

Huxley laughed. "Your confidence in our escape is commendable, but you didn't see what they are capable of. Those ... *Things* ... continue to study us, but for what reason I cannot say. I have lost everything. Denied my future; robbed of my past. Yet I remain fearful; not for myself but for the world we know."

"You say you were in there for three days," Jack reminded him. "How do you account for the quantum time shift?"

"I can't. At times a sickness overcame Seth and I, our vision strangely affected and our pocket watches frequently stopping for no good reason. During such episodes we saw the shadow-figures appear around us, and it is my humble opinion that they were the residue—spirits, if you like—of the Elder Things, residing in the same space as us, but perhaps in a different time." He clutched at his beard, trembling. "Don't you see? It's all true. The Cthulhu Mythos, the Necronomicon ... Everything Lovecraft had foreseen."

"How did you escape?"

"We discovered a maze of catacombs beneath the city, leading us to this cave and daylight. We thought we were safe, but the storm brought those *things* in pursuit. It was too much for Seth, taking my gun and ending the nightmare once and for all. You appeared shortly after and the creatures withdrew. Why? I don't know. For how long? Who can say?"

The wind moaned outside, piquing Jack's attention as wisps of snow penetrated the cave, settling on his hand. He watched the flakes reduce to water under the warmth of his surging blood, considering the effects of global warming on the mountains, eventually exposing the city the way it had already exposed this cave.

It was all about time and space, Jack realised, sensing the rip in both just as his hand grew heavy. He frowned, his focus waning as another wave of sleep surged through his being and his arm fell across his chest. Huxley's eyes were fixed on him, his expression turning to concern. "Don't sleep," he said. But there was no fighting it this time as Huxley's warning and Jack's consciousness faded to black...

And in an instant, the nightmare sparked to life.

He was running through an infinite tunnel beneath the alien metropolis, feeling the city's mass bearing down on the passageway with the weight of time itself. A curious, diffused light filtered down through a row of ports in the ceiling as a pulsating, machine-like whine emanated from the surrounding stone walls. He stumbled through into an immense antechamber and stopped, breathless, peering up at the great columns etched in alien hieroglyphs.

When he turned to peer back into the tunnel he saw the lights extinguishing one at a time as a veil of darkness accelerated towards him. Just beyond the pale, heavy footfalls resonated through the foundations as the torrential unseen bore down upon him. His heart pounded as the horror pursued him through the subterranean twilight. Glimpses of the great beast's form penetrated the light seconds before the darkness overcame it. Although it was enough to arouse Jack's curiosity, he knew that to conceive of its true form would only tempt madness. This builder of cities; this guardian of the Elder Things; this Shoggoth.

He collapsed on the floor as the last ceiling light blinked out and a grand door of stone slid closed behind him. There was a brief moment of silence before the beast slammed into it with a thundering roar. He could hear its breath on the other side as claws scratched at the edges, testing its integrity before falling patiently quiet. Jack knew it could wait. It had been waiting for centuries.

He stood and backed away from the door. A soft light radiated from a single orb suspended high in the ceiling, barely bright enough to cast a shadow. A row of solid slabs stood in the centre of the chamber, commanding Jack's attention. As he stepped closer, the orb flared brighter and he could clearly see the horror on each platform, the remnants of the Huxley expedition, man and dog alike, dissected, explored, flesh opened after The Elder

Things' cruel experiments, exposed spines and skulls attached to pulsating organic umbilical cords hanging from the ceiling.

A thunderous moan resonated from the other side of the door, drawn out and oscillating in pitch like a hellish whale song, then somewhere distant, its call was answered. He stepped closer to where a naked cadaver lay, skinless. The torso was peeled open, the internal organs placed beside the body still attached to the host as the heart beat steadily on the warm slab. *Alive*! He grimace at the bloodless display, leaning over the broken puzzle, its lidless eyes glistening under the harsh light as its lips parted to speak. "Wake up," it said, and slapped his face.

The pain snapped him back to consciousness, back to the ice cave. He lashed out, seeing Huxley kneeling over him, his bandaged hand raised to strike again.

"You can't sleep," Huxley said, slowly lowering his arm. "It's the Elder Things," he said. "It's how they cross the divide."

Jack fell back into his sleeping bag as Huxley stepped away. *So real*, he thought, recognising that his trembling wasn't because of the cold. "How long was I out?" he asked.

"Seconds."

"Seconds? But ..."

"Time is irrelevant to *them*," Huxley said. "Hours, days, years ... They can pass in a lifetime or a heartbeat."

The GPS screen lit up, its beeping startling Jack. He frowned. *It couldn't possibly pick up a satellite through the stone and ice*. He snatched it from its perch on the backpack, watching as the latitude and longitude readings cascaded in various readings, the time and date profile doing the same.

The knot in Jack's stomach tightened as the moaning wind outside altered into an inhuman cry, the earth trembling around them as the sound pierced the mountain. It was the same surging wail he heard from the Shoggoth in his dream. Cupping his hands to his ears, Jack noticed the wide-eyed look of dread grip Huxley.

"*It's them*!" Huxley bellowed, running toward the opening.

"Come back!" Jack cried, clutching the gun, stumbling to his feet in pursuit. But Huxley had stopped beneath the arch of ice, staring out at the blizzard as the unholy sound promptly pervaded back into the storm.

"They're here," he said in a whisper, all hope draining from his expression.

Jack saw the shadow figures begin to appear within the white-out—hundreds of them—standing sentinel as one alone drew closer and clearer. After Huxley's story, the realms of possibility had been questioned, and after his own dream those realms seemed imminent. Now this ...

There was no doubt about what he was witnessing, yet his mind struggled to rationalise it as his heartbeat quickened.

The approaching figure was Seth, his arms open as if to embrace, each erratic step splintering the film of ice that coated his body. The gaping hole in his face pulsated, moist and sucking, smelling like sulfur. He shambled past as if Jack was invisible and stopped in the entrance, coal-black eyes staring into Huxley's. Jack knew the definition of bravery. It was simply fear hanging on for one more minute, but when he looked into Huxley's eyes he realised the man had no minutes left.

Jack stirred. Maybe—*just maybe*—he still possessed the minute he needed to be brave.

He drew the gun in trembling hands and pushed Huxley aside, pointing into the pit of Seth's face as he realised this nightmare was just beginning. The Seth-thing began trembling as its head tilted back and a string of tentacles erupted from the pit, twisting as the body turned inside out in a pulsing mass of flesh and knotted bone. It expanded in size until the entrance was obscured, each leg dividing until four spider-like limbs supported its swaying body on clawed feet. Fear gripped Jack's body, his minute of bravery ticking by. *Time is irrelevant to them.* Huxley's words were never clearer. Jack's finger paused on the trigger, gun sight wavering as the creature's tentacles explored the cave's interior.

"Shoot the wretched thing," cried Huxley.

It was like a switch in Jack's mind, travelling down his arm, squeezing the trigger. The two remaining bullets found their mark as the Shoggoth's chest split and peeled back in a jagged row of teeth. An unholy roar emanated from the pit, shaking the cave's walls in a shower of splintered ice. One of the tentacles whipped the gun from Jack's hand as another swept his legs from beneath him and he fell heavily. The creature scurried up the walls to the ceiling, where it hung above Huxley. Another moist tentacle wrapped around Huxley's body, constricting in a decisive crunching of bone. Huxley's body collapsed, lifeless, blood pooling, freezing crimson in the carpet of ice. Jack noted the final expression in his eyes. It was release. The creature then turned toward Jack and he scurried to his feet, a moan of despair escaping his opened mouth as the last grip of sanity seeped away in a stream of warm liquid down his legs. The thing reached out and touched his cheek, curling as it gently caressed. Jack stepped away, backing into the wall, waiting for the final act. How would he die, tentacle or teeth? *Or does this thing have yet another method?*

Its mouth opened wide, drawing a great breath before extruding a deep wail. Its form then shifted once more, falling from the ceiling, morphing back into the shape of Seth, dead human. Jack turned to look out into the blizzard, seeing the gathering shadows—the Elder Things—drawing closer. He stepped out into their midst, walking among them as they encircled him. He no longer felt the icy wind on his face, or even the heavy clothes against his skin, for he had surrendered his senses, his sanity, when the Shoggoth showed itself within Seth's body. Whatever happened next would be the Elder Things' doing. One stepped forward and Jack felt himself breathe its shadow-form deep within his lungs, the creature's essence surging through his own life source, populating his veins and nerve cells, his body now its vessel. He closed his eyes for a moment, and when he opened them again the other shadows were gone. He smiled as the storm fell silent and the snow stopped falling, realising that his sinister traveller was more than just one. They were legion, and he was their host.

He sat in the snow, the sky clearing. Soon the chopper would come for him; soon he would be home on the great fertile southern land. He thought of the waves on the beach he often surfed, and of the sea, joining the continents; the sea where the Elder Things had migrated and great Cthulhu resides in waiting. Jack closed his eyes, imagining the sound of the surf and the kiss of the sun on his flesh.

The legion stirred, and he knew they approved.

VANGUARD

AARON STERNS

I

Storm clouds blacken the sky like the end of the world. The air howls.

Detective Michael Booker glances up as he braces at the library doors and rain razors his eyes. The looming clouds swirl in a great lazy vortex, like a forming tornado over the city. The air crackles with building electricity. He'd never seen anything like it before.

Hasn't got time to worry.

"Ethan! Where are you?"

The radio hisses empty.

"Goddamnit, where's our backup?"

The base commander comes in like the voice of God: *"Soggies on site."*

They'll still be minutes away. "Library, inner courtyard of campus. I'm heading in."

"Negative. Wait for Alpha Team—"

Michael slaps the radio off and shoulders the frame. There's still no movement from inside. He darts in at a crouch, silhouetted against the doorway for a heart-stopping eternity.

Darkness swallows him. His torch barely cuts the blackness and he has to move more slowly than he wants, clearing each passing corner and blind spot.

A great dragged smear of blood coats the carpet of the foyer, miring a frantic fly in its gore. There are two more pools nearby.

He stares at them, then follows their trail into the building, finger hovering on the Glock's trigger.

Something shifts in the shadow of a trolley of books and he takes cover.

"That's not my blood, in case you're worrying." Ethan tries to smile, shifting a leg to show the soaked carpet beneath him. "This is mine."

Michael's partner slumps against the wall, a spreading stain darkening his shirt.

"Jesus." Michael drops to his knees and clamps the flow, putting his bodyweight into the pressure. "Damn it, I told you to turn back."

Ethan hisses. "And I told you…we were underestimating this. It's not one man…it's a group. A…cult. I shot one of them there." Ethan motions at the doorway of the men's room across from them. A body lies slumped half-inside, toes pointing to the roof. "Fucker ambushed me. A…lookout."

"A lookout? For what?"

Ethan shakes his head, face tight with pain. "There was this one guy: huge, crazy hair, no shirt. Skin covered in something—not tattoos, but…scars maybe. He seemed to be orchestrating them. He sounds like the description Armitage gave us of…that homeless guy casing the place."

"Armitage is dead."

Ethan stares at him. "But you—"

"They're all dead. The whole floor." He looks at the drag marks.

"Security guards I think."

"How many guards does this library need? And why take them?"

But Ethan's barely listening. He leans back, eyes clenched shut.

"I read this all wrong," Michael says. "Didn't believe you. And now…" He breaks off, having to look away from the pain on his friend's face. He feels a directionless anger threatening to overwhelm him. "We'll get the bastards, Ethe. The Soggies will—"

Light blinds them. Michael whirls to train his gun and half-a-dozen muzzles point back from the entrance. Special Operations Group Alpha materialise out of the night like hi-tech, black-clad ghosts.

The team leader—a lethal bullet of a man with an M4A1 like an extension of his arms—doesn't move to help. "Position?" he whispers.

Ethan points a bloody finger into the darkness ahead. "They were dragging them down there. To the back rooms I think—"

The leader nods dismissal and the team float past, gunlights on their MP5s and sweeping Bennelli shotguns scything the way. They disappear into the main reading hall and their glow fades.

"Yeah, you take over guys," Ethan says and leans back, eyes pinpricking with pain. The shot's missed his renal artery, as far as Michael can tell, but there might be organ damage.

"*Closed door at rear. Special Collections room. Engaging,*" the radio crackles.

"*Roger, team leader,*" the base commander says. "*Ready, ready.*" There's a pause for last-minute contingencies. Then: "*Go go go!*"

A distant boom rocks the floor beneath them as the concussive force of a door blast shakes the building.

"*Contact!*"

"*Roger Team Alpha. Engage at will—*"

Then a massive explosion eclipses everything. From where they crouch at the front of the library the two detectives feel a wave of hot air sweep over them. The sound is nearly deafening. Screams echo down the corridor. Then comes the sound of gunfire: short controlled bursts.

Executions.

"What the hell—"

But Michael's cut off by the radio: "*Status, Alpha? I repeat, Team Leader Alpha: what's your status?*" There's no response to base. Then: "*Bobby, what the fuck's happening in there?*"

Michael hesitates. Ethan pushes his hand away and stamps the flow himself. "Go."

Michael runs to the corner and glances back. Blood's seeping through his partner's fingers.

"Go, damnit!"

Smoke hangs like mist at the back of the vast main room of the library from the blown door and the flashbangs the SOG had thrown. A weird quiet has descended inside the building. All he can hear are the last moans of the dying, the distant sirens from outside, a chopper somewhere overhead too far away to help.

He edges closer, gun sweeping the smoke, and then the fetid air clears and he sees the bodies littering the doorway. The SOG team lies torn and shredded in a tumble of broken limbs and useless equipment, many with single bullet holes in the chest or head. One man coughs his last—the team leader, Michael thinks—and blood gouts over his dimpled chin. Then he's still.

Michael stares at them. There's nothing he can do.

He can only make sure whoever they're up against doesn't get away.

He edges to the frame and peers around. More bodies lie blasted across the floor inside the display room. All motionless and ripped apart, smoke swirling above the strewn body parts. Priceless manuscripts smoulder inside shattered glass cases.

But the scale of death's not what takes his breath away. Beyond the SOG team, in the murk at the back of the room, are the dragged security guards and ambushed library researchers. It's just a wall of flesh at first, and then Michael makes out hanging arms and draping breasts, genitals like dark fruit. Clothes lie discarded in piles to either side. The dead have been stacked in a pyramid of meat against the wall, an intricate, interconnected pattern of blood and shit-stained nudity rising halfway to the ceiling. Like…like some sort of door.

The smell of cordite and leaking corpse gases and…something else, something sulfuric nearly makes Michael vomit. His vision swims with the stench.

Then he sees the figures come out of the gloom. Beneath their coats of smeared blood both men's skin glint with weird silvery symbols of etched scars. One of the two carries a jerrycan and hand-held blowtorch, a slung AK bumping against his shoulder as he races to complete whatever insane ceremony they've dreamt up. The other man—tall, wild hair like a dark shock, messiah beard—intones gibberish from an ancient and mottled book in one hand that's almost hypnotic in its rhythms, like some innate pre-language. In his other hand he clutches a dripping curved knife.

Michael—enraged, in shock—doesn't even bark a warning as he brings up the gun.

Then the cult leader reaches into the shadows beside the wall of flesh and drags forth another figure: a girl, her thin naked back marred also with the intricate knife cuts. He raises the knife. "Forr'e wgah'n c'ftagh—" the man begins to roar, then breaks off sensing Michael about to fire.

He can't take the shot. He'll hit her.

And in that moment of hesitation the second man realises he's there and spins, bringing up the AK. Michael gut-aims and drops him and the blowtorch tumbles into a stack of torn books and ignites. He flashes back to the leader and sees a sliver of skull above the girl's head and takes the shot. The man's brains disappear in a cloud of blood.

The fire's taken hold and the room goes up with a roar and Michael stumbles back with the heat of it. Then he hears a scream and looks to the girl charging at him with the knife, face twisted with hate in the smouldering air and he brings up the gun too late as she comes at him as she fills his world.

Michael stares out the window at the sleeting rain, lost for a moment in the torrential weather.

"Mike, you with me?"

He jolts. "Huh? Yeah, we're clear."

Ethan glances across as he drives, hands tightening on the steering wheel. Michael ignores him and continues scanning ahead for suspicious cars, planted obstacles, some sign they'd been leaked. It's almost impossible to see anything. Bloody Melbourne weather. It'd been sunny this morning. They should've delayed.

"If you're gonna space on me—"

"I said I was ready, didn't I?"

"Yeah, it's gonna be a hoot," Ethan says.

Michael notices his friend has one hand unconsciously cradling the old bullet wound to his stomach. He feels a twinge in his neck in sympathy. The burns lacing his chest and stomach ache to be itched.

He checks the side mirror for the other two SUVs streamlining in their wake. "Convoy's holding. No perceived threats." But it doesn't distract Ethan. Michael grits his teeth, knowing his friend's been holding this back the whole trip.

"Damnit, Mike. You didn't have to come back. You could've taken a pension. You have a family—I don't. You could've stayed home with Rachel and Isla—"

"Rachel knows why I have to do this," Michael says quietly. "So should you."

Ethan doesn't say anything for a long moment, then: "It wasn't your fault, Mike. You're going to have to accept that one day."

Michael keeps glowering at the streaking rain.

The air turns frostier inside the car than out and neither talk as they finally near the isolated coastal city of Warrnambool. Even though they're low on petrol they take the bypass; Port Herring's only twenty K's or so further on and they'll make it fine on what's left. They can always take targeted runs out later to refuel.

There's little other traffic travelling the shipwreck coast. A few hire cars persisting through the storm to the Loch Inn Gorge—site of early Australia's most famous maritime disaster, and now reduced to a tick-off tourist trap on the Great Ocean Road—and that's about it. Michael can be thankful for that much at least. If they'd tried the transfer on a weekend it would've been a nightmare.

The once-thriving whaling village of Port Herring sits slowly dying in a sheltering inlet gouged into the coastline. Tuna trawlers—the only industry still viable in south-west Victoria—crowd the bay, rocking in the storm like play-toys in a baby's bath. As they rip through Michael does a quick mental recon, noting supermarkets and a servo, but also, more importantly, medical facilities and the police station. The rest of the town seems just a collection of broken-down buildings and empty lots. A couple of locals in hoodies hunch beneath a bus shelter and stare balefully at the sleek cars as they pass. Michael gets a glimpse of heavy brows, a harelip, dark scowls, little opportunity.

"Must be something in the water down here," Ethan says. "Makes you fuck your cousin."

"They are your cousins."

Ethan laughs and the mood lifts a little. Then Michael's radio crackles.

"*Two minutes out,*" Simmonds says from the Principal's car.

"Roger, Commander. Advance team heading in."

Michael signals an unmarked road ahead and Ethan grins. "Last chance. I can keep driving."

"And what's beyond here? Adelaide? No thanks."

They laugh. Then Michael unholsters his gun and Ethan sets himself. He takes the corner hard, sweeping ahead while the other cars continue on.

Michael grips the handrail as they bounce down the unpaved road, the rain reducing visibility to maybe ten metres. Then the weather abruptly eases and the safehouse appears ahead. Michael takes in as much as he can of the surrounds as they stream towards it.

He can see why the property had been chosen. The old, two-storey free-settler homestead—old by Australian standards anyway, probably going back to 1850, maybe even 1840—sits high and alone backed against the drop-off cliffs, its array of windows like eyes watching over the empty farmland stretching inland. The long driveway is clear of trees and runs stark and open down from the road above; a frontal assault would be seen a mile off.

They idle in the driveway a moment, then Michael nods and they hit their doors.

"I've gone over the layout. It's solid," Ethan says as they run the perimeter. "Cameras to the four winds. Two on the tree line, two in the back covering the side road and beach. Weakest spot's here where the trees are closest, I reckon, but there's twenty metres of open ground on crunching gravel to cover to get to the house. Infra-red'll pick up anyone coming down through the trees long before then anyway." He points beyond the twisted tea-trees to the overlooking hill. "Escape Route One is along this ridgeline up to the main road, assuming the driveway's compromised. But we lose the whole front—" They circle the house and head for the drop-away cliffs, the biting Southern Ocean air hitting them as they look over. "We can go on foot down this path shaded by outcrops, hug the cliffs. I miss anything, boss?"

Michael stares at the beach below. The sea roars.

"You think crooks are gonna send frogmen in dinghies?"

Michael glances at his partner.

Ethan rolls his eyes. "Fine. I'll get the techies to put a camera on the water. Forgot how paranoid you get."

"That's what we're paid for."

"What we're paid for is to sit on our arses the next two weeks and listen to each other fart."

Michael smiles and is about to turn away when he sees something glint dull silver on the sand below. A dead fish has somehow beached itself up near the rocks at the cliff base. The tideline didn't even make it that far, so how the hell did it get there? Had it shimmied all the way up? Michael edges closer to see more clearly.

And then the fish spikes down dark prehensile arms and flops forward.

Michael almost pitches over the edge, vision lurching.

"You okay?" Ethan says, grabbing him.

The dead fish lies unmoving below. And armless. Shifting shadows play over its skin; that's all the effect was.

"Yeah, of course," Michael says and turns to go.

Ethan keeps hold. "You said you weren't on meds anymore," he says softly.

Michael stares at him.

"Your eyes are like pin-pricks."

"I told you. I stopped that shit months ago."

"C'mon, Mike. I took them myself, remember? The dreams, hallucinations—you can't be out here dealing with that—"

Michael pulls away. "I'm clean. Okay?" He heads back to clear the house before his friend can say anything else.

The rambling building—'Dalkeith House' reads a faded

inscription on the front door—is big for a safe house. Maybe too big: four bedrooms adapted to shared quarters, a couple of living areas for endless rounds of cards and a big kitchen downstairs; an entire separate eco-space upstairs for the Principal and the minders. And never the twain shall meet. The décor's a bit old and musty, but it's a mansion compared to some of the locations Michael had worked in. He'd once done a wiretap in a caravan with redbacks in its cupboards in Ballarat's dead winter. Didn't sleep a wink the whole two weeks. Thought his balls were going to get frostbite, if they didn't get bitten first.

The moment they've cleared the last room Michael calls in the rest of the team, not allowing a chance for any more helpful chit-chat. He and Ethan stand either side of the driveway, weapons low but safeties off as they scan the surrounds. Michael can feel his partner's eyes on him.

Then the dark SUVs gun down the driveway in a billow of dust and the job takes over. Michael's hair whips as they flash past. The pair of SUVs pull up as close to the house as possible, screeching gravel, and the two fat surveillance guys—Tommy and Robbo—tumble out of their car first to provide cover, followed by some new kid with scared-rabbit eyes Michael had never worked with before.

Finally the team commander—a huge bear of a man called Simmonds they'd worked under before, and who'd always been an officious prick—emerges from the other car and scans the area. He glances at Michael and frowns, then gives a quick nod into the car and a rangy whippet of a man snakes out followed by a heiffer liaison officer—Jess, Michael thinks her name is—and the two check the surroundings one last time.

Michael's heart pounds. His throat has gone dry.

Three. Two. One—

The whippet-man reaches in and ushers out the Principal. Michael can barely see through the tight crush of bodies. He notices the others peering for a look.

Then there's a gap and he sees a thin arm glistening with scars—then the girl appears, dwarfed between her two minders as she's shielded ahead. She looks back between the crowd of limbs and locks on Michael. His chest prickles at the sight of her.

He expects a look of pure hatred, the same zealous mania he'd seen that night.

Instead she seems scared, somehow lost and bewildered. Her eyes plead with him through the tangle.

Then she's gone.

"Yeah, fuck you too, bitch," Ethan says and motions everyone in.

"Should be paying us more so I don't shoot her meself," Robbo mumbles. "Fuckin' cop killer."

He notices Michael staring at him.

"Sorry, chief," the techie says and slinks past.

Michael follows, his own righteous anger unravelling now at the look she'd given him.

II

"The only name we have for her is Sara," Simmonds says, standing at the head of the table in the downstairs kitchen. Beside him stands the girl's minder—a lean, dangerous man called Vilks, so ramroad straight he was either ex-military or actually had a stick up his arse. Michael had seen him walk the perimeter before the briefing, the man not realising he was being watched as he crouched at the corners of the property teasing a handful of dirt and staring out at the surrounding land like some watchful animal marking its territory. Once satisfied with the location he'd returned to the house, giving Michael in the doorway a look that sliced through him. A look like he's giving now. "An attempt was made against her at the city watch-house, so she's finally agreed to testify—"

"At Command?" the young kid, Ted, asks. "That place is crawling with cops."

"Maybe that's why," Simmonds says and Robbo squirms. "We have to get her through to trial. We don't know anything about this group. After underestimating them once already," Michael looks up at this, "we won't be doing it again. We need everything she can give us. I know you will all act professionally, even those of you who were there." He stares at the two detectives.

As the commander runs through protocols and contingencies Michael simmers, looking away down the hall at the stairs to the upper floor.

The glimpse of her still troubles him. He'd been so certain of her insanity, had demonised her like the others, but what if she'd been brainwashed? What if she was sitting up there scared, quiet, only now beginning to understand the consequences of what she'd done?

He imagines his own daughter years from now. What if she fell in with the wrong people? Believed others' lies. Is that all it takes?

He glances at the control room at the end of the corridor. Tommy's already in there spreading over the sides of his chair, settling in for an eight-hour shift. Michael can see the bank of screens over his shoulder for each camera, including the one Michael'd just had to convince Simmonds to place overlooking the water. Fuck it. It was worth pissing the commander off to demand it. Should've been a given.

He's about to look away when the screen stutters. He jolts forward.

"Booker? Something to add?"

"Huh?" Michael glances at the rest of the table. Everyone's watching him. The screen down the corridor is clear now: water rippling a washed-out infra-red green. For a moment he'd thought he'd seen—

"Then I'll keep boring you, shall I?" Simmonds gives him a look of death and continues the briefing.

Michael tries to stay focused but the damage is done. As the others clear out afterwards the huge commander pulls him aside, his breathing like a bull in the enclosed room.

"I want you to know I was forced to take you," Simmonds says, towering over him. "I fought it. But you got friends higher up it seems."

"I had nothing to do with that. I'd left the job—"

"So it's not a personal vendetta then?"

Michael breathes through his teeth. "I'm not a threat, if that's your concern."

"She and her friends did a lot of damage to you. Killed ten SOG in front of your eyes. You can forget all that?"

Michael tries to keep his voice low. "I'm just here to see this through. We don't even know who they are or what they were doing. Or if there's any more freaks out there who believe the same shit. We need her cooperation for that. We don't need her dead."

Simmonds stands breathing heavily, weighing that up. "I think you're here because you fucked up once already, and now you're trying to make up for it."

Michael has to stop himself from punching that big ugly nose.

"Step wrong I'm throwing you off," Simmonds says, too-close. "Screw the blowback. And after your bullshit with the camera—" Michael realises he means commanding the extra one for the beach, not the glitch he'd just imagined, "—you keep your fuckhole shut from now on. I don't care how you think this op should be run." He leaves, taking the oxygen in the room with him.

"What'd El Commando want?" Ethan asks when Michael returns to the team's quarters to unpack.

"Pissing contest. I let him win."

"Good," Ethan says with relief. "Keep it that way. About before—"

"Don't sweat it."

Michael bumps fists and heads into the shared bathroom to store his toiletries. He makes sure the door's locked before fumbling open a bottle of Xanax, standing holding the sink waiting for it to hit. His pounding heart finally settles, but when he looks up his reflection in the mirror wavers and for a second he's not looking at himself but someone he doesn't recognise, someone older and broken. And then he blinks and it's him again, albeit with darker bags under his eyes than he's used to. He stands swaying, unsettled by the vision.

But he's lived with these…skips…for months. That's the trade-off with the medication.

He's about to head out when he feels something in his pocket. He brings out the cross on its golden necklace and stares at it a moment. Then puts it back. That stopped giving him solace long ago.

He stashes the baggie behind the pipes and washes the fear-sweat off his face before heading back out to Ethan's scrutiny.

"**W**e're eating alone?" Ted asks, jerking a thumb at the second floor.

"They'll prepare their own meals," Simmonds says. "Not your concern."

"Bit unsociable, innit?"

The commander gives the kid a look that could melt plastic. Ted flinches as if struck.

Michael stands in the doorway smelling the dinner. Robbo sees him and grins, leaning over the bubbling pot dripping sweat. "Spaghetti marinara, Mikey. Fresh clams, calamari. Better than your Nonna makes."

Michael's stomach churns at the memory of the crawling fish on the beach. He hopes no one retrieved it for the meal.

"You two: hourly patrol at twenty-one hundred." Simmonds points at Ethan and Michael without bothering to look at them, then grabs a bowl and heads back to his room to bone up on procedures or what-not.

Ted salutes once he's out of sight. "So who we up against?" he asks the table. "This chick's group are religious nuts, right? But why hit a university? They don't like people learning?"

"We're not up against anyone," Michael says. "No one knows we're here."

Ted blinks at him. "Yeah, of course. I didn't mean—"

"This your first detail?"

Ted shifts uncomfortably. "I worked three years vice, four on the streets before that. I know my shit."

Ethan tries to smooth it over. "He's just being superstitious, mate. No sense wanting something to happen just because we're out here. As for the cult—" He raises an eyebrow at Michael:

Who's it gonna hurt? Michael shrugs: *Okay.* "Like Simmonds said, we don't know jack shit about them. We've had this girl six months and she's still a mystery. It was only luck we ever found out anything about them. We'd been investigating a series of break-ins at universities across the country. There'd been two deaths: one a history academic in Canberra who must have stumbled in on someone ransacking his office. All of his books were torn apart. Another a tenured professor in Wollongong who'd been tortured."

"Tortured? For what?"

"We thought it might've been part of the illegal book trade. We'd been working this guy called Armitage, a professor in linguistics at La Trobe. There'd been an attempt at their library— they had this huge collection of rare books under armed guard—"

"Armed guard?" Robbo asks, forgetting to stir the sauce.

"Weird, right? That's why we thought the book trade. Based on the previous MOs we figured the library'd be hit again— whoever was doing this didn't muck around—so we went back to interview Armitage on a hunch."

"And then it all went to Hell," Michael says.

The table looks at him. "Sorry, man," Ted says. "I heard you guys got banged up pretty bad." Michael turns away, seeing him glance at the deep scar on his neck.

"Well, she's gonna burn for it," Robbo says and slops a serve of spaghetti in front of Michael. Then he realises the faux pas. "I mean...she's gonna pay."

Michael almost vomits at the smell of the seafood. Not wanting to show how unsettled he is he reaches for his fork, but as his arm is obscuring the bowl he thinks he sees a length of calamari tentacle convulse on top of the pile. He drops the cutlery with a clang.

The red-soaked calamari arm lies still and curled on the mass of clam shells and pasta. He imagines it sliding down his throat, unfurling and gripping with its suckers.

He pushes back from the table. "Sorry. I...don't like seafood."

Robbo stands stricken in the middle of the kitchen, his apron barely containing his stomach. "Since when?"

"It's okay," Ethan says and grabs Michael's helping. "More for me. Forget about the bitch upstairs." He grins at Ted. "You wanna hear a real war story?"

Michael hesitates at the door and Ethan gives him a glance; lets him know he'll cover for him. This time.

Michael stands staring at himself in the mirror, gripping the sides of the sink. Whenever he closes his eyes he sees the tentacle constrict, remembers the shadowy fish spike down its arms. And then he's back in the library as the world falls apart around him. He can't take much more of this.

He flushes the pills.

Michael tries to maintain watch on the trees, the horizon, but his gaze keeps being drawn to the muffled light of the second-floor room like a tongue seeking out a rotting tooth. He shouldn't have agreed to the assignment, should've listened to the psych evaluations saying he was hiding his post-traumatic stress, should've listened to Rachel when she first reacted with horror at the idea of him returning to the job—and a job where he and Ethan would have to protect the very person who'd nearly killed them.

He's so distracted he stumbles as he rounds the east corner of the house. The scuff of gravel must carry because Ethan— patrolling the inroad north—alerts everyone over the radio.

"You okay, Mikey? Falling asleep out there?"

Michael glances up at the silent camera underneath the big colonial's eaves and keeps walking. "I'm fine. Just stubbed my toe," he whispers into his throat mic. "East side clear." He resists the urge to wipe the sweat from his face and already regrets flushing the medication.

"East side clear," Tommy repeats from the control room. *"Go on, Ethe."*

"Yeah, you gotta hear this shit," Ted chimes in.

"So we come in through the back door of this dim sim factory,"

Ethan continues, as Michael finds a blind spot to catch his breath, *"and we'd been told the triads had been dumping there for years, so we expect half-ground bodies sticking out of meat vats. But instead we find this iced-up guy in one of the back rooms with this dog—what sort was it, Mike?"*

"An Afghan," Michael says, staring at the window.

He'd wanted to watch her stew. See her frustration at incarceration. That was the real reason he'd agreed to the assignment.

He wanted that much revenge.

But now... Now he knows that won't help him. Simmonds was right. He'd underestimated the cult, hadn't stopped the slaughter at the university, had even underestimated the girl and she'd nearly killed him. And now he'd pushed himself to return to the job when he wasn't ready.

"Yeah, an Afghan. A dead Afghan. So we burst in and this little Asian guy's naked and he grabs a cleaver. But he's still in the dog—"

"Holy shit!" Tommy blurts.

Ethan laughs. *"Yeah. So the first shot hits the dog's head, and it must've spasmed around him because—"*

Michael unhooks the earpiece and lets it hang with the night-vision goggles bobbing around his neck as he continues past the house to the cliffs. Without the chatter in his ear he can hear now the freezing southern waters crashing and rumbling out in the spreading darkness like some great monster and he closes his eyes and latches onto it. The wind scrabbles at his face and a smell washes over him of crisp salt and...something else. Something metallic.

Beckoning rain.

He looks up. The clouds hang so low they're almost about to fall. Distant thunder grumbles, beckoning release. Electricity bolts and crackles across the underside in little bursts.

He shudders at the memories it triggers, has to tell himself: *you're not back there, it's only a storm.* But his heartbeat keeps skipping and he forces himself to look back down.

There's something out on the water. A silhouette against the horizon.

Though he squints he can't make out the shape fully, and although he hates the night-vision glasses—they always made him nauseous, like he's seeing the world through someone else's eyes—eventually he relents and snaps them up. The headset whines like an insect burrowing into his ear.

The night swims with green.

And at the reaches of the night-vision's range: a yellow blob of heat of a figure. The man stands wavering on top of the water, staring into shore.

Michael instinctively clamps his eyes shut, disbelieving.

When he opens them again the figure is gone. The churning surf is a line of white, the sea stretching beyond a featureless mass of dark green.

Michael forces himself to breathe again and jams his earpiece back in. Ethan's still yabbering about the raid.

"Tommy," Michael cuts in. "The water."

"Huh, Mike? Hang on… Nah, camera six don't have shit."

Sweat streams down Michael's brow. He feels it splash off the metal jut of the glasses. The sickly illumination nearly makes him vomit as he strains to scan the rolling waves.

"How many targets, Mike?" Ethan asks, voice ragged as he runs to his location.

Michael hesitates, and then Simmonds blasts in over the airwaves: *"I'm in the control room. Screens are fucking clear. Do we have a breach, damnit?"*

Bile tickles Michael's throat as the world drowns in green.

"Negative. False alarm."

"What do you mean, negative? What did you bloody see?"

Pounding footsteps sound behind him. Ethan's as out of shape as he is and he rests his hands on his knees as he clips up his goggles and scans the water.

"Must've been a glitch," his partner eventually reports. "First night jitters."

"You blaming the tools?" Tommy splutters.

"You are a tool, couch boy," Ethan quips, but he's looking at Michael now.

"*If only we had a couch in here. Fucking ergonomic chairs, my arse—*"

"*Both of you shitheads: report in now.*"

Michael barely hears Simmonds as he stares out to sea, fighting the nausea of the glasses, needing some explanation for what he'd seen.

Then it's too much and he rips off the goggles and his throat mic and throws up what little's in his stomach.

Ethan unhooks his own mic, then kicks some gravel over the steaming vomit.

"I'll leave tomorrow," Michael says, staring at the ground.

"It'll take a few days to flush out the system. Try to ride it out."

Michael looks up at his friend. Ethan meets his eyes without flinching.

"I know why you have to be here. I may be the only one."

Michael stands there a moment. Then he says what he's been trying to avoid all this time. "She left me, Ethan. Took Isla. Said she couldn't cope with what I'd become. Couldn't let our daughter be affected."

Ethan takes this in. The storm threatens. "Then this is all we've got."

Michael lets himself be led back to the house.

"**L**emme see your night eyes."

Michael hands Tommy his goggles, eyes fixed on the monitors over the techie's shoulder. The other cop notices.

"There was nothing, Mike. I even rewound the feed."

Michael nods and looks away.

"Maybe it was a glitch," the techie concedes, even though he doesn't have to. "Too much light filtering in. I'll get you a new pair."

"Thanks."

Michael waits for him to head to the storeroom then skips back through the infra-red footage. He knows the answer even before he does it. There's only the washed-out sea of light green endlessly rolling over itself.

"Did you see something or not?" Simmonds fills the doorway, glaring at him.

Michael's not sure if he'd been caught. "Must've been a spike. I'm changing the headset."

The commander enters the cramped room, crowding Michael as he frowns at the monitor. Michael can smell the rot of the man's stomach ulcer. Had he seen—

"You know the damned protocol—if there's any chance of breach we evac and ask questions later."

"I understand the drill."

"Yeah? Then maybe you want something to happen to justify you being here. That's why you're jumping at shadows."

"That's not what happened."

Yet maybe he's right. Maybe Michael should excuse himself from the mission before anything else goes wrong. He doesn't know if he can last a few more days, doesn't know if he believes in anything enough anymore to keep going—

"I'm not going to let you fuck up this mission because you're too invested. Like I said: I don't care if the girl did request you on this—"

Michael looks up. "Wait. What?"

"Only way she agreed to testify. And the only reason I'm still putting up with your bullshit." He stabs a finger into Michael's chest, right in the agonising centre of the burns. "But I'll override it if I have to."

Tommy trots back in after Simmonds is gone and slaps a new pair of goggles in Michael's hands. "Here you go, tosser. Don't break this one."

Michael blinks at him. Then at the glasses. "Thanks."

He steps back into the hallway and has to rest against the wall before his legs give out. His vision blurs with the after-effects of the night-vision, the stress of the reaming, Simmonds' revelation.

The door at the top of the stairs beckons.

He heads back to bed and lies staring at the shifting shadows on the roof until the distant cracking of the waves draws him down into darkness.

Rachel snuggles back against him and he smiles through half-sleep at the heat of her body against his, the softness of her skin beneath his draped arm, and as he leans in to kiss his wife's biteable shoulder he sees beyond her a shadow in the doorway: Isla looking at him over her clenched bunny—timing it as perfectly as ever—and he sighs smiling and shuffles room, patting the bed so his daughter can clamber in dragging her threadworn sleep-toy; and as she burrows in alongside them she glances back at her father, giggling. *"Forr'e wgah'n c'ftaghu Avanhara!"* she whispers and her eyes have become black voids in her skull and in them is something unfathomable and hidden and yearning—and Michael wakes, heart pounding, a terror strangling his breath. He sits there in a pool of sweat until Ethan's snuffling across the room brings him back to the reality of the safehouse and he can force himself up.

In the bathroom his skin itches like a thousand mosquitoes biting him and he rips off his shirt and stares at the angry red mess of his body in the mirror. The puckered burn wounds snake the length of his torso like mottled raw meat. His untouched face looks surreal perched on his ruined body. He remembers the first time Rachel had seen his wounds. The hidden recoil in her eyes that'd only gotten worse over the long months of angry rehabilitation.

That brings the dream back, and the anxiety punches into his chest in an instant. He fumbles for the stash of medication before remembering it's gone.

The panic clutches at his throat and threatens to collapse his heart. He can smell smoke and when he closes his eyes he can see flames overwhelming him, feel the heat grab at his skin.

Eventually his breathing deepens and the room stops pulsing and he's able to open his eyes and look in the mirror again. He'd never been able to beat it before.

You can do this.
You have to.

Michael can feel eyes on him as he enters the kitchen, but no one says anything about the false alarm. Robbo must be on shift now, because Tommy sits eating vegemite toast by the bucket and wiping sleep from his eyes with smeared fingers. Beside him Ted hunches over a half-finished shopping list. Ethan—already dressed—looks up from the fridge and Michael nods. Ethan gives a small smile of solidarity.

"Heya, Mike," Tommy yawns and continues dictating: "And cigarettes. And matches."

"Yeah, yeah. Hang on," Ted says and scrawls the additions.

"And some more Coke."

"Two bottles not enough?"

"You don't have to stay up all night."

"Alright, settle."

"You asked what they need upstairs?"

Ted rolls his eyes. "I gotta do a patrol in three minutes—"

"I'll go." Michael yanks the list before he can keep whining.

"Hey, thanks, mate. Grab some Milo if you can." Ted glances at the others. "I can't sleep without hot Milo."

"Your mum stir it with her dick for you, too?" Tommy asks around a gobful of toast.

Michael heads out, avoiding Ethan's look, hoping he doesn't try to follow.

He pauses at the base of the stairs to calm his shaking hands, part of him still wishing he had the security of the medication, knowing he was right to rid himself of it. Then he heads up.

"Supply run, Jess," Michael calls as he knocks. "What do you guys need from town?"

There's no answer and he pries the door and peers in.

The shower's running in the front room and he heads over to the kitchenette and opens the fridge before anyone can question him being up here, barely glancing at the food stocks as he surveys the sparse living area. He'd been through on the first day, but he's surprised now to realise there's no television, no books, not even a pack of cards. And he thought it was boring downstairs.

He hears a muffled sound from the darkened hallway threading off from the loungeroom. Then an angry voice.

The door at the end is ajar and he sees a shadow move across the gap as he gets closer. At first he just makes out the shoulders of the minder—Vilks—hunched and threatening. And then the man shifts to the side and Michael sees the girl kneeling on the floor at his feet. Her shirt is off, her back a mess of sigil-like patterns and scars like a rippled coat, like his own ruined skin.

Vilks holds a knife to her throat.

Michael slams in and whips out his gun. In that instant he sees the man is pressing the flat of the heated blade against a line of scars on the girl's collarbone, leaning over her teeth bared.

"You will tell me where the book is—"

Michael centres his head: "Put down—"

Metal against the back of his own neck: cold and deadly. He senses the unforgiving press of a metal barrel.

"You first," the liaison officer, Jess, says in his ear. He can smell the shampoo on her.

Vilks rounds on them. "You let him up here?"

"Fuck you," Jess flares back. "I can't take a shit?"

Michael stands frozen, staring down at the girl. She gathers up her top and covers herself, scooting against the bed. Her eyes so white and wide in the low light of the fireplace. She's younger than Michael remembers: maybe eighteen, nineteen, tiny as she huddles before them.

He looks at the minder with naked hate.

The man doesn't even blink. "You don't know anything. *Detective*."

III

The girl crouches staring at him.

"Please," she says.

Michael stares down the barrel of the gun.

"Move and I put a bullet in you."

"Who are you?" Michael demands of the two minders. "You think you could get away with this for weeks? There's half-a-dozen cops downstairs."

The man doesn't react.

"You take me out. And then what? You can't cover that up. You going to kill everyone else?"

"If I have to."

Michael looks from him to the woman. Neither look like backing down. "You're insane."

"You really don't remember, do you?" Vilks asks.

"Remember what?"

"What she did to you."

Michael stares at him, uncomprehending. Then at the girl. She's looking at him now with heavy-lidded eyes, wary. "She attacked me—"

"I not know what I was doing. They drug me—" she says quickly and Vilks scoffs.

"She tried to sacrifice you. Even as you both burned."

Sara looks like a cornered rat. Her eyes flick to the door and Jess steps closer.

Michael stares at her, fighting the memory. Then it comes: Leaving Ethan huddled gut-shot in the corridor. The smothering smoke. The bodies of the SOG team in the doorway. Then flashes: a wild-haired man with scars all over his body holding something in his hands and intoning incoherently. A wall of flesh at the back of the room: formed of dragged security guards and library researchers. Raising his gun as the man senses him and turns. Then the girl rushing at him and slashing the knife even as he aims at her. That's all he's ever remembered.

But now there's something more: he's on his back as she scrabbles above, hair alight, yelling something he can't understand as she strains down with the knife, and he's trying to stop it but the blood's leaking strength from his throat, and even as their clothes catch fire she still puts all her weight against him and he stares up at her crazed face, willing to sacrifice herself if it means killing him, and he knows he will die here.

He stares at the girl, hand to his neck.

Her lips roll back in a sneer. "I should have ended you then, *cockroach.*"

"Enough," Vilks commands, but it's like something unleashed in the girl.

"Your whole species lurches from one generation to next in an endless succession of ignorants, all oblivious to the tenuous hold you have on this earth! You believe you are born into privilege: the rulers of the planet. Yet after so many thousands of years you are still no closer to understanding your place here, or your purpose. We inherit this world by default. And its rightful owners have spent their exile engineering their return—"

Jess crosses the gap and leans in. The girl shrinks back, suddenly fearful.

"You can denounce your humanity as much as you want," Jess says. "But you still feel the pain of one."

There's an amulet around the girl's neck: a curved triangle with an eye inside. As she says this it seems to glow brighter. The girl gives a hiss of pain.

Michael stares at it. That's not possible.

"The book," Vilks says. "The one they came for. What did she do with it?"

Michael keeps staring at her. She watches, waiting to see how much he remembers. "That's why they broke in? Some book?" Michael can barely picture it. "The man had it—we think he was the cult leader. He was reading from it. It...it dropped when I shot him. She was... she was screaming before she attacked me, trying to put it out. It must've burned. I don't fucking know. Why?"

"If it burned why do the clouds gather? Why do the stars align against us?"

The girl laughs.

They're all stark-raving mad. Michael glances at the corridor. He could yell, but then what? Vilks shoots him and the others hear the gunshot and come running, but then he and the woman would fortify themselves up here. And if pushed they'd just kill the girl. He'd die for what? He needs some way to distract the guy, but there's nothing up here of help. If he can get back into the loungeroom maybe he could kick a chair at him and—

"He is no use to us," Jess says. "Like I said. His mind is closed. He holds you back." Her finger tenses on the trigger.

"Fuck you, you crazy bitch," Michael spits at her.

At least that gets her attention. It's a bit hard to dehumanise someone when they're throwing your insanity back in your face.

"You're all whacked out on drugs. Brainwashed by some God-complex sicko or something. You think my mind's closed? Well, maybe that's because I'm not nuts." He needs to take control of this, stop them spouting their rhetoric to each other—

"Aren't you?" Vilks asks. "You dream night after night: seeing into the other world. And still you don't believe."

Michael stares at the righteous certainty in his eyes, Jess's finger tight on the trigger. Jesus, he has to get out of here.

Vilks takes the gun from the female officer and she steps in to grab the girl.

"We will prove to you they are not dreams," the man says.

Sara struggles as Jess slides a bright-red knife from the fireplace.

"Scream," the woman says, an inch from her eyes, "and I bring you agony." The amulet flares.

She steadies the girl's arm.

"Wait—stop!" Michael says and steps to intervene despite the gun pointing at him. Vilks nearly pulls the trigger.

"Damn it, stay there," Vilks commands him. "And watch."

Sara grits her teeth as the heated blade draws towards her held arm. Michael can smell the promise of searing flesh: a sick-sweet earthiness that churns his stomach.

"Don't let them—" the girl says, but the gun holds Michael where he is.

The girl tenses as the knife approaches as if she's about to spring away and Jess says a hissed word Michael can't hear and Sara freezes rigid. The amulet glows red-hot now. She can only stare at the blade descending towards the intricate carving on her bicep.

Jess continues to intone something over the girl's moaning

and then Michael gasps and stumbles backwards. His mind lurches and threatens to shut down, and he claws at the air as he hits the bed and falls to his knees.

The scar had moved. As the heated knife presses the girl's skin the interweavings of tattoos and scarification devolve as if trying to flee, retreating to untouched parts of her body. As soon as the knife is removed the intricate lines seep back to their original positions like pooled mercury. There's no burn mark.

Sara stares at him as if a cornered animal. She bares feral teeth.

"You should have helped me. *Cockroach*."

Jess slaps her. The girl's head whips to the side. Then she licks the cut on her lip and looks at him again. She smiles bloodied teeth.

Michael sits shattered on the couch in the living room. He reaches up to touch the cross at his throat, then remembers it's still jammed in his pocket. He debates taking it out, even though what he's just seen and heard should destroy his faith once and for all.

"You are a religious man, yes?" Vilks asks sitting across from him, gun forgotten on the chair beside. He shakes his head. "There is no God. There are only the *gods*." He skins his sleeve to show the dark scars disappearing up his arm. "The *Avanhara* teach us this is the sign of our faith. For our flesh is not our own. It belongs to the divine ones. And only they can give us power over ourselves—"

Michael stares at him. His blood freezes. "Wait...the *Avan*—"

"The *Avanhara*. The Vanguard. The ones who will usher in the true owners and destroy us all. At first I sought out the cult: its name whispered only on the lips of the dying, in the shadows of battle, whispered by the insane. I was born into war in Chechnya. I watch my family tortured, my only love years later raped and killed by Spetsnaz. I wanted world to suffer as I did and I followed their teachings. But then the visions came, night after night. The glimpses into our future. And...and even I with my hatred could not let this come to pass—"

"The *Avanhara*," Michael repeats, barely hearing anything the man's said. "It's…it's impossible. I've only heard that—"

"In dream?"

Michael stares at him, unable to speak.

And then something flashes across his vision: his daughter's face opening out in his dream and this time he sees within a vast void of impossible, writhing flesh and seething, otherworldly forms sliding over each other. A glimpse into the waiting dimension. He hears a distant, hateful keening almost beyond the hearing or sanity of the human and slams back against the couch, staring at Vilks with horror. It takes a moment to adjust back to reality.

"Yes," Vilks says. "You are beginning to see the truth. The forces against us. If Vanguard discovered I was still alive they would slaughter me where I stand. Their depravity knows no end. The girl herself was the most favoured wife of Khemenov — the leader you killed—kidnapped off street when young and brought up in teachings of the cult. She stole back into her house years later and killed her parents to rid herself of ties to this world. She is most zealous of all and will do anything in her power to see the end. That is why she key for us. She must know. The *Avanhara* have waited hundreds of years for the Alignment to come again. That is why book must still exist. It cannot be so easy." He leans forward. "You must remember—"

"I can't—"

"Have you listened to what I've told you? What you have seen yourself? Try, damn it."

"All…all I can remember is the fire. And then…" Even saying this much causes his heart to spike, makes him long for the soothing spread of Xanax, of anything he could find so long as it numbed his mind to all this.

He searches the past. She's above him pressing the knife to his chest and he has both her wrists and he knows he's going to die, knows he can't fight much longer—he's so weak as the fire licks at his arms now, running along the skin and catching hold. He looks to the side and sees what's fuelling it: the book too close, its leathery cover nearly touching him. He tries to edge away and the girl screams down and there's a shadow forming around her shoulders and her eyes have filled with blackness.

He sits gasping at the memory. "The book was burning. Next to me."

Vilks studies Michael. "But you didn't see it destroyed? You don't remember anything else?"

Michael shakes his head and Vilks breathes frustration through his teeth, trying to think.

"Attempts have been made to burn it before. I know it cannot be that easy. We can only think she was able to pass the book off to someone first. Or perhaps hide it in a sliver of time. She was taken into custody immediately, yes? So perhaps she has not been able to speak to her people yet, to tell them of the book. The attempt at the watch-house, we think that was not to silence her, but to break her out."

Michael stares at him. "This book—"

"Written by a madman, it is said to bring insanity to all who read it. And yet it is believed to contain terrible truths, which only one with his mind open to the other world could have transcribed. I have read copies only, deliberate misprints to shelter its existence—omitting the Enochian calls necessary for the end rituals—but even those copies contained enough of the original manuscript to be dangerous. They detail rites that, conducted at right time in history, at weakest conjunctions of the dimensions—those places already touched by the hand of divine ones—will bring about our end. It is said that the book is bound in the skin of its own creator, after he bled himself out over its pages, and has survived every attempt to destroy it over the centuries as it waits for its ultimate use. Even I, when in Vanguard, did not know when this time was. Until now. But I believe the window begins to close. The weather, the stars build to something ... They will try to find her again before it is too late. Other than Simmonds, no one in your force apart from the men in this building even knows we are here. Nowhere in your safe house—"

"Simmonds knows about this?"

The man nods. "As much as he needed to be convinced. He

was resistant to you being here. But the girl herself insists, for what reason I do not know. I begin to think now it is because you know something you not yet remember. Or else she thinks you take pity on her and try to save her. As for others, Simmonds picks those he thinks he can trust without having to tell them anything. People he has worked with before. You have too, yes?"

"Ethan was my partner for years. He nearly died that night at the university. He had no more idea than I did. And I've worked with Tommy and Robbo many times." He looks up. "But there's a new guy I've never seen before."

"Watch him."

"Simmonds vetted him though."

"The Vanguard have people in power throughout all societies: politicians, police, lawyers, all watching, waiting. You must be careful who you trust."

"Jesus. So, all that's stopping them is you two?"

"The numbers of those who resist are so small now. After Armitage and the others died we are spread thin. I dispatched some of those left as decoys to other safehouses—I believe the Vanguard cannot hit us all at once. Now I wonder if I should have consolidated us all here." He looks haunted and scrapes the stubble on his chin with a weary hand. The toll this has taken on him must be great. "We can only hope we not followed, and no one betrays us. The barrier will protect us from vision at least—"

"What barrier?" Michael has a flash of him pausing at the corners of the property that first night, crouching while he considered the vulnerability of the location. Or placing something.

Vilks nods, seeing the recognition in his eyes. "The talismans will protect us against attack. At least for a while. Perhaps that will give us enough time until the window closes. Or for us to break her and find the location of book. Until then you must ensure none of your men suspects, nor are they allowed contact with the outside world."

Michael takes this in, mind reeling with it all, not sure how much he believes, not sure how much he can refute. Then he nods.

He leaves the floor with the sounds of quiet torture in the back rooms following him. He shuts the door as he leaves.

Ethan waits at the bottom of the stairs. "I thought *el commando* said upstairs was a no go?"

Michael hesitates, then heads down. He taps the shopping list. "Too late now. Man, that Jess heiffer can eat."

"I'll give her something to eat."

Michael smiles as he passes, heading back to his quarters to get ready for the next hourly patrol. When he glances back Ethan's still in the shadows, watching him.

Michael retraces his steps to the edge of the trees. The thick bush stretches up over the ridgeline in an impenetrable tangle. He almost wishes he'd brought the night vision goggles, but the infra-red camera behind him has a better view anyway. He knows Robbo will call out anything.

Vilks had hidden his work well, but there's a small scuffmark near the outermost tree, a twisted redgum. It'd be impossible to see if you didn't know it was there: a slightly raised mound like an extension of tree root. He wonders what's beneath the soil.

Can only trust it will protect them.

"Found something?"

Michael spins. Ethan raises his hands. His throat mic's off, gun in the holster.

"Whoa Trigger. You telling me you didn't hear me? Should I be worried patrolling with you?"

"Sorry." Michael lowers his Glock and wipes his brow, checking himself too late. He takes off his own mic. "Still spacing, you know?"

Ethan clocks the sweat at his temple and looks away. "Just a couple more days, mate. Try not to see any dancing clowns in the trees until then, hey? Or at least don't call it in."

Michael tries to return his smile.

"You need to head back? I can take this." Ethan's looking at the base of the tree, tracking Michael's gaze.

"No, Ethe," Michael says quickly. "I haven't checked the beach yet."

"Hopefully there's no walking fish."

"What?"

Ethan looks up, puzzled. "I said, hopefully it doesn't rain. Just a coupla minutes more. Then I reckon it's going to bucket." He points at the threatening sky.

Michael starts to head off, making sure not to glance at the ground and give away the bump again.

Ethan stays where he is. "You sure you're okay, man?"

Michael nods, hating the lie but wanting to get back to the safety of the house. Now that he knows of the Vanguard he doesn't like being out in the open. He imagines faceless cultists lining out of sight beyond the trees, waiting for whatever this barrier thing is to fail. Even the fact he's thinking of a barrier freaks him out. The way the scars moved on the girl's arm...it's like the veil has been lifted from the world and he can never go back to the way things used to be.

"Getting sick of this place already," says Ethan. "How about we scope out town in the afternoon? At least that'll be a break from the same four walls."

Shit. "I might postpone that until tomorrow, give me a bit more time to hole up."

"Oh," Ethan actually seems disappointed. "You know I grew up near here? Been meaning to get down this way again for a while. We're right near the Loch Inn shipwreck. I used to hear about it when I was a kid."

Michael glances up at the clouds again as Ethan rabbits on. The guy has missed his calling: he should be a writer, or an entertainer in an old folks' home.

There's something unnatural now in the symmetrical swirling above. Yet another confirmation he didn't want. He starts to head off but Ethan's in no hurry to leave the treeline.

"You probably know the early free-settler ship that smashed on the rocks near here in one of the huge storms that wrack the coast, despite the nearby lighthouse, right?" Ethan continues, oblivious. "But did you know two people survived? A young deckhand and a girl. They sheltered in the nearby gorge until found days later by the first farmers to have claimed land here— the Bouchers. They still have family around here. People thought it was romantic, hoping the two would become a couple. Instead, neither could speak, traumatised by what they'd seen. They just kept drawing something in the sand. A spiral, like this—"

He crouches and inscribes in the earth with a stick. Michael takes a faltering step towards him. He's perilously close to the tree. "Let's go."

Ethan looks up at the edge in his voice.

"Feels like the DTs, man," Michael explains. "You've got to go easy on me for a few days, remember?"

Ethan doesn't move. "You gonna tell me what's going on?"

Michael should've known how hard it'd be to hoodwink him. They've been partners for years. He hesitates, wondering if he should try to explain the truth. But he doesn't know he believes it himself yet; how can he convince someone else? Even someone he considers his closest friend in the world.

"You know what's going on, Ethe. I can barely think straight out here."

His friend frowns with that sceptical expression he always gets talking to crooks. Nothing gets past the bastard.

Fuck it, he's going to think I'm truly crazy, but here goes—

Then Ethan reaches out with the stick and smoothes away the sand either side of the lump beneath the tree. Whatever's beneath now stands out in stark contrast. He contemplates it a moment.

"That's a shame, Michael. I was hoping you would be more cooperative."

He stands and turns to him and his eyes have become black pits stretching back infinitely into his skull.

IV

"**N**o!" Michael cries. But he's too late to stop Ethan taking a step and kicking at the lump. A carved piece of stone emerges like a buried toad. Thunder cracks above and the earth shudders beneath them. A ripple of dark electricity pulses out over the trees.

And then the shroud falls. Some sort of invisible protection circling the grounds of the house in a huge arc burns away into the air and leaves them open to the world beyond.

Figures stand amongst the twisted tea trees and towering gums. Shoulders misshapen beneath their hooded sweatshirts, hands hanging asymmetrically, their faces almost subhuman and devolved. They look like…like some of the townspeople they'd seen on the way through.

Ethan smiles. "Strange that I lived so close to here and never knew the truth." His tone is as conversational as ever. Michael reaches for his gun but Ethan whips his out first and shakes his head.

"No, Michael. You know, many things have been sent to this out-of-the-way little country to be hidden—like the book itself, in fact. Ancient artefacts were often stowed on early settler boats, sometimes warping the minds of all on board. The crew of the Loch Inn tore each other apart, you know that? That's not in the history books. The two that survived were said to have joined in union as they huddled in the cove riddled with madness. Nine months later a child was born, but it was not a child like anything on this earth. Something born instead from the depths of the sea, from out of space and time. And when the *Avanhara* swept in they cultivated its line and let it breed and spread through the area. That is why I chose this house—or at least let Simmonds think he was choosing it—the house where that first baby was born."

Michael stares at him. "So you—"

Ethan scoffs. "I'm not so lucky. No, I knew as little as you before my death. But then my world was opened." He lifts his shirt, grinning, the gun trained on Michael never wavering.

"Did you think I could survive that gunshot? I was just fortuitous they have numbers everywhere—including at the hospital that worked to save me."

His stomach puckers inwards like a great toothless mouth, the sucking dark pit stretching to the very edges of his body. And as

Michael stares in disbelief something deep within scuttles with anger at the encroaching light.

Michael falls to the ground, scrabbling backwards. Ethan drops the shirt and advances, stopping him.

"You left me to die. But then you always have to be the hero, don't you, Mikey? Even if it costs your own life, or those around you. What does it feel like, now, to know it was all for nothing? That everything you ever did led to this moment of failure."

Michael stares up at the vast, seething clouds, so dark they're turning day to night. The figures move down through the trees, seeking to bring about the end of whatever their plan is. He begins to despair.

His gun's only a foot away. Ethan sees him glance at it. "Don't bother."

"I won't let you get to her." Michael tenses to spring, knowing it will be his last act. His wife and daughter flash before his eyes one last time. *I'm sorry.*

"The girl?" Ethan seems surprised. "I don't need the girl—"

Ethan's neck explodes like paint splatter. He staggers backwards and clutches his throat. A second bullet whistles past Michael and blossoms a hole mid-forehead. Ethan gives a fleeting look of betrayal before the awareness goes out of his eyes and he keels backwards. Something screeches in his belly.

Vilks runs towards them, hair whipping in the wind. The first drops of rain hit his shirt like bullet holes. "Get away!" he yells to Michael.

A shape presses against Ethan's clothing, seeking another host perhaps. Then Simmonds is next to Vilks aiming his gun. The boom is so close Michael's hearing buzzes. He can't hear the next shots but can see the implosions of blood and matter erupt from Ethan's gut. And then the thing animating his friend dies.

Vilks is yelling at Michael, dragging him to his feet. He's pointing to the house and Michael staggers after him. Simmonds covers them, firing into the trees and Michael looks to the right as he runs, seeing the figures now threading between the dark trunks towards them.

They'll never make it in time. There's too many of the Vanguard streaming towards them.

Vilks pushes Michael and runs back, ripping off his shirt. As Michael stumbles on he sees the man draw a knife down his forearm. Michael's hearing kicks in to hear him intone something: *"Iä'ai fm'latgh!"* it sounds like, but there's something weird in his voice—like it's being spoken at multiple octaves—and then his entire arm ripples as the dark snakes of his scars respond. He raises the arm and then pile-drives his hand into the dirt.

A shockwave launches out across the ground, flattening grass and whipping gravel up like buckshot. The first of the darkened figures punch backwards as if hit, slamming onto their backs or against the thick trees. The rest stagger with the force.

"Go!" Vilks says, pulling Michael on.

"The cars," Michael says as they near the house. Then he falters as he sees the hoods of each are propped, the wiring within ripped out like gizzards. Ethan must've sabotaged—

"No. We must get to the girl!" Vilks pushes him on to the open door.

Ted and Robbo are standing inside, guns drawn. "What the—" Robbo starts to say but Simmonds just barrels past him followed by Michael.

Michael turns to slam the door shut but Vilks pauses at the threshold, kneeling with both hands in the dirt. He's saying something beneath his breath and the sigils on his back respond in unison. Ted and Robbo freak out at the sight, stumbling backwards and even Simmonds looks terrified, unaware of the true nature of what he's been enlisted in. Vilks ignores them all, even ignores the screeching mutated townspeople as they run in.

He slowly stands raising his arms, and a dark translucent film pulls from the ground and slides into the air. It extends to the edges of the house and around as far as Michael can tell, like a protective membrane around the whole building. Vilks thrusts his hands up and the sheath keeps rising beyond his reach, up and over the roof. The outside world blots out.

Then Vilks slumps, exhausted and Michael has to help him inside. The other police retreat like he's possessed.

Tommy sticks his head out of the control room. The video screens flicker and protest behind him. "It's going haywire—" Then the screens blow one by one. "Shit! We're blind!" The techie stares at the men with their backs against the wall staring at Vilks. "What's going—"

Then the power goes out. Darkness descends in the house, made worse by the barrier suppressing outside light. Michael can barely see Tommy at the other end of the corridor now.

"The girl…" Vilks croaks.

They must've left her upstairs with Jess, and Michael starts to race up. Simmonds grabs him.

"How did he—"

"We haven't time. We need to secure the house."

Simmonds stares at him, mouth working soundlessly like a fish. Then he slams his trap shut and nods. He can work it out later.

They race up the stairs. The door's ajar.

Jess isn't there to meet them. They move cautiously through the darkened living area. Michael hopes she's got the girl secured in a back room. Unless…

Unless the liaison officer's a traitor too. Michael's still reeling from his partner's betrayal, remembering what Vilks had said earlier about not trusting anyone. What if she's played Vilks just as Ethan played them? She could have used the distraction to smuggle the girl out.

A body lies in the darkness of the back room. Michael edges closer, gun drawn as he moves into the room.

She wasn't a traitor at least.

The woman's throat has been cut in a jagged frenzy of hatred. Long diagonal burns streak her face and Michael realises the girl took the time to heat a knife and return the torture before escaping. His stomach lurches. The amulet that had restrained Sara has been jammed into Jess's mouth. Tufts of burnt skin still cling to the underside.

"We're too late."

He almost gives up then. The girl could be anywhere by now: on foot protected by the swarm of attackers outside. They'd have to fight their way through first, and then there's no telling which way she's gone.

Even now she could be leading the Vanguard to the book. And then...then what? The end? Did he really believe the girl they'd been guarding held the power to destroy the world?

How could he not after everything he's seen?

Simmonds stares at him. "Where has she—"

There's a shout from downstairs.

"They're trying to get in!" Robbo races from window to window, freaked out.

Shadows gather against the dark seethe of plasma. One of the figures places their hands against the surface of the barrier and a crack of light blasts them backwards. But still more come and at each jolt the defence becomes weaker. The figure closest places his spread fingers without fear against the membrane. Energy pulses and eats away at the curtain.

Robbo steps back and fires. The bullet rips through the translucent wall like butter and into the figure. The shadow falls backwards. But there's more lining up around the house.

Michael aims at one, then glimpses something out of the corner of his eyes: a figure on the inside of the back door, hands pressed against the barrier trying to force their way out.

"Stop!" he roars running towards the girl, bracing for a shot.

Sara spins and her eyes are black and endless. *"C'uln 'bthnk k'yarnak Shoggor!"* she hisses and something forms above her shoulders: a shadow beyond the material realm clinging to her back, its dark streams of smoke whipping like tentacles and shifting in and out of polarity.

Michael freezes and it's like something from his dreams. He's held by the sight.

The girl smiles a terrible smile and the writhing tentacles scent him, rearing back to strike. "You are mine now," she says, and it's like she's whispering in his ear, the words worming their way deep inside his brain.

Then Tommy runs up beside him. "Holy shi—" he shouts as he raises the gun to blast the shit out of her.

Her face twists with hate. Before the policeman can fire she clutches her hand at him and the dark tendrils whip across the gap. The techie screams as they envelop him and lift him into the air. He fights the barely-substantial bonds but he's held tight. Robbo tries to grab for him but the smoke-tentacles squeeze possessively, then raise Tommy higher and start spinning him in mid-air. His screams are cut short by the whipping funnel. Blood sprays as his flesh strips from his face and arms and his bones rip apart. Then he's dropped and sprays a devolved splatter of meat over the men closest and the walls of the hallway. All that's left is his torn body steaming in the crumple of his clothes.

Robbo screams and turns to run, knocking Michael's aim. His bullet slams into the wall beside her. She turns back to him and reaches her hand and Michael feels time slow, trying to drag the gunsight down to her face.

Vilks moves past him, cutting a deep line across his scarred chest. Before the girl can react he palms the blood and flicks his fingers at her.

The droplets are like bullets. They punch into her and she screams as they acid-hiss their way into her skin. The shadow tendrils retract screeching.

Vilks continues to whisper something, cupping his hands out to either side and the girl goes rigid as his blood works its way through her. Her veins pop out in dark riddled lines beneath her skin. She's paralysed.

"Traitor!" she screams. "*Tarakan!* Let me go!"

Vilks' eyes have also turned black as he walks towards her, hands controlling. Sweat beads his brow. Every moment he holds her exposes him to the other world, Michael realises. Every minute brings him closer to madness.

"I must…keep her here," Vilks says. "Protect the barrier. We only need to survive…until the window closes. It could only be hours."

"Hours? You can't keep—"

"Go."

The cops look like little children in the hallway, adrift in incomprehension. The smell of Tommy's still-warm body fills the house. "Plan C Breach," Michael barks, pulling them back to reality. "Escape avenues lost. We're under siege now. Protect all points of entry—"

There's a crash from the control room down the interlocking corridor and he can see a shadow pushing its way in through the window, stretching the membrane inwards. He starts to run towards it and senses Simmonds alongside him.

Then he realises one of the policemen hasn't moved.

Ted brings up his gun, aiming at the back of Vilks' head.

Don't trust anyone.

"No!" Michael cries, spinning and lunging to grab his arm. He's too far away. His fingers grasp air as he falls.

Ted squeezes the trigger, face twisted with hatred like the girl's, like Ethan's.

Then something ripples beneath the skin down Michael's arm. A shadowed line darts out, almost imperceptible in the darkness.

Ted jolts to one side as he fires. The bullet blasts Vilks' shoulder open and he pitches forward. The girl drops, free, but crouches staring at Michael.

Then Ted's turning, aiming at him even as blood spurts between the fingers against his neck. Michael grabs him and the man howls at his touch. It's like Michael's hands are dipped in fire and they sink through Ted's skin to the bone. He falls screaming.

The world swims with darkness. Something's wrong with Michael's eyes, and he knows with horrible certainty that they have become as black as the girl's.

He focuses on her and sees fear in her eyes as she backs against the door.

"Stop her!" Vilks croaks.

She turns and strains through the membrane. It stretches and elongates around her face. Michael raises his hand, barely even understanding what he's doing, but is too late. She falls through, swallowed by darkness, and then the barrier stutters, beginning to dissolve.

Ted kicks to the wall and props himself against it, holding his mangled arm and crying out in agony. Simmonds takes a step and places his gun at the man's temple.

"Where is she going?" he yells but Ted just chokes back vomit long enough to look up at him.

"You have failed, cockro—"

Simmonds puts a bullet in his brain. Ted crumples.

Michael looks up to see the commander and Vilks staring at him.

"What's happening to me?"

Vilks starts to speak and blood bubbles over his lips. He chokes it back. "Once you have seen into the other world…there is no return. That night…when she attacked you. She made you part of the ceremony. When you did not die you gained…their knowledge. She knows this…must have wanted to use you…but now you can rival her." He tries to rise and fails. "You have to go after her."

Michael stares at him. "But I don't even—"

Robbo cries out, pointing to the control room. "They're getting in!" He pumps his shotgun and runs to intercept two cultists pushing through the membrane as if it's giving birth. Michael moves to help and Simmonds grabs him.

"No. Stop her." He heads instead for the control room, drawing the shadows along the windows away from the back door. The shotgun booms, but then Robbo screams as one of the cultists ducks under the buckshot and comes at him. Simmonds runs in firing, but they'll never be able to fight them all off.

Vilks grabs Michael's arm. "Use this. You will know how." Michael gasps as he gouges his blade into the skin of Michael's forearm: a triangle with an eye in it. "The Elder Gods still watch over," he says. "The masters who banished the evil ones. Maybe they will take pity at the last. Now *go*."

Michael pauses at the door to glance back. Vilks kneels, head down, intoning something as he draws the light of the hall into him. It's like a supernova forming in the middle of the house. Michael hasn't time to wonder what he's doing.

The barrier is like hot glue. It burns his eyes, his hair, his skin. It feels like it's seeping down into his bones. And then cold air hits him and he's lying in the dirt.

A deformed shadow running around the corner of the house

turns back at the sound. Michael instinctively punches out a hand before it can attack. A whirlwind of dust whips up and tears through the man. He falls shattered.

Michael stares amazed. Then he sees a distant figure disappearing over the ridge beside the beach.

Hate spreads through him. He takes off at a run after the girl.

The wind screams and pulls at him as he nears the cliffs. Rain begins to hit his face and he looks up at the circling clouds. The vast whirlpool has become a giant spiral, just as Ethan had drawn. Michael stares up, mesmerised, almost lost in the unnatural movement. And as he watches, the centre of the forming tornado breaks apart and reveals the sky beyond. Even though it must still be daytime, there's only blackness beyond. Stars glitter from countless light years away.

Then the stars begin to move. Impossibly, he sees the pinpricks of light begin to circle also, forming a sister spiral. He can feel his mind being pulled up into madness. The end must be near.

A roar of fury sounds behind him. He looks back to see the figures surrounding the house, and they see him too. The shimmering dark barrier has almost fallen—broken and tattered in parts—but now they ignore it and break off after him. He stumbles at the sight, knowing he'll never be able to fight them all.

And then a light begins to pulse from within the house. The air seems to suck inwards and the closest of the townspeople are pulled off their feet. The rest look back to the gathering supernova inside.

The house bulges with light. Michael runs and leaps behind a rock.

Then it explodes. A lightwave pulses out into the night ahead of him and the sound hits like thunder. Then there's just the crash of the waves from the water ahead, the sound of the wind through the trees. The night is still.

He stumbles out and looks back at the shattered house. It's been levelled: just a flattened black shell buying him precious minutes more.

He turns and pushes on. As he nears the path hidden beneath

the outcrops he has a moment where his resolve almost leaves him. He can hear a strange skittering and for some stupid reason glances over the nearest rocks. His mind lurches. Covering the beach are thousands of crawling deformed fish, many with arms or almost-human bodies—failed offspring of the townspeople perhaps. Amongst them are twisted giant starfish, rearing their suckered legs at the sight of him. Dripping translucent jellyfish crawl over the mass, trying to climb the cliffs.

As he stares the other dimension takes hold of his mind. The world swims with blackness.

And then his sanity almost collapses.

Everywhere he looks shadows seethe beneath the surface of things, not just within the creatures filling the beach, but the rocks, the plants gripping the sides of the cliff, the circling gulls. The divine ones are not lurking beyond the stars at all. They're here, they've always been here. Mere psychic inches beneath the veneer of reality. Always striving to bridge the gap, collapse the thin veneer between the dimensions. Writhing, shadowed forms filled with jealous hate churning beneath every element of matter in the world.

Then he sees a flash-succession of images he barely understands: a vast city stretching across the ocean, of massive interweaved structures that hurt his mind with their impossible angles and distorted dimensions, the streets filled with rivers of blood-sacrifice; something lording above all this, rearing its huge bulk against the water, then the air buckling and crackling around the bizarre mass, a screech of betrayal as a dark void opens and with a thunderclap sucks it into the depths of the ocean and out of this world. Then he sees from the eyes of the shadows moving alongside us, watching the earth through a filmy veil and raging for what has been lost.

And the girl will let them regain it.

The realisation almost strips away the last of his resolve. Somehow he continues on, but the sound of the skittering beach stays with him long after he's left it behind. He is now the only one who can stop her.

The path twists and Michael nearly loses his footing in the

darkness numerous times. The breaking rocks yawn death below. It takes everything in his power to keep concentrating. He sets his sights out to sea, on the silhouetted monoliths of the Twelve Apostles—a series of marooned towers of ancient rock—using them as a guide. The coastline cuts in ahead and he hears roaring waves. It must be the Loch Inn Gorge, conception place of the evil now infecting the area, a site where the junctions between dimensions are weak. The girl must have already hidden the book there somehow, or perhaps has some way of accessing it from there. A silhouette against the cliff ahead moves down into the chasm.

He stumbles, losing his footing.

She's too far ahead.

He can feel the stars above increase their orbit. Soon they will lock into place and open the gateway.

He can't make it in time.

He's failed.

He stares out over the ocean and for a moment pictures the ancient city. He has to shut his eyes, and as he does he thinks of his daughter, Isla, remembers her happy birth, the burning hope he once had for her, the meaning she brought to his life. He remembers the first time he met his wife Rachel at a party Ethan had dragged him to, his friend grinning as he'd pushed them together on some pretext of a conversation. The many years they'd shared together.

He had a chance to save them.

Not just now, but that night in the library. He'd had the girl in his sights and hesitated, thrown by the memory of his daughter perhaps. If he'd just shot her then…

The guilt is like fire through him.

The rocks beckon.

He deserves to die, after everything he's done wrong. He was too resistant to believing any of this, kept fighting its unravelling of his reality. And now he has cost them all.

He almost jumps. Then he looks down at the sigil carved into his arm: the sign of the Elder Gods, Vilks had said. Gods before those who covet this world. He can feel his skin itch as the symbol ripples and strains to be used.

Perhaps it senses the last of his will. He has to keep trying. Even if he's been wrong it's all he's ever known how to do. That's what makes him human. And maybe that determination to keep fighting for those he loves is what sets him apart from those filled with evil who value nothing.

Even though its myths mean nothing anymore he brings the cross from his pocket and places it around his neck. Maybe it's just to show faith in himself.

He keeps running, pushed on by the pulsing symbol on his arm, the necklace around his throat.

Sara stands in a great spiral etched into the sand in the gorge below. She's naked, her body rippling and undulating, hands outstretched.

There's something at her feet: a book, ancient and half-destroyed by fire.

Michael stares at it and remembers the leathered cover resting against his arm, burning them both, remembers her straining to kill him then seeing the book, turning to it, reaching out to save it—

Then the vision's gone and he has to steady himself against a rock. He doesn't know how she saved it. Vilks had said something about being able to hide it in a sliver of time. Maybe she's been waiting until now, distracting her enemies until the final moment before her escape. Just like that night they had underestimated her, hadn't foreseen the extent of her plans.

Well, he's not underestimating her now, and he won't let her succeed. Her actions drawing him into this have also given him a power. And now he'll use it against her.

He creeps down the rock face as she continues to intone something, her back to him. The wind rises and nearly rips him off the cliff. The surf thrashes and draws out to sea as if readying for a tsunami.

She is in the final stages. A dark mist crackles around her, building.

Michael hits the sand and feels his anger fill him. He knows instinctively he has to get her out of that circle. He briefly considers shooting her, but there's something about the mist that makes him realise nothing of the natural world will impact on her.

He has to use the darkness against her.

He tries to remember her words, and then they slip into his mind like they've always been there, waiting, part of his DNA, part of the gift given to him by the Elder Gods when they spawned humanity after banishing the previous rulers of the earth.

"C'uln 'bthnk k'yarnak Shoggor!"

The world shimmers with blackness as his eyes open. He sees beneath reality. Power pulses above his shoulders and seeks release.

The girl spins, sensing the disturbance in the air, and then she shrieks with anger. Her own spirit-guardian rears to defend her.

But Michael moves too quickly. He flares out a hand and a shadow rips through the air and punctures the smoke around her head. Something beyond this world cries as its hold is torn from her. He attacks again, again, and with each strike the shadow form is pulled backwards. Until finally it's ripped away and dissolves back into the night.

Sara stands naked and defenceless, darkness surging within her but not enough to draw against him.

He raises both arms to the heavens. *"Iä ai fm'latgh!"* he roars.

And drives both hands into the sand.

A deep fissure cracks towards her. She screams and turns to flee and the shockwave hits her back and smashes her across the rings of the spiral and out of its embrace. Her thin naked body flails across the sand in a thrash of limbs, and then she's still.

Michael looks up, but the clouds still circle, the stars within their centre revolving in unison. He stares at the spiral: the book clings to its position at its apex, even without the girl there protecting it. Vilks had said that it had survived innumerable attempts to destroy it over the centuries.

But now, now when it is at its most vulnerable, its essence laid bare as it tries to bridge the gap between the dimensions—

maybe now is the one time it can be truly rid from this earth.

Michael thinks he knows how to do it. It will mean his own destruction, but he is at peace with that now.

For you, my daughter.

A dark mist still hangs over the book and a bolt of black light shoots out at Michael. The eye sigil on his arm flares and a whipping tentacle lashes out to deflect it. Vilks has given him everything he needs to end this.

As he walks and more bolts shoot out at him, struck aside by the smoke manifestation protecting him, he begins to draw in the light of the surrounding sky towards himself. He can feel himself get heavier as the essence of the night, the surrounding cliff-face, the sand beneath his feet is leeched and stolen into him. The hatred of the darkness within life threatens to overwhelm him with each passing second, but he just needs to control it a few moments more. Enough to unleash it in one massive implosion as he holds the book to himself.

Sara stirs and looks up to see him step towards the spiral. He sees the surprise on her face, and then he's sucking the dark from her too and she screams, arching back against the sand.

Michael feels the immense power flooding him. He only needs a few seconds more.

He's mere steps from the spiral. The book flutters ahead, its pages flicking in the tearing wind. He imagines it scream.

It tries one last attack, unleashing a massive bolt of black power.

He bats it aside. Then steps into the spiral to claim it.

He's suddenly pulled rigid. Pain floods through him. The Elder God sigil on his arm burns with light, and then it flakes into flared matter and drifts up into the night, leaving him defenceless. He can't feel the smoke-essence at his back. The darkness within filters back out into the world.

With terror he feels himself being dragged towards the centre of the circle. The book continues to flutter, and then it upends and tumbles away into the night.

He takes its place.

Sara stands at the edge of the spiral, one arm broken, face

stripped raw from his attack. She's smiling.

"I needed you to open yourself to the darkness. Only you could do that."

"What's...happening..."

"In time, Michael." She gestures behind him and he's able to move his eyes only to the cave at the back of the gorge, some thirty feet away. It had yawned black when he'd stolen into the canyon, but now he can see shapes within. Then there's a strip of moonlight and figures move out of its entrance: naked Vanguard walking towards him.

But the cave mouth itself continues to ripple as if filled with something, and as the moonlight gets stronger he sees now the hidden wall of flesh. A gateway like the one that night at the university.

"No!" he struggles.

"There was only one way I could smuggle the book out, Michael. It has its own defence mechanisms. I didn't even realise what it was doing at first. Then I understand and realised how brilliant it would be. All I would need do is convince you to guard me. And then I could use you whenever I needed. You were the perfect hiding spot." He tries to resist listening to her, but her words keep coming, destroying him with their revelations.

"You are the book, Michael, and its sacrifice. *You* are the Vanguard."

"No," he cries, but he senses the truth of it, and then that whole night comes flooding back and he feels the book merging with him, draining into him. The invasion like being raped.

"All that is left is for you to make way."

So there is still a chance left. "Never," he croaks. It has to be willing. He doesn't understand why, doesn't care, but it's all he has to cling to.

Then he sees something that strips the last of his sanity.

A figure within the towering flesh gate: dark hanging hair, a small mole on one draping breast—a mole he remembered teasing with his tongue the first time he'd seen it—long legs that had wrapped around his waist so many nights.

It can't be.

Sara laughs and her voice cuts him. He tries to move even a finger, filled with such violent hate his head's almost bursting as he froths at her.

She nods, eyes shining.

"Your daughter too," she whispers and points at a smaller form on the wall below, and then something breaks within him. The last of his resistance leaves. The last he had to fight for.

He barely hears her as she prepares for the last of the ritual, barely registers the other cultists joining her circle.

"Give yourself to their embrace, Michael. Let their wonders cleanse you from the agony of this world."

The pain within him is too great to hear her beyond that and he doesn't feel anything anymore. His mind draws out into the darkness, into the other world that has so surely destroyed his own.

Everything he has done has been wrong.

He barely feels the lizard skin of his burns sloughing from his chest and stomach, revealing pink newborn flesh beneath that blisters and darkens before coalescing into letters. The black text races along his body: down his arms and hands, along his stomach and chest, across his back, up his neck and face, but he only faintly registers any of it. His broken mind floats above, staring down at his twisting form as his screams drown out the thunder.

Sara is intoning something he no longer hears and the gateway in the cave responds, the bodies he can no longer look at devolving and merging together, then forming into dripping light.

The sentient, clinging light creeps out over the sand and to the spiral, enveloping the shell of his body. The earth shudders and opens, and the waters out to sea part in preparation. The monoliths of the Apostles fall in a shuddering line.

And as his ribs break apart and lift up from his body one by one, becoming great fingers of the fist pushing through him, Michael finally lets his mind escape into the darkness and he sees no more.

BIOGRAPHIES
(IN ORDER OF APPEARANCE)

STEVE PROPOSCH, CHRISTOPHER SEQUEIRA & BRYCE STEVENS are the co-editors and creators of the Cthulhu Deep Down Under (CDDU) concept. Their recent decision to collaborate on a rolling series of anthologies under the group moniker 'Horror Australis' reflects their belief that the most exciting opportunities for southern-equatorial genre fiction lie ahead. Works by the members of this team in collaboration include co-editing Terror Australis: The Australian Horror and Fantasy Magazine; Bloodsongs magazine (published internationally); and horror comics under the Sequence Publications banner that included contributions by each of them. Two more CDDU volumes, as well as Cthulhu: Land of the Long White Cloud, are set for release in 2018-19.

STEVE SANTIAGO became a fan of all things weird at an early age and that attraction has never stopped. He graduated with a BA in Graphic Design and has over 20 years of experience working as a full-time graphic designer in California. The past few years he has been able to devote most of his time to illustrating and photoshopping covers and interior art for anthologies, magazines, ezines, CD covers, board game art and concept art for a Lovecraftian film. As a freelancer, Steve has created art/designs for clients from as far away as Australia, Germany, Hungary, U.K., and the Netherlands.—illustrator-steve.com

LINDSAY C. WALKER always had a passion for drawing, and absolutely adored monsters. She grew up loving movies such as *Labyrinth, Dark Crystal, Gremlins, Star Wars* and anything by Harryhausen. She began a career in comics in 2008, illustrating the cover art for her favourite super-hero, *The Phantom*, for Moonstone Books, however, Lindsay's ability to draw decreased due to crippling pains brought on by fibromyalgia. Although crushed by the diminishing of her illustration career, she moved on to writing. Lindsay said she was pleasantly surprised when asked to draw for *Cthulhu: Deep Down Under* and felt she couldn't say 'no' to the request. Lindsay also returned to some *Phantom* illustration which saw print for both Hermes Press in the USA and Frew Publishing in Australia. Lindsay was a transgender woman. She passed away in 2016, and is survived by her partner Kim and their three daughters, Ariel, Heloise and Evelyn.

[eds—Lindsay's art and professionalism were outstanding and the editors were sincerely saddened to hear of her passing. They thank Kim Ross for allowing Lindsay's work to be published here.]

RAMSEY CAMPBELL is one of the most respected, lauded, and awarded writers in fantasy. He has won multiple British Fantasy and World Fantasy Awards and several Bram Stoker and International Horror Guild Awards. He is the author of such classic works of horror and dark fantasy as *Obsession, The Face Must Die, The Nameless, Incarnate* and *The Influence*, and, more recently, *The Darkest Part of the Woods, The Overnight* and *The Grin of the Dark*.

JANEEN WEBB is a multiple award winning author, editor and critic who has written or edited ten books and over a hundred essays and stories. Her short story collection, *Death At The Blue Elephant*, was short listed for the 2015 World Fantasy Award. Janeen is a recipient of the World Fantasy Award, the Peter MacNamara SF Achievement Award, the Aurealis Award, and the Ditmar Award. She holds a PhD in literature from the University of Newcastle, and divides her time between Melbourne and a small farm overlooking the sea near Wilson's Promontory, Australia—janeenwebb.com.au

DMETRI KAKMI is a writer and editor. His memoir *Mother Land* was shortlisted for the New South Wales Premier's Literary Awards in Australia, and is published in England and Turkey. He edited the acclaimed children's anthology *When We Were Young*. The ghost story 'The Boy by the Gate' was reprinted in *The Year's Best Australian Fantasy and Horror 2013*. *Haunting Matilda* was shortlisted in the Aurealis Awards Best Fantasy Novella category in 2015. His essays and short stories appear in anthologies. He lives in Melbourne.

LUCY SUSSEX was born in New Zealand. She has edited four anthologies, including *She's Fantastical* (1995), shortlisted for the World Fantasy Award. Her award-winning fiction includes books for younger readers, and the novel *The Scarlet Rider* (1996, reprinted 2014). She has five short story collections, *My Lady Tongue, A Tour Guide in Utopia, Absolute Uncertainty, Matilda Told Such Dreadful Lies* (a best of), and *Thief of Lives*. Currently she is a Fellow at the State Library of Victoria. Her 2015 *Blockbuster!: Fergus Hume and The Mystery of a Hansom Cab* won the Victorian Community History Award.

JASON FRANKS is the author of the *Sixsmiths* graphic novels, a satire about a family of suburban Satanists who have fallen prey to the GFC, and the occult rock'n'roll novel *Bloody Waters*. He is the writer of the *Left Hand Path* comic series and the editor of the *Kagemono* horror anthologies. Franks' work has been short-listed for Aurealis and Ledger awards. His second novel, *Faerie Apocalypse*, will be available in November 2017 from IFWG.

KAARON WARREN is a Shirley Jackson Award winner and World Fantasy Award nominee, and has lived in Melbourne, Sydney, Canberra and Fiji. She's sold many short stories, four novels (the multi-award-winning *Slights, Walking the Tree, Mistification* and *The Grief Hole*) and six short story collections. Her most recent novel, *The Grief Hole*, won a Canberra Critic's Circle Award for Fiction, a Ditmar Award, the Australian Shadows Award and the Aurealis Award. Her stories have appeared in Australia, the US, the UK and elsewhere in Europe, and have been selected for both Ellen Datlow's and Paula Guran's Year's Best Anthologies. She is a Guest of Honour at World Fantasy Convention in 2018 and Geysercon, NZ, 2019—kaaronwarren. wordpress.com

STEPHEN DEDMAN grew up (though many would dispute this) on the outskirts of Perth, Western Australia, far enough away from any bookshops that he had to make up his own science fiction stories. He is the author of the novels *The Art of Arrow Cutting, Shadows Bite, Foreign Bodies,* and *Shadowrun: A Fistful of Data,* and more than 120 short stories published in an eclectic range of magazines and anthologies and reprinted in his collections *The Lady of Situations* and *Never Seen by Waking Eyes.* He has won two Aurealis Awards and an Australian Science Fiction Achievement Award, and been nominated for the Bram Stoker Award, the British Science Fiction Association Award, the Seiun Award, the Sidewise Award, the Spectrum Award, and a sainthood. He taught creative writing at the University of Western Australia, and has been an associate editor of *Eidolon,* the fiction editor of *Borderlands,* the book buyer for most of Perth's science fiction bookshops, an actor, a game designer, a book reviewer and an experimental subject. He enjoys reading, travel, movies, talking to cats, and startling people.

WILLIAM TEVELEIN is a Brisbane-born, Manhattan-based writer and editor whose fondness for all things Lovecraftian (particularly his adjectives and ellipses) has flourished for more than four decades. 'Liam' spent his twenties as a bookseller, his thirties as an editor, and his forties as an author and journalist. Now in his fifties, he is working on the next logical step, i.e. to become a fictional character as soon as possible. It is a process he finds strangely comforting. His novels, *The Visitants* and *First*

Frost, and an anthology of short fiction, *A Dimension Down The Road*, are available as e-books on Amazon and as rather nice paperbacks published by Ramble House—ramblehouse.com

CHRISTOPHER SEQUEIRA is a writer and editor who specialises in mystery, horror, science fiction and superheroes. His short stories, articles and comic books have been published in Australia, the UK, the USA and Canada and include flagship superhero work on *Justice League Adventures* for DC Entertainment, *Iron Man* and *X-Men* stories for Marvel Entertainment, and *The Phantom* for Australia's Frew Publishing. He edited the recently released anthology *Sherlock Holmes: The Australian Casebook* (Bonnier Publishing), and has two forthcoming anthologies— *Sherlock Holmes and Doctor Was Not* and *Cthulhu: Land of the Long White Cloud* (both for IFWG Publishing Australia).

B. MICHAEL RADBURN has been writing successfully for many years and has published more than a hundred short stories, articles and reviews in Australia and overseas. He was an award-winning short story teller before his move to novels, which freed him to further explore his characters, as well as the natural and supernatural environs in his work. The hauntingly beautiful surrounds of his rural Southern Highlands holding are often the inspiration for those stories. Through the late '80s, Radburn was Publishing Editor of the iconic *Australian Horror & Fantasy Magazine* and founder of Dark Press Publications. He has won several Melbourne University Literary Awards and more recently was short-listed for the Henry Lawson Festival Awards. *The Falls* is Radburn's current novel, the second book featuring Taylor Bridges after *The Crossing* (soon to be a major motion picture). He is also the author of *Blackwater Moon* and his forthcoming novel, *The Reach*, is due for release in 2018.

SARAH ELLERTON is an illustrator, comic artist, programmer and systems engineer currently based in Sydney, Australia. She began drawing in 1998, and slowly expanded from simple character fan art to creating her own fully-fledged characters, and stories in which to reveal them. She is available for commissioned illustrations and graphic novels—arts-angel.com

AARON STERNS is a rare writer who is comfortable in both fiction and film; not only did he write *Wolf Creek 2* (Best Screenplay, Madrid International Fantastic Film Festival 2014) but he is also author of prequel novel *Wolf Creek: Origin*, described in early reviews as "one of the best serial killer novels out there... destined to be considered a classic in future years." Sterns' short fiction has appeared in such anthologies as the WFA-winning *Dreaming Down-Under, Dreaming Again* and *Gathering the Bones*. He is currently working on a number of screenplays, including an adaptation of 'Vanguard', and a novel—aaronsterns.com